COURT OF MIDNIGHT

Twisted Fae Book Three

LUCINDA DARK
HELEN SCOTT

Cover Design by FrostAlexis Cover Design

Editing by Your Editing Lounge

Proofreading by Jean Bachen

❄ Created with Vellum

ACKNOWLEDGMENTS

FROM HELEN

I would like to thank you most of all, as the reader, for giving us a chance to entertain you and invite you into our world. Thank you so much. I hope you enjoyed it! A big thank you to our cover designer, FrostAlexis Art & Design, for helping us bring this book to life. Big hugs and thank yous to all our editors and beta readers for helping us polish this baby up.

Thank you to my family for helping me pursue my dream and putting up with my wandering mind. Last, but not least, thank you to my husband for pushing me to share my stories with the world and to trust that other people out there have minds just as weird as my own. Thanks for putting up with me every day, babe. You're amazing!

FROM LUCINDA

Thank you to all of the people who've helped Helen and I bring this book to life. Cress has been so much fun to write and Helen has been an amazing partner, so patient and understanding. You're awesome, babe. Seriously. I think Cress is a combination of your sassiness and my internal dialogue.

Another thank you to all of our alphas, betas, editors, proofreaders, designers, and readers. Without y'all, this series would not exist.

CHAPTER ONE

CRESS

I paced from one end of my tower cell to the next. I'd never felt this trapped before. I didn't like it. I couldn't see the sky. I couldn't feel fresh air on my skin. I felt like I was suffocating and in the dark no less since I'd been given no light. There wasn't even a damn window. Tyr—Orion's rotten bastard of a brother—was the cause.

As if my thoughts had summoned the creature straight from Death's realm, the door to my prison rattled and opened and he stepped into the entrance, framed by the firelight behind him. Oh, how I wanted to run him through with one of the Princes' swords. I wanted to claw his eyes out. Punch him in the throat. Kick him in the balls.

I took several steps towards him, intending to do just that when he held up a hand and invisible manacles encircled my arms and legs, stopping me from moving any further.

"I can understand your reasonable anger, Cress," Tyr said as he stepped into the room. He lifted a hand, the movement a shadow across the floor at my feet. Within seconds, fires erupted around the room—clinging to lanterns that had been hung there previously but had gone unlit. "But you won't harm me—or rather, I won't allow you to."

I narrowed my eyes on him. "What?" I snapped in challenge. "Are you scared of a little girl?"

He chuckled as the door behind him closed. "Of course not. Give me just a moment," he replied calmly.

Fuck his calm! I wasn't calm. I was angry. Angrier than I'd ever been. I listened to the sound of keys jingling in the lock as the door was relocked. Only then did Tyr lower his arm and the invisible bindings disappeared. I didn't even hesitate. I continued my forward momentum, brought my foot back, and nailed him right between the legs.

"Fuck!" He went down on his knees, throwing a hand out at me. A wave of power hit me and propelled me backwards. My spine hit the stone wall, and I winced as I slid down. That was going to bruise. I didn't care. It'd been worth it to kick him right where the sun didn't shine. So fucking worth it.

"You are a feisty one, I'll give you that," he wheezed. "Seems my brother chose well for his mate … and his friends' mate."

I clenched my teeth against the pain in my back as I got on my knees and leveraged myself up. I stood and held my ground, my hands balling into fists at my side. Already I could feel the soreness in my back. It was going to make sleeping really painful, I knew. "Why would you do this?" I demanded, ignoring his comment. "Why would you take me? What could I possibly have to help you gain anything? It's clear you're in this for power. Right?"

"Right." He nodded and I took some pleasure in the fact that he still looked pale. When he stood, he did so slightly hunched as he moved further from me and back towards the door to lean against the wall alongside it.

It didn't matter. I'd done what I wanted. I knew there was no way I'd get much more than one hit in. I was effectively trapped here. And even if I did manage to escape, I knew nothing about the King's castle. Sure, I'd grown up in Amnestia, but I hadn't ever left the small abbey I'd been raised in until I'd met the Princes.

"It's more than that, little Changeling," he said gruffly.

I narrowed my gaze on him and waited. Slowly, ever so slowly, Tyr straightened his back and looked at me. "I admit," he said, "originally, I was bored."

My mouth dropped open. That couldn't be right. He couldn't possibly be telling me that he did all of this— betrayed his race and his *brother* because he was bored. As if sensing my thoughts, he grinned ruefully.

"I'm sure my little brother has told you very little, if anything, about his home Court. The Court of Midnight is as secretive as it is powerful," he said. "We are taught from birth to play the game and play it well."

"What game?" I demanded. "Life and death? That's no game."

Tyr tilted his head and slowly lowered his eyes until they had passed over the rest of me. "There is a reason we keep to ourselves, a reason why ours is the Court called upon for action and war, little Changeling." I snarled, hating it when he called me that. *They*—my Princes—could call me that, but he couldn't. He ignored the sound and continued. "The Court of Midnight possesses old magic, ancient and dangerous magic. We were the ones called upon when Courts of old needed to be taught a lesson."

When Courts of old needed to be taught a lesson ... My lips parted and shock rocketed through me. He couldn't mean what I thought he meant. Did that mean ... was his Court—Orion's Court—responsible for the loss of the Brightling Court?

A cruel, twisted sneer lit his face. "I can see you understand," he said. "Midnight is the power that steals all other magic. We are not life. We are death incarnate. With such power comes a great deal of tediousness. What does one do when you have all of the power of the world, hmmm?"

My muscles jumped and shook. Anger poured through me, and yet, I couldn't move. I simply stood there and watched him, cautious, confused, and yes, even a little scared. It wasn't a Fae that stood before me but a monster.

"Orion, of course, was always a little different. When heirs are young, they are sent away to other Courts to begin their training. He met Sorrell and Roan at the Court of Frost and Court of Crimson and when The Crimson Queen decided to step down from her Court to give her son some ruling experience, well, it came as no shock to me when Orion leapt at the chance to join him. He always was a weakling."

"He's not weak!" I snapped. My skin heated. My face flamed. Something deep within me burned with the agonizing heat of the sun and it made me want to melt his smug face off. "Orion is one of the strongest, bravest men I know. If anything—you're the weak one."

Tyr's eyes widened for merely a fraction of a moment before he burst out laughing. "Truly amusing," he barked. "I almost believed you there for a moment myself."

"You should believe me," I said through gritted teeth. My hands clenched into fists. I wanted so badly to hit him, but I didn't trust that it wouldn't come back to bite me in the ass. "I'm serious."

"I'm sure you are," he replied, sounding arrogant in his sarcasm, "but you keep interrupting me. Don't you want to know why I did this?" He waved his hand to the stone prison.

I clamped my lips shut.

He grinned. "There, now, that's better. Keep your pretty mouth shut and you might just make it out of this alive," he offered. *I'd show him a pretty face.* I bet his face would look a whole lot prettier with a couple of bruises. My previous anger towards Ariana held no candle to the fury I felt for this man.

"Now," he continued, "as I was saying. Yes, I began this endeavor out of boredom—the whole betrayal thing really adds some spice to life, don't you think? Humans are so easy to manipulate. They ignore magic that's right before their eyes." He lifted his hand and a flame so dark it was blue danced at his fingertips, illuminating his face in a grotesque mass of shadows and dancing light before it disappeared. "They'll believe what they want to believe and if you use it against them, they aren't even smart enough to realize."

Tyr pushed away from the wall and took a few steps into the room. I didn't move. In fact, I felt my body lock up as I pushed back against the wall, wanting to stay as far from him as possible. "Then a grand idea appeared before me," Tyr said, throwing his arms out wide. When he smiled this time it was too tight with a maniacal gleam in his eyes. "Why control only humans? Fae are just as easy to control? What if I could control the world? Everything!"

I frowned. My brows drew down low and I shook my head back and forth. I didn't understand. "What?" I blurted.

Tyr lowered his arms. "It's simple," he explained. "All I have to do is let them kill each other. I won't even have to lift a finger or dirty my hands. I am the player and they are my pawns. All I need to do is push them into place and let them finish the work. Afterwards, I'll be able to rule over the remains with no opposition. And you—" He stopped and turned to me. "You came along at the most perfect opportunity."

A sick feeling of dread curled in my stomach and I swallowed reflexively.

"My brother has no idea the power he wields," he confessed. "And I made sure to keep it that way."

"The scars..." I whispered. "You did that." His tone was too smug, too proud for it not to be true.

He shrugged. "If he wasn't strong enough to beat me once, what made him think he could do it again?"

"He can beat you now, though, can't he?" I asked. That was why he'd tortured him as a child, I realized. Because he knew the kind of power Orion would grow into. I'd never seen it myself, but I'd felt it. And Orion was backed by Sorrell and Roan. They were each powerful on their own, but together ... they were unstoppable. And that's why he'd needed me.

"All I needed to do, once I'd understood the kind of power you held over them, was incite them."

I felt so foolish. So stupid. *But how could I have known?* I lifted my arms and curled my fingers into my hair. *No no no. This couldn't be happening. Was I the reason that they would be hurt?* I knew that was true in the deepest parts of my soul.

"I lied before," Tyr admitted. *Shocker*, I thought as I released my hair and glanced up. Except it wasn't. It really wasn't. "You won't make it out of this alive. Your death will instigate the next part of this war. The final part. And from the ashes, I will rise."

I was disgusted. Horrified. And utterly at a loss. My lips parted but no words emerged. What could I say? What could I do? Nothing. I could do and say nothing that would stop the course that he'd set.

Tyr grinned again, recognizing the emotions on my face. "Be overjoyed, little Changeling." This time, when he said that name, I didn't flinch. "You'll be the reason I finally get my wish. You'll be the very pawn used to decide the next God among humans and Fae. Me. Fitting, don't you think? All those years ago, I was ordered to kill the entirety of you and your brood. Yet here you stand before me and finally, my task will be carried out."

"What?" I gaped at him. "What do you mean you were ordered to kill me?"

He arched a brow. "You still haven't figured it out?" He laughed, sounding more than amused. He sounded crazy. Deranged. Completely cut off from sanity. He stopped abruptly, turning and striding towards the door that led to freedom. He knocked once, twice, three times before turning back to me. "You are the last heir to the Brightling Court, Cressida," he said. "You are the Brightling Princess and it was my duty to slay you. You escaped once. You won't escape again. Instead, you'll be used to hand the world over to me. Who knows?" He chuckled again as the door was unlocked and pulled open. "Maybe you're technically a Brightling Queen now since your mother is long dead. At my hands, too."

"Wait!" I jerked forward as he stepped out and the door closed behind him. I slammed into the wood, feeling the hit shake me to my core. I wanted to know more. No, I *needed* to know more.

"Don't worry, Cressida." Tyr's voice drifted through the wood. "Like I said, you'll be leaving here soon and you'll be joining your true family in the afterlife."

I sank against the door, turning and pressing my back to it as my bones trembled. My knees hit the cold, dirty ground and I curled into myself as his words echoed in my mind over and over again. I closed my eyes and let darkness take me into oblivion.

CHAPTER TWO

ROAN

he was gone.

S The thought beat at me like the heat of the sun, unrelenting in its force. Wave after wave of heated anger pulsed through me. We had fucked up. We'd missed it. And Tyr was a fucking traitor. Perhaps he didn't know yet that we knew where he'd taken her, but just before the portal had closed, I'd glimpsed a hint of where they'd landed. The human Kingdom, and not just any place, but the Royal human palace.

When I get my hands on him, I'm going to burn him to ash, I swore silently.

The urge to track her down, to save her from whatever Tyr was planning, was almost uncontrollable. My bones and muscles vibrated with the desire—it swelled up even beyond the initial shock.

I looked to Sorrell and Orion. Silence echoed between us as we made our way back to the Court of

Frost's castle. A darkness had overtaken Orion. For all of his Midnight powers, he'd never truly appeared as though he was a part of their Court. He'd been too compassionate, too sane, too gentle. He was anything but that now. Even in his silence, I could sense the dark force within him. There was no denying it, no hiding it.

And surprisingly, Sorrell wasn't much better. No matter how much he preached against Cress, his anger was nearly as potent as mine. His very skin was whiter than ice, nearly blue as frost crept up over the side of his neck, inching forward. Every step he took left a path of ice in his wake. None of us could control it—the emotions swirling within our bodies demanding restitution.

"We need to get back," I said, stopping in the corridor just outside of the Court of Frost's throne room. "We have to go after her."

Neither of them said a word, but their strides did slow and stop alongside mine. I closed my eyes and forced my anger back. I grabbed each of their arms and yanked them along with me. Shoving until they both slammed into the wall.

"Wake *the fuck* up!" I yelled. "We are in no position for this. We need to figure out what we're going to do. We have to form a plan of attack." Cress was depending on me, she was depending on *us*.

Sorrell blinked at me, a light seeming to reenter his eyes, though not fast enough for my liking. Orion remained expressionless.

"It's time to fucking go," I gritted out. When, once again, neither of them said a word, my Royal fire burned out of control, and for the first time since I was a child incapable of controlling my powers, I lost it. I roared as fire licked against my scalp, and turning, I slammed my fist into a nearby stone wall. So many turbulent emotions were pent up.

I didn't think. I just reacted to all of it. I pivoted, grabbed onto Orion, and yanked him towards me, shoving my face into his.

"You think this is going to help Cress?" I demanded. "It's not. We need to go out, find her, and get her back. And I swear to you, Orion—throne brother of mine or not—I will kill your blood brother if it's the last thing I do. I will not settle for less. He took what is mine."

Orion blinked and I could feel something seeping from his pores as a darkness wafted over my skin. "Ours," he rasped.

For a moment, relief poured through me. "Yes," I agreed. "She's ours, and we need to get her back." I took a deep breath and fixed him with a look. "Don't make me do it alone. I need you." I knew he cared for her as I did. There was no one else I would want at my back than my throne brothers.

"You are not going alone," Sorrel said as he stepped up alongside Orion and me. His cool, icy gaze traveled over us both. "I'm coming as well."

Orion didn't look at him, not even when I took my hands back and released him from the wall. The three of us stood in a semi circle and there was a jagged piece of us missing—a piece I hadn't realized was so important until that moment. Her. She was everything. And perhaps I'd just been claiming her as my fiancée and future Crimson Princess to protect her in the hostile frozen Court of Sorrell's ancestors, but the truth was, I expected to marry her. I wanted her. *They* wanted her.

And there was nothing that would stop us from taking her back.

I dragged in a lungful of air. "We must speak to the Queens," I said.

Sorrell and Orion both nodded, and together we turned and moved towards the throne room.

We stopped just inside the entryway and my eyes widened at what I saw. The Frost and Crimson Queens sat, side by side, entertaining their guests from their thrones, seemingly unconcerned, or perhaps unaware, of what had occurred at the Run of the Gods. It didn't take long, however, for them to notice our presence.

"Roan," my mother bid me, lifting her hand towards me as she beckoned me to her side. "Is the Run over already?" Her lips tilted up into a half smirk and already, I sensed her thoughts. She likely believed that our early arrival must have meant that I'd called off the engagement. That assumption was far from the truth.

"There has been a breach in our security," I stated, not moving from my spot. Orion and Sorrell remained vigil at my sides. "Cress has been taken by Tyr into the human realm. He's working with the humans."

Gasps echoed up from those present in the room. Sorrell's mother jerked her head towards me, her cold blue eyes narrowing. "What is the meaning of this?" she demanded.

"It's exactly as he said," Sorrell answered. "Cress has

been kidnapped. We are leaving at once for our Court and we will be going after her."

"All three of you?" my mother demanded.

"Yes," Orion replied.

There was a moment of silent shock from both of them and before either could think to order us to stay, we turned as one and left. Orion went one way and Sorrell another. We didn't have to speak to know our plans. Each of us would pack our belongings and leave by horse within the hour. There would be no sleep or stops along the way. We had to make it back to our Court with all haste.

I arrived at my chambers and was already beginning to pack when the door was unceremoniously flung open and the Crimson Queen came storming in.

"This is an absolute outrage," she snarled as she approached. "How dare you come into my throne room and disrespect me by leaving without my leave—"

I turned and pinned her with a look. "It is not your throne," I reminded her, my voice sharp with cruelty. "You chose to remain in Alfheim, and therefore, you hold a seat in that throne room, but make no mistake. This is not your Court, mother," I said. "You no longer have one."

She gasps. "I am your mother," she said, shocked. "How dare you treat me this way? I demand that you stay here and apologize."

I snorted, shoving another item of clothing into the bag in my hand. "You cannot stop my leaving," I replied. "I will find my fiancée, and as soon as I have her in my arms once more, I will make sure that she is protected."

The woman before me rolled her eyes. "That child does not deserve this level of loyalty, Son," she replied. "If anything, this only proves that you should marry Ariana. It's clear that your Changeling was likely having an affair with Tyr. You know how humans are, easily seduced by—"

A snarl worked its way up my throat and I dropped the bag in my hand, turning on her so abruptly that she stumbled back a step. "She is *not* a human!" I yelled. "We are leaving. We will find her. And when I do, I will marry her and make her the next Crimson Queen once I have come of age. I may be a Prince now, but make no mistake—unless you plan to kill me—there will come a time when my power far outweighs your own."

"You would defy your mother, your Queen?"

"Without hesitation. No one takes what is mine and lives to tell about it. I will have her back and have Tyr's head on a spike."

"You wish to start a war between the Court of Crimson and the Court of Midnight? Fine. But do not expect any assistance from me or Adorra."

"I never have," I snapped, returning to my task.

"The Court of Midnight is dangerous," she continued as though I hadn't spoken. Try as I might to ignore her words, they pierced into my mind as she hurled them at me. "They will tear you apart as they do their own young!" she exclaimed. "And you would go willingly into the battle for a girl with no wealth or status or talent. You have lost your mind."

The door to my chambers opened and Sorrell and Orion both stood there. Their packs rested against their shoulders as they looked into the room and spotted us. They must have heard her proclamations because, without hesitation, Orion stepped inside and fixed her with a look.

"We will tear my brother apart," Orion said, a dark sinister aura coating his skin like smoke as it twined around his hands and up his arms. His eyes practically glittered with the Midnight danger my mother spoke of.

In typical fashion, my mother ignored him and addressed me instead. "Is she really worth all of this? What is she other than the byproduct of a forgotten line? There is nothing special about her, no good breeding, no family to speak of, no money, no power. She's just a momentary entertainment. Now she's gone, probably run away with Tyr, and you should let her go. Please, for the love of the Gods, marry Ariana; she has everything that your Changeling lacked, plus she is an excellent example of how Fae women should behave, unlike that child you brought before us who talked back to her queens."

"She is not a child, that I can guarantee," I said coldly, lifting my bag and slinging it over my shoulder. "And while she may not be the typical Fae noble, to us she's better, she's honest, and not trying to use us for her own gain. She's stronger and more special than you think, and that's exactly why we are going to get her back. Ariana has no place in the Court of Crimson. As of this day, she has been exiled. She will remain here in the Court of Frost and if you refuse to house her, you may cast her out, but she will never be welcome in my Court again."

Sparks lit the ends of my mother's hair as she scowled at me. "You are a fool," she snapped. "You would leave The Court of Crimson open to a human attack if you leave to follow that girl."

"That is no longer any of your concern," I said, shouldering past her as I made my way to my brothers. "We can handle our Court ourselves."

I didn't look back as I left the room, feeling Orion and Sorrell following as we made our way to the stables. As Orion disappeared to find stable hands to assist in readying our mounts, I sucked in a lungful of icy air and pushed it out in a rush. Seconds later, I felt the niggling of eyes on me. Turning slightly, I caught a glimpse of the very bitch I'd exiled.

"What do you want?" I asked, calling Ariana from her hiding place.

After a moment, she gave up pretending and slowly slid around the corner, her eyes turned towards the ground.

"Spit it out," Sorrell snapped, just as through with her as I was. "We don't have all day."

"Is it really true?" she asked. "That I won't be allowed back into the Court of Crimson?"

"You put my betrothed at risk, you attempted to kill her, and only by her mercy are you even alive," I growled. "Yes, it is true. If ever you show your face in our Court again, I will have you shackled in silver and then burned at the stake."

Her head jerked up and she took a step forward, her hand reaching out blindly. "Roan—"

Without stopping to think, I took the few steps to

reach her, raised my palm, and backhanded her across the face. Ariana fell to the ground, her hand coming up to cover her face as tears tracked down her cheeks. A hollowness filled me. Something twisted and dark. Cress would have been so angry had she seen my actions, and yet, I didn't care.

"Do not speak to me so disrespectfully, peasant," I snapped. "I am a Royal and you are nothing. I am a future King of the Crimson Court and you will address me as such. If I ever see your face again, I can promise you nothing but pain and misery. Your home is now the Court of Frost. You are not welcome anywhere else."

I turned my back on her and walked over to my horse as Orion and two stable hands came around the opposite corner, each with a mount in hand. There wasn't a single feeling of remorse, I noted, as her quiet sobs followed me. Sorrell didn't say a word as we each took our steeds and headed out. A sick sinister feeling coated my every movement and I blinked, turning my nose down and sniffing at myself. But no, I had to be imagining it. Every ounce of hatred I had for Ariana, every modicum of disgust, had finally seeped out of me. It was only my anger that had caused my actions.

Still, my eyes slid towards Orion as he mounted his horse and took the reins. Regardless of my behavior, we had more important things to attend to. Our focus needed to be on getting back to the Court of Crimson and then to the human realm. Cress was waiting.

CHAPTER THREE

SORRELL

The Court of Crimson appeared over the hill and, as if the others felt the same renewed sense of urgency at the sight of it, our pace increased. With just the three of us, we'd managed to keep our mounts through the Pass and were now so very close to our Court and our way back to the human realm. Sweat slicked the back of my neck as my mind rolled with thoughts, possibilities, and plans.

How long had Tyr been preparing for this betrayal? His treachery didn't come as a surprise, but ... my gaze slid to Orion on the other side of Roan. Cold fury burned hot inside my core. He would regret his deception, that much I would make sure of.

The front gates of the Court of Crimson opened and I slowed as Roan passed through first, then Orion, and I brought up the back. Roan rode towards the stables and we followed. I slipped from the saddle, handing the reins over to a stable hand without a second thought.

"The Lanuaet," I said as I turned towards the castle's front entrance. Orion and Roan followed behind as we made our way into the front corridor.

"Your majesties!" a familiar voice called out.

"Groffet." Roan stepped forward as the short dwarf hobbled towards us.

"How—" The old man stopped and adjusted the spectacles at the end of his bulbous nose, glancing behind us. "Where is the Changeling?"

"She has been stolen," Orion stated, his voice lowering. I cut a look towards him as the scent of ash and doom intensified in the immediate area.

Groffet's eyes widened and he glanced back over his shoulder as if waiting for something to appear. "Should I tell the..." He let his sentence trail off, but we knew who he meant. Cressida's human friend.

I gritted my teeth. "No," I said with a shake of my head. "We will be moving the castle today. Make sure she remains with you. Do not let the girl out of your sight."

Groffet nodded but remained right where he was. "Do you have the energy to move the castle?" he asked a moment later.

I saw Roan's back stiffen before I felt mine do the same. My jaw clenched. The answer was not an easy one. Truth be told, I wasn't sure if we could or if we did, what the results of the strain on our bodies would be. It didn't matter. We had to get back. We had to find her. Though we'd cut our trip short by traveling with just the three of us on horseback—it had still taken us nearly a day and a half to return. Added to the fact that none of us had slept or eaten much since the Changeling had been taken … we were not at our most powerful.

"It will happen," Roan stated before pushing past the dwarf. "We will find a way."

With that, he took off. Orion didn't hesitate to follow him, and I was left standing between their retreating backs and Groffet's knowing look. I leveled him with a glare when still he hadn't said anything. "Speak your piece," I commanded. "And then be gone."

He sighed, shaking his head. "If you overexert your strengths—even between the three of you—it may damage your magic abilities," he stated. "You're all still young. You are powerful, but none of you have yet come into your full potential. If you damage your bodies now, you may never reach it."

I knew he was right, loathe as I was to admit it, but it no longer mattered. I would push my body to the brink of death if it meant saving that damn Changeling. She had weaseled her way into our Court, into my throne brothers' beds, and into our lives. When I didn't respond, he heaved another great sigh and turned around to waddle away.

My feet carried me to the Lanuaet chamber where Orion and Roan were already waiting. As soon as I stepped inside, their heads lifted and their eyes met mine.

"We will need replenishment when we get there," I stated as we gathered around the orb above us. It buzzed with barely repressed magical energy. The feel of it was like lightning grazing my skin as I moved closer.

"You may take a lover," Roan grunted as he lifted his arms, "but I will not."

"*No.*" The word barked out of my mouth, harsh and violent. Roan's arms paused and his head turned towards me. He arched one singular brow. "I will take matters into my own hands as I suspect you will as well."

"It will not be enough," Orion said.

No, it wouldn't. Masturbation only did so much for the healing of sexual energy, but then again, I had waited long enough—repressed my attraction to the Changeling long enough—that nothing else would do now. There wasn't a single body within the walls of our Court that I wanted but hers, and I'd finally decided that I would have it or no other.

Orion took a step closer to the Lanuaet. I closed my eyes and lifted my arms. Already, I could feel the orbs need to devour. "To the human realm," I said, reopening them and fixing my gaze on the clouded magical element hovering just out of physical reach. It had all started with this sacred piece of Fae energy. The Lanuaet had landed us in the middle of Amnestia and we'd found who was likely the last of her line. This time, it would bring us back to her or her back to us. Either way, it didn't matter so long as she was within our reach once more.

"To the human realm," they repeated back.

At once, the orb began to glow and spin. The floor beneath our feet trembled and swayed as the castle reacted to the Lanuaet's power. I stood my ground as the world grew fuzzy, my vision blurring into obscurity. Sweat beads slid down my back until the droplets became rivers, soaking through my shirt, making the fabric cling to my skin. My muscles strained and my hearing disappeared completely as my magic was sucked from my every pore.

Pain rocketed up my spine, daggers in my temples. None of it mattered.

None of it but *her*.

CHAPTER FOUR

CRESS

I heard the footsteps before the keys in the lock. My head jerked up from its resting place upon my knees as the door to my prison swung open. Unfamiliar guards strode inside. I glanced behind them, but there was no Tyr. On shaky legs, I tried to stand. My heart thumped in my chest.

"What's going on?" I demanded. "Why are you here?"

"Turn around," one of them commanded.

"No!" I took a wary step back and glared at them. "Not a chance."

One of them removed a sword and brandished it at me. "We were told to bring you before his Royal Highness. King Felix has commanded that you be presented. He did not say you had to be unharmed. Come with us willingly or else."

I hesitated. "W-why do you want me to turn around?"

"You must be restrained," the second one said, producing a pair of thick metal cuffs.

I swallowed nervously. "Is that silver?"

He nodded. "Of course."

Shit. Shit. Shit. My mind whirled with thoughts. What to do? My eyes darted to the half open door. There was no way I'd be able to make it past them and out the door before they caught me, was there? And even if I did, what could I do? Never in my life had I been inside the King of Amnestia's palace. I didn't know where I was. There were no escape routes in my mind. Only this ever increasing need to flee.

My throat burned as I slowly turned and presented the guards with my back. The sound of scuffed boots thudding against the ground as they approached ratcheted up my fear. For a split second, a thought crossed my mind.

If only Roan or Orion were here. Dear Coreliath, I'd take even Sorrell's grumpy self. A single tear escaped and slid down my cheek as I felt my hands being pulled behind my back and locked into the restraints. Before turning back around, I sniffed hard and turned my face against my shoulder, wiping the evidence of it away. This was not the time for crying.

The guards led me out of the cell I'd been locked in for the last few days. To the right, there was a long, steep staircase. One went ahead and the other lingered at my back. I kept my head facing forward, but took the opportunity to examine my surroundings. Every several feet there was a slit window barely wide enough to fit an arm through, and certainly not a body. They would offer no escape, but they did at least give me a glimpse of the outside world.

Dark gray storm clouds hovered above us. The scent of ash and smoke was on the wind. *What was happening out there?* I wondered. I wasn't given the chance to think about it too long because as we reached the bottom of the stairs, I was pushed towards the right and down an even longer but straight corridor.

My bare feet scraped against the cold ground and I shivered as a chill stole over me. We stopped before twin arching doors made of a deep red wood. I tilted my head at the front of it. Unlike doors I'd seen in both the Court of Crimson and Court of Frost, these had been horribly burned. Yet, it looked like it had been … purposeful? Because within the burn marks, I could see a scene taking place before me. Like a tapestry or painting but in wood.

A great human King with a sword in one hand and the head of a Fae in the other. The image made me gasp and step back. A heavy hand fell on my shoulder and pushed me forward as the doors were opened and I stumbled under the urging until I fell onto my knees, wincing as the stone beneath cut a gash across one.

The scent of blood lifted to my nostrils and I lifted my head a moment later, meeting the cool, calculating gaze of my kidnapper. Tyr stood to the side with a smirk on his face and his arms crossed. He leaned against the side of the King's throne while the King himself glared down at me as if I were nothing more than a bug who'd made its unfortunate way into his food.

"So," he began. "This is one of the Fae responsible for the chaos in my Kingdom."

I blinked, but before I could respond, Tyr answered. "She is, Your Majesty," he said politely before throwing a wink my way.

Narrowing my gaze on him, I wanted nothing more than to throw him my middle finger or perhaps introduce his balls to my kneecap. Bloodied or not, I bet it would hurt. I turned my face to the King.

"That man is a Fae, too," I stated, nodding towards Tyr. "I'm not bad. I've never hurt anyone. You have no reason to keep me captive."

There was a moment of silence before the King lifted one large bushy eyebrow. "You claim that a member of my Court is a Fae?" he inquired, his voice a low rumble.

I straightened my back, not turning my gaze away. "I do."

He scowled. "How dare you, you vile piece of trash," he snarled.

"It's the truth!" I snapped. "He brought me here through a portal he created!"

"This man is one of my most trusted advisors. He has been with me for years. I would know if he were a despicable Fae," the King snapped.

"Well, that's obviously not true," I deadpanned. "I mean, he *is* a Fae and yet, you don't believe it. Why would I lie about that?"

"To try and save your own skin of course," he replied.

"What? My own skin? What have I done?" I yelled. "Nothing! I haven't done anything!"

"You are guilty of treason."

I shook my head violently. "You're making a mistake. Sure, okay, yeah, maybe I'm Fae—technically, I'm a Changeling. I was raised with humans—"

"In a convent, yes?" he interrupted me.

My head tipped back as I eyed him with confusion. "Yes," I said. "How did you—"

The King waved his meaty fist and an unfamiliar man clad in armor—like the guards had been—stepped forward, handing him a scroll. "The orphan Cressida," he stated, opening the scroll and reading from its contents. "Over a month ago, I received reports that the village that protected the convent in the hills of my Kingdom had been attacked by a female Fae and she had been chased away, but not after stealing a human child."

Nellie wasn't really a child. Then again, I didn't believe arguing that point would do me any good, but still, I shook my head. "I was raised there!" I insisted. "I didn't even know I was a Fae until the castle appeared!"

"You masqueraded as a human, deceived the people of my Kingdom, and will be sentenced to death." The King's cold eyes lifted and met mine as he snapped the scroll shut. My lips parted in shock.

Death? No. Nononono. Death was not in the plans. "You're making a mistake," I insisted. "I'm not a bad Fae, I'm good—"

"Bah!" He handed the scroll back to his soldier. "There is no such thing as a good Fae."

I frowned. "That's not true!" My hands tightened into fists within my cuffs. My skin grew heated. My breath came in ragged pants as panic began to set in. I strained against them and felt an unfamiliar burning sensation. A fog swirled in my mind and my energy suddenly left me in a rush. So quickly that had it not been for one of the guards reaching forward and clasping my shoulder, I would've fallen over. Turning my cheek, I glanced over my shoulder.

What was happening to me? Why couldn't I think straight?

"I see the silver cuffs are coming in handy," Tyr said with a small chuckle.

I whipped my head back around and stared at him. He'd done this? He knew what silver did to Fae. Wait? This was silver and it was weakening me. Had it happened? Had my powers finally come to the fore-front? The physician at the Court of Frost had said my Fae powers were weak, practically nonexistent. Could I … I considered what to do, but no matter how heated my skin grew, as soon as I felt a tingle of magical energy pour into it, it was quickly washed away by the effect of the silver.

"I'm innocent," I mumbled. "I haven't done anything wrong."

"You are Fae and you are no innocent." The King strode down the steps of his throne until he stood right before me. My head fell back onto my shoulders and I looked up into his older, scarred face. *What had he done to receive those scars?* I wondered. *How many had he killed in his effort to rid the world of Fae?*

It was wrong. Why couldn't he see that? Fae were part of nature. They were neither bad nor good. Just as humans were neither bad nor good.

LUCINDA DARK & HELEN SCOTT

"You destroyed a large portion of the countryside of my Kingdom, little treacherous Fae girl," he said coldly.

I had? It was growing harder and harder to think.

"In one week's time, you will be presented to the public and at dawn on the seventh day, you will be executed. Your death will mark the final battle between humans and Fae. With the help of my advisor"—my head sank forward and turned until I could see Tyr, who watched me with sinister amusement—"we will finally be rid of your dangerous race and, with your extinction, we will usher in the Age of Mankind."

Genocide. That's what he was talking about. The extinction of an entire race of creatures. The only ones who might escape would be those in Alfheim. Actually … with Tyr on the side of humans, perhaps even they weren't safe. What did he have planned? I had to find out.

"What—" I began, but the King waved his hand, cutting me off.

"Take her away," he ordered.

Hands gripped my arms and jerked me up. I bent over, breathing hard as sweat slid down my temples. An aching started at the top of my spine and ricocheted up through my skull.

"With one of your magical orbs, we will destroy you and your kind," the King called after me as I was pulled from the throne room. "Enjoy your last days on this Earth."

Despite my weakness, I struggled against the guards' grip. My vision blurred. "No!" I yelled. "You can't! He's not human! It's all a trap!"

I argued. I fought. I struggled. But the throne doors closed behind me as I was hauled up and over a man's shoulder and, just before the black creeping at the edges of my vision overtook me completely, I saw the image of a human King with the head of a Fae. My mind replaced the burned portrait of a generic head with that of first Roan's then Orion's and finally Sorrell's.

No matter what, I had to stop this.

CHAPTER FIVE

ORION

B y the time we got back to the Crimson Court, I was ready to throttle anyone who got in my way. We needed to move the castle, so that was what we did, just the three of us, dragging it back to Amnestia. I couldn't lie, it was harder without Cress there.

Well, if I was being honest, everything was harder without her.

Moving the castle seemed to drain us all more than usual, and since we weren't about to go to bed with any of the other Court ladies it meant that it was going to take us a while to recover our power after such a taxing task. We each sat there for a while after we'd landed just trying to gather ourselves together.

"We should check on the human girl," Roan said quietly.

The three of us pushed to our feet and began to make our way to the library. I wasn't sure if it was just me, but the hallways felt so much longer and darker. Even though we were back in Amnestia, we didn't have a plan on how to find Cress, and every time I even thought about it my mind went on the fritz, panic and darkness clouding it.

Finally, the large wooden doors of the library loomed in front of us and my legs almost gave out in relief. The trek from the Lanuaet to the library had never felt so long before. As I looked at my throne brothers, I knew I wasn't the only one feeling the effects of getting the castle out of the Fae realm and back to Amnestia.

When we pushed the doors open my heart stopped as I saw Nellie, in all her human glory, sitting there chatting with a young Fae male. The three of us froze as we each took in the scene before us. Nellie and her Fae companion looked up at us as we entered, the blood draining from the male's face.

"What is he doing here? And with her?" Sorrell said, stabbing a finger in the direction of Nellie and her companion as Groffet came around the desk area.

"I-I-I've helped Groffet in the past, my Lord," the Fae male said, speaking up unexpectedly. From the looks of him, pale and rather scrawny looking, I'd expected him to cower, especially in the face of Sorrell's anger, but he didn't. He may have been a lesser male, but he was brave and stood his ground, something I found impressive.

"Ash is trustworthy. He has helped me on many occasions, and I know he wouldn't betray us or Ms. Nellie over there. He'll keep his mouth shut if he knows what's good for him," Groffet said as he crossed his arms over his chest, daring Sorrell to disagree with him.

Of course none of us did. We were all smarter than that. Disagreeing with Groffet when he felt strongly about something was like yelling into the wind. It might be heard, but it didn't stick around. Nor did it change a damn thing.

"Fine," I growled before either of the others could say anything more.

Roan stepped in and leveled both Groffet and the male Fae, Ash, with a dark look. "We need to speak with the…" He flicked a glance between them and surprisingly, instead of saying "human" he spoke the girl's name. "We must speak with Nellie."

"What's wrong?" she asked, and then she seemed to realize something. Her eyes roamed between us, scanning for something—Cress—and when her search came up empty, a worried frown turned her lips down. "Where's Cress?" she asked.

A dark, sinister feeling stabbed me in the gut, and having felt this particular emotion many times before, I could easily place it. Guilt. The vile creature clawed at my insides, laughing as it reminded me that this girl's friend, someone we had—*someone I had*—sworn to protect had not returned with us. Nellie's gaze pleaded with us, as if she could sense the onslaught of bad news and still hoped that her instincts were wrong.

It shredded something inside me to confirm her obvious fears. Except, I didn't get the chance. My answer was interrupted by another.

"She was taken." Sorrell's voice was icy as the

temperature of the room dropped. A wave of cold air washed outwardly from his figure, visible only in the way Nellie shivered and stepped closer to her newfound friend. His anger was palpable.

"What do you mean t-taken?" Nellie stuttered, eyes round, luminous. Lost. I gritted my teeth when she shook her head and seemed to suck all of that fear back inside herself as she took a step towards us, a brighter fury coming forth. "Where is she?" she demanded. "What's happened to her?" Were she Fae, I suspect, the fire in her eyes might rival even Roan's. Unfortunately for her, however, she was not. The girl possessed no magic, and in our Court, she was nothing but a guest— the guest of a lost Changeling who had been stolen from us—and she was precariously close to the edge of both of my throne brothers' tolerance for humans.

"The fault is mine," I said quietly. "It was my brother that took her." My blood brother. The wicked soul that he was. Cruel. Senseless. And soon to be very, very dead. I sucked in a breath before continuing. "Tyr is using Cress to get to me, *to us*," I corrected, "and because of my inability to predict his behavior, she's now paying the price." Nellie's eyelashes flickered as she stared at me in cold shock. "We will figure out how to find her," I assured the human girl. "Of that, you can be sure. I will find Cress and I will bring her back." I turned to Groffet and swelled with breath as I spoke to him directly. "And I have come to request your assistance with this matter."

"It's *not* your fault," Roan snapped before Groffet could reply.

Blinking, I glanced in his direction only to find him

glaring at me with a burning rage. Of course he would not want to blame me. Roan, for all his faults and arrogance, would not blame me for what was so clearly the result of my failures. Cress's abduction, however, *was* my fault. Tyr was *my* brother. Everything he did was to get to me, or to get around me, or to torture me somehow. Why? I didn't know. All I knew was that it had been this way since I was young. Perhaps it was simply how Midnight Fae were, and I was the peculiar one for not falling in line. I never should have let him see how much Cress meant to me.

When I returned my gaze to the human, Nellie was watching me, her eyes glistening in the low light of the library as silent tears streamed down her face. "What's he going to do to her?" she asked shakily.

I opened my mouth to respond, but nothing came out. There were so many cruel things Tyr was capable of. Things I, myself, had experienced, but for some reason when I tried to think of them—it only made me sick. I didn't want to tell this girl the horrors I'd known at the hand of my brother, and the possible torment Cress could be going through even as we spoke.

Roan saved me. "He enjoys mental games," he said. "But Cress is strong. She knows we would never leave her with him. We're going to get her back before anything can happen to her, so don't worry about it."

"Something bad has already happened," Nellie replied. "Cress is gone!" Fat tears began to slide from the girl's eyes as she inhaled trembling breaths, looking like one strong push would break her into a million pieces. I couldn't say I blamed her. I didn't. The mere sight of her, so distressed and horrified over her friend's disappearance made the sick feeling in my gut even more painful. I closed my eyes and relished in that pain. I deserved it.

When I opened my eyes again, anger and despair warred on the human's face. Her words, however, had pushed Roan too far. The icy chill of the room faded as Roan's rage grew hotter.

"We will get her back," he insisted. "She will be fine. Cress will return and when she does, she will become my bride. I will ensure that nothing and no one ever thinks to take her from my side again."

"Our side," Sorrell muttered a beat later. No one agreed, but neither did any of us deny the statement. The fact remained that Cress had become our center in a short amount of time. She was wild and reckless. A breath of fresh air that we so desperately craved and needed after having been locked in our Courts for too long. Perhaps ... a thought occurred to me. Perhaps the hatred between humans and Faekind had finally reached its peak. Gods knew we were tired of the war. It could not go on forever.

But before we could focus on that, we needed to get her back. Cress was our utmost priority.

"Bride?" Nellie stared at Roan in shock, her mouth agape. "You're going to marry her?" She didn't even comment on Sorrell's quiet statement. Perhaps she hadn't heard.

Roan nodded once. "Yes. Cress is Fae whether or not she was raised by your people, she is ours now, and ours she will remain."

The Fae male, Ash, rushed forward and took Nellie's hands in his before he turned her to face him. "The Princes will figure it out. I'm sure they are just as upset as you are. Trust them to get your friend back," he said quickly, his gaze flicking up to us as if to sense whether or not his words were accepted. When his eyes landed on mine, I nodded once to assure him.

Nellie looked up into his face, her tears falling harder, and then, with a surprising amount of strength, she crushed herself against the male's front and openly sobbed. Without a second thought, Ash scooped her up so she was cradled in his arms, her own tangled around his neck as she buried her face in his chest and cried. After a beat, he lifted his gaze from her head to the rest of us. "May I please take her back to her chambers?" he asked gently. "I promise to stay with her and ensure she rests, if it's permitted."

Groffet was the one that answered. "I think that's a sane idea," he said with a huff. "Take the girl back and watch over her, Ash." The male nodded and hurried from the room, bowing slightly to the rest of us as he passed by. "Now then." Groffet lifted his head and narrowed his eyes at the three of us. "Come, let us propose a strategy to retrieve the Changeling."

The three of us—Sorrell, Roan, and I—followed him as we moved towards the library's main open area. Roan immediately plopped down next to the fire. Sorrell wandered over to the open window, and I took my place in one of the three nook seats set within the walls surrounding the space. With the wall at my back and the open space in front of me, I felt marginally enclosed, as if I were sitting within the wall, itself, watching the scene before me even as I channeled my inner thoughts to calm and focus.

"The Changeling was taken," Groffet said the words, but they were not a question.

Regardless, Roan answered. "Yes."

Groffet nodded and hobbled over to a table stacked high with tomes and volumes. He grunted and muttered beneath his breath as he searched, pulling book after book and checking their contents. If he found one satisfying, he set it on the ground and if it wasn't, he tossed it.

"Let's see," he began. "You could try and track her? Scry for her?"

"Already tried that." Sorrell's tone was biting as though he was insulted that Groffet would suggest something so simple.

"And what about the Midnight Heir?" Groffet asked, one bushy brow rising as he glared back at the Prince of Frost. "Did you attempt to track him?" Silence. Groffet huffed out a breath before selecting a particularly hefty looking volume and moving over to the three of us. "If he's the one that took her maybe tracking him will lead you to her?"

"Tyr has protections around him at all times to prevent that from happening," I said. "It always drove our mother insane..." That is, before she actually *had* gone insane.

Groffet harrumphed at that statement, slamming the book he carried on the ground in the center of the space and flipping it open. He paged through the contents.

More muttering emanated from the small, old man, but none of it was sensical. Finally, he grunted and stopped flipping the pages. His head turned from side to side and after a moment, he lifted it.

"What about a dream spell?" I didn't have to look at the others to know that they had perked up some. Groffet noticed our captured attentions and nodded. "Yes, I think that might be good."

Sorrell took a step into the center, his arms falling away from his chest. "Someone cast one on me while we were at the Court of Frost," he announced.

Roan growled. "Why didn't you say something?" he demanded.

Sorrell didn't look at him as he replied. "I assumed it was my mother. She used to do things like that when I was a child," he explained. "It was her way of … teaching me a lesson. To say she was unhappy about Cress's presence in our Court would be an understatement. Though she didn't show her irritation as well as the Crimson Queen, my mother is not our ally."

"Do you think she could've helped Tyr?" I asked, curious. I doubted it, but I wanted to hear his response.

Sorrell's eyes found mine and he shook his head. "No. She doesn't approve of Cressida, but she has never once trusted a member of the Midnight Court. She wouldn't be working with Tyr. I suspect he's working on his own."

I nodded.

"Regardless," Roan said, bringing us back to the main point, "what would a dream spell do? We can get into contact with her, but what if she doesn't understand what's happening? Dream spells aren't always easy to perform."

"It still has potential," Groffet replied. "And whoever goes will need to be very careful with her. She is still unused to Fae magic. Treat her as though her magic is still in its infantile stage."

The only issue that remained was that none of us were particularly skilled with dream magic. Dream magic wasn't forbidden, but it also wasn't encouraged, for a reason. It was dangerous. Dreamscapes were fickle and confusing places. One wrong turn down a dark memory or a mind that was too clouded, and the caster might end up trapped in the other person's mind.

Forever.

The decision, though, was easy. If there was a chance we could get into contact with Cress, an opportunity to save her, then there was no real question as to if we would do it or not. I lifted my gaze and met each one of my brothers' before centering my attention on Groffet. "I'll do it," I announced. "And you're going to teach me, old man."

CHAPTER SIX

CRESS

The feeling of arms holding me awoke my senses. Fast. *Running. Trees blurred past. The arms that held me, however, were warm and I felt ... safe.*

Why did I feel safe? *I wondered.* Who was holding me? Was it one of the guys? *No. It didn't feel like one of them. The arms encircling my frame were much more slender than any of them. They felt almost feminine. And whoever it was that held me, did so against a soft chest. I tried to open my eyes but found that when I did everything appeared in dark and light tones of blacks, whites, and grays. Like the whole world had been leached of color.*

"How much farther?" a soft, female voice asked, her tone shaky and ... scared? It was hard to hear. The scent of something pungent and something sweet permeated the air around me and there was a sudden rush of air as if a small wind tunnel had opened up and sucked me and the woman holding me through it.

"Not much farther," a male voice answered. He was close by, the sound of his voice soothing, but there was no disguising that he, too, was uncertain of something. His tone, although strong, was tight—as if pulled taut from some sort of strong emotion.

"Henri," the woman called. "Henri!"

"Keep going, Marcella. We have to. They're tracking us."

"We can't keep running," the woman said, her fear much stronger now as she slowed to a walk and then stopped altogether. "Not with her."

Who was 'her?' *I wanted to ask. The woman above me sniffled and something wet hit my forehead and slid down the side of my face. Why was she crying? For some reason, I didn't like hearing this woman's pain. It made something in my chest tighten. I wanted to tell her everything would be okay even if I didn't know exactly what was going on.*

"Marci." The man's voice grew closer and then the warmth I felt being cuddled into the woman's breast was increased as he wrapped his arms around both her and me. "It's going to be okay, but we have to keep moving."

The woman continued to cry and other than a few breathy gasps, she kept her pain and sorrow and fear to a quiet murmur. When she finally regained the ability to speak, she pushed back against the man with one arm. My eyes flickered between the two of them. I could make out their heads, bent over mine, but not their features. It was as if someone had blurred out what they looked like and left only the vaguest of outlines for me to draw information from. What I could tell, though, was that they were both looking down at me.

"We have to leave her behind," the woman said.

Silence. Then, "Are you sure?" The man sounded strained as if it cost him to even say the words, to even consider the woman's claim.

The woman shook her head. "No. I'm not sure of anything anymore," she whispered in the darkness of the forest. "I thought we could trust the Courts. I thought our friends would survive. I've thought so many things, Henri. I don't trust my instincts anymore. But I think ... this time, maybe ... her best chance is away from us. With the humans."

That's when it hit me. Who these people really were. What this was. It wasn't a dream. It was a memory. Why had I recalled this now? What was the point of this memory surfacing after so long? I couldn't make sense of the reason, but the truth of it could be felt in the fires of my veins. I knew these two people. These were my parents. My real parents. It all became too much for me. I opened my mouth—to say what, I didn't know—but before I could say anything, a horrifying squalling noise erupted from my throat.

"Oh, no, my dear." Marci—the woman, my mother—shushed me, rocking me in her arms back and forth. "Oh, you poor thing. I know, my darling. It's scary, but trust me—trust us—we love you. We only want what's best for you."

"We want her to live," Henri, my father, said. "And if we're going to do that, we need to find a place to leave her, now, before they catch up with us."

"The humans," she said. "They'll take her in."

"We can't say what she is," Henri replied.

My mother's head shook. "No, we won't even see them." She started moving again. "There's an abbey not far from here. We can leave her there. On their doorstep. The nuns of Coreliath will take her in."

"Hold on." The sound of heavy footsteps stomping back to the two of us sounded in my ears. "If we're going to do this, my love, we have to protect her from them as well. The humans will take her in, but she'll start showing signs of her magic soon. We have to..." He trailed off, the hoarseness of his voice becoming too much for him.

"Yes," my mother finished for him. "You're right." Another tear fell onto my face. "Alright then." She reached out and took his hand, drawing him closer, once more, to the two of us. "Then let us cast it."

A wide, masculine palm landed gently on my cheek. My father's thumb stroked down my smooth skin. "Our little Princess," he murmured. "How I wish things had been different for you. How difficult your life will be. I hope one day, you can forgive us for this."

Forgive them? What were they going to ... I screamed as I felt something moving in me as they began to speak. Their words were hard to understand. I didn't hear them with my ears but in my mind as something wove into my body, beneath my skin. Far beyond the recesses of my mind, I heard a door slam. Was that real or was it my imagination?

Everything grew heavy. My limbs. My eyelids. Darkness encroached. A weight landed on my chest, and suddenly my mother's arms fell away and I descended into a dark oblivion.

"Cress?" a voice called out to me in the darkness. "Cress, are you there, sweetheart?" I recognized the sound. It was someone I knew. Someone I cared for. Who? Where was I?

Two strong arms came around me, lifting me back out of the shadows, and I gasped as my eyes popped open. Orion's face appeared over me and as I sat up and looked around, I realized my memory had faded. No longer was I in the forest with the man and woman. I was sitting in a stone room, not unlike my cell except there was no furniture and no door. None of that mattered right then because Orion was there!

"Orion!" I launched myself into his arms, clinging tightly. He returned my embrace without reserve, his arms banding around me as he squeezed me right back. "Oh, I'm so glad you're here," I whispered thickly against his chest.

"Of course I'm here," he said after a moment. "I'll always come for you when you need me."

I let myself have a few more moments with him, but when I realized that this wasn't exactly reality either and it wasn't possible for Orion to be locked in a stone room with no entrance with me, I pulled back. "What's going on?" I asked. "What are you—"

"Cress." He stopped me, his dark eyes looking down at me through even darker lashes.

I didn't need to say it, but I did nonetheless. "This isn't real," I whispered. "Is it?"

He shook his head. "This is merely a dream. I'm here because we're searching for you, Sorrell, Roan, and I. I need you to give me some information about where you are. Anything can help. Do you remember—"

"I know where I am," I interrupted him quickly.

His brows rose in surprise as if he hadn't expected that. "You do?"

I nodded. "I'm in Amnestia," I said, and then with a sharp inhale, I told him the next part. "I'm in the King's prison tower," I admitted. "Tyr's working with King Felix. The King has no idea that he's a Fae. Orion, it's bad. Tyr's planning to let the humans and Fae destroy each other. I don't know how long he's been planning this, but there's going to be a battle—"

"Shhhh." Orion's heavy hand stroked down the side of my face as he quieted me. "It's going to be okay." His eyes were sharp when they connected with mine. "Go slow. Tell me everything, and then when you wake, know that we are coming for you."

"He's going to execute me," I said, my lips trembling. I hadn't wanted to admit it before, but sitting here, in Orion's lap, my fear was impossible to disguise. I couldn't deny it or hide it any longer. "On the seventh day of my imprisonment," I continued. "At dawn. Orion … it's coming soon."

"No," he growled the word, palming the back of my head and bringing me closer until his forehead pressed to mine. "We will not let that happen."

"But—" He didn't let me finish. Orion's lips crashed down hard on mine and he swallowed my words, draining my fear with his mouth. His tongue moved against mine and I felt myself caving to his ministrations. My whole body rocked into his and before I knew it, my fingers were sinking into the silky dark strands of his hair. I clambered onto his lap, sliding my legs around his waist until the familiar feel of his cock pressed against my core.

Orion pulled away long enough to emit another growl as he pushed his hips up into me, as if he couldn't even help himself. "I'm sorry, Cress," he said, his voice trembling. "So fucking sorry. I will find you. I will save you. Believe me, sweetheart. I will—"

"I do," I said, cutting him off.

Orion tilted his head down, closed his eyes, and kept going as though I hadn't spoken. "When we free you," he said. "I'll leave." Ice washed through my veins and I reared back,

47

shocked. "I'll make sure you're safe and then I'll make sure I'm never the cause for something like this again."

Anger and pain sliced into my chest. I pressed my lips together and fought back the sting of tears as water filled my eyes. "Orion." I cupped his face. "Orion, look at me."

His eyes opened.

Sucking in a deep breath, I pressed my lips to his in a soft, feather-light touch. And that's where I held them as I spoke in a soft whisper. "Your brother's actions are not yours," I urged. "You are not your brother. This is not your fault."

"I—"

"No," I snapped, cutting him off. I wouldn't let him say it again. I couldn't bear to hear it. "Stop it. Don't pity yourself. Don't act the martyr. Just get off your ass and come get me because, Orion, I'm scared. I'm scared and I fucking need you. Please don't leave me."

His hands clenched against my sides as if he wanted to pull away, but something—hopefully words— was preventing him from doing so. "I love you." The words were so quiet, I almost didn't hear them. They were like the sound of a bird's wings beating against the wind. There with each breath he took, but so natural, a person could forget its existence.

"I..." A tear broke through the surface and slid down the outside of my cheek. "I love you, too." I pushed him back. "Now hurry up and come get me."

He nodded, his eyes meeting mine. "I will," he said "We will. We're coming, Cress. Just hang on."

Another tear slid down my opposite cheek and Orion's eyes tracked it. "Okay," I whispered. "I'll wait."

I leaned forward, just wanting one last kiss. One more to hold me until I could feel his arms around me—for real.

The kiss never came.

CHAPTER SEVEN

ORION

Lips untaken were the most delicious of fruit, and that last kiss would have been the sweetest, had I not been ripped away. Dream magic was fickle like that. It was dangerous and never quite as easy as it sounded once one was encompassed in another's mind. The user never knew how long they had or when they'd be snapped back to their own reality.

My heart seized as I came back to myself in the present. Sweat dripped from my pores and slid against my temples. The urge to go to her was beyond anything I'd ever felt before. I counted each breath I took as I fought against those instincts.

I hadn't gotten the chance to kiss her, but even if I had, one single kiss wouldn't have been enough. I needed more—the weight of her in my hands, the warmth of her body pressed against mine, the scent of her filling my nose. I craved it all. Despite coming back to the world of awareness, without her, all of my senses felt dulled. But my objective had been fulfilled. We now knew where she was. The darkness that had been haunting the edges of my vision receded slightly.

Breathing in and out through my nose, air flowed into my lungs and left without leaving me feeling like I was breathing in jagged pieces of glass. The dream magic dispersed and the darkness was pushed back as I recalled the way she'd looked when she'd seen me. The beauty of her sunshine colored hair and those wide eyes. *How was it that in the course of only a few short months, I'd fallen for her as hard as I had?*

When I finally opened my eyes, the library was dark, but I was not alone. Roan and Sorrell waited just a few paces away, watching me with their brows lowered and a deeply rooted concern in their expressions. Unlike them, I could see in the darkness—it was where I'd been born and it was where I belonged. Fires flared to life, illuminating the room, as Groffet lit a few candles. I forced myself into a sitting position, reaching up and wiping the sweat from my brow.

Groffet's little body waddled to another part of the room as he continued to light the rest of the candles along the walls. Roan grunted. "Enough," he snapped, and suddenly all of the candles in the room flared to life.

The old man shot him a look that—had anyone else attempted to deliver the same harsh glare, they'd find themselves in iron chains in the dungeons. Groffet, though, was far too valuable and he knew it. Roan drew all eyes to him as he pushed away from the wall. "Well?" he demanded. "How did it go?"

Three pairs of eyes settled on me expectantly. I opened my mouth to speak and coughed. Dry and hoarse, my throat felt as though I'd not drunk water in ages. Groffet hurried over and picked up a pitcher, pouring me a glass before handing it over and stepping back. I drained the liquid, gasping in relief. Dream magic had so many irritating side effects, but I should count my blessings that I hadn't gotten lost and ended up sleeping for months, years, or worse. I should count myself lucky that I hadn't ended up dead.

"Orion," Roan said. "Did you find her?" His leg bounced up and down in front of him as though he was struggling to restrain himself. He ran his hand through his hair and pushed it back, away from his face, squashing some of the smaller flames that had flickered to life as he spoke.

"I found her, but we have a problem," I said. The hoarseness was not yet gone and I had to stop and swallow around the crusty feeling in the back of my mouth. *Problem* was an underestimation of what we faced. We had a fucking catastrophe on our hands.

"But she's alive?" Roan asked.

"Yes." I coughed again and again, had to take water from Groffet, before the feeling of being suffocated by sand and dust finally receded.

"Get on with it," Sorrel snapped. "Where is she?"

"She's being held prisoner." How could I explain the rest? The words stuck in my mind, right on the tip of my tongue. I turned my gaze down as I clutched the sides of the small settee I'd laid upon before passing into the spell. Wood creaked under my fingers as I clenched hard. "Tyr is with the human King. She's being kept in a tower within the castle." Had Tyr not considered that we would find her? I wondered. Or was he planning on it? I couldn't say. I didn't know what he was thinking at all.

"She's alive, though. We can save her as long as she's still breathing."

I hated to destroy the relief in Roan's voice, but it was necessary. I lifted my head and met his gaze, letting him feel the weight of my stare. "Tyr is antagonizing relations between Fae and the humans. The King's planning a battle of some kind."

"Like the Queens..." Sorrel said, his gaze straying away as he considered my words.

The worst part had yet to be spoken. "They're not just holding her," I said. "They're planning to execute her on the seventh day of her imprisonment."

A brief echo of silence descended and then all of their wrath broke loose. Fires erupted across Roan's scalp at the same time Sorrell's head snapped to the side and the roaring heat of my Crimson brother's fire was doused by the icy chill of his anger.

"He's going to execute her?" Sorrell roared. He stormed forward, grabbing me by the front of my shirt. His fingers clenched into the fabric and I could feel icicles forming in my lungs as he breathed in my face. "Next time," he hissed, "lead with that."

"What the fuck are we going to do?" Roan panted, his fires burning bright and fizzling out as the icy coat that was taking over the room lingered in the air above us.

"We don't have much time," I said as Sorrell released me and allowed me to stand.

"We have to move the Court again. We need to get to her. We cannot fail."

I agreed. Cress needed us, all of us.

Roan gritted his teeth and turned his back on us. His long legs ate up the distance as he paced back and forth. Sweat collected on the back of my neck and spilled down my spine with every pass he made near me. I could feel the burning fire of his emotions—untamed, uncontrolled. Wild—like him and the depth of his feeling for a unique little Changeling.

"That's the problem, though, isn't it? How are we going to move the Court again to be close enough to the King's castle to rescue her if we're all drained? Gods, how are we going to keep it hidden from the humans?" Sorrell argued. "The very second we land in Amnestia, they'll be on us like flies on cow shit." He shook his head. "We need to strategize."

He was right, we did need to strategize, but I couldn't, not when my mind was filled not just with Cress's smile, but with my own fear. I closed my eyes and recalled the image of her just before it had slipped away. In my mind's eye, I saw her before me once more. Her face was hardly illuminated, most of it cast in shadow but I could still see the way her lips trembled as she told me of her impending execution. It wouldn't happen. I would not let it.

My eyes opened. "I will return," I said abruptly.

"Orion, wait! What about—" I didn't stay to hear anymore. The doors slammed against the stone wall as I pushed out into the corridor. I couldn't take the chance that they wouldn't allow me this time—time that I very much needed. My footsteps sped up until I was well out of range.

She had been in my arms, and though I knew it had just been a fantasy, it had still felt real, and it had felt like a piercing blade through my chest to be ripped away from her again. My brothers only had to suffer through that once. It was so much worse the second time. I hadn't realized it would be like reopening an old wound and infecting it with poison. That poison slowly seeped into my mind—telling me all sorts of horrible thoughts.

Would we get to her in time? What if we were too late? What if? What if? What if?

My legs moved faster and faster, as if I could outrun those questions. I wove through the halls and up and down stairs as I headed for the one place that was mine —not part of the Castle that I shared with the others, not a public area or somewhere that anyone could simply intrude—but my own safe haven. And the first place where I had taken Cress.

The door loomed in front of me and I reached out, shoving the wood as I slammed into my chambers, turned, and locked the door. Breath was released from my chest like a cork being pulled from a wine bottle. Relief—if only for a brief moment—touched me. And then there was nothing but anger.

I took two steps into the chamber, turned, and

slammed my fist into the door. My knuckles split and pain radiated up my arm, but nothing could compare. Nothing could dampen my rage at this whole situation. Cress's abduction. The impending execution. Tyr.

Never before had I felt the same darkness that I knew was in him make itself known in me. My brother was a monster, but for years, I'd simply let it lie. He was my brother—my blood. A part of me thought that perhaps if I never admitted it, I wouldn't have to claim that piece of myself. Because as true as it was, his blood and mine were the same. His powers and mine were connected.

If he wanted to destroy the Fae and the humans then he would. And perhaps I wouldn't have cared as much as I did had it not been for his involving Cress. Whatever he had planned, it was no good, I knew that. His anger at me for forsaking the Midnight Court had caused this and therefore, I had caused this. But Tyr was smart enough to know that in taking Cress, he had earned himself no reprieve. There would be repercussions. We would come for her.

Pulling my hand away from the door, I stared down at my bruised and bleeding knuckles even as my magic worked to heal the minor damage. A heavy breath left me and I headed for the stairs, tipping my head back as my garden came into view. The very garden where I'd first lain her down and made love to her. Halfway into the garden area, my legs gave out and I crashed to the floor. Exhaustion hit me, seeping into my bones. When my hand came out to steady my weary frame, I realized that as much as my magic was trying to close the wounds—I was depleted.

I needed to replenish my magic's source. I needed to *fuck*.

But there were no women to have. No other could make me even hard enough to get the job done save for one and she was far from my grasp. My fingers clenched and scraped against the floor as I turned and laid back. No, this was a solo job. Was it as good as sharing my magical energy with another? Of course not. But it was better than nothing.

I brought up the memory of the two of us together, on that first night. My lips twitched as I recalled her nervousness. The shimmer of her sunshine hair around her shoulders as she had looked up at me with such fascination. Such a funny little creature, our Changeling. Who would have known she would come to mean so much to each of us?

My hands slipped to the waistband of my pants. I pushed them down and out of the way, raising my hips to aid the process along. I remembered the feel of Cress's soft skin against mine as she had sat astride me, grinding her pussy against my cock.

I palmed myself, gripping my shaft and slowly working my hand up and down as I let my memories and imagination run free.

My hands touched her thighs, slowly tracing upward as I held her in place for my cock to push against her folds. I could feel her heat through her clothing, and I wanted more. The soft fabric of her dress bunched in my hands and I pulled, tearing it away from her form, revealing her to me.

"You ruined another dress! This is why I wear pants. Less likely to get them torn off," she said with a huff. The smile at the end let me know she didn't really mind though.

"Maybe I'll have to start tearing your pants off you, as well, then." I grinned as the top of the dress fell away. Roan and Sorrell were there with us. Their mouths descended on each side of her neck and her head fell back in pleasure as a groan escaped her perfect lips.

I pushed up onto my elbows and sucked one of her nipples into my mouth, flicking it with my tongue and grazing it with my teeth until it was as hard as stone under my lips, then I did the same thing to the other. Her hips began to buck and grind against me and her breathing sped until I knew she was already on the edge of her first orgasm.

When I pulled away she whimpered at the loss of my touch which only made my cock throb harder. I slid my hands under her hips and lifted her slightly until the head of my cock pressed against the wet heat of her folds. I eased myself into her inch by inch and relished the hot, vice-like grip her pussy had on my cock.

Her moan as I filled her almost made me lose it right then and there, like it always did. I had to sit still for a moment, even with her squirming on top of me, as my throne brothers teased her. Finally, the tight sensation I felt right before I came passed and I ground my hips up against her, making her release a throaty moan.

I began to move against her, thrusting up into her heated core with ever increasing speed until the sound of skin smacking against skin was the only thing that filled my ears. My body ached as I filled her over and over again, needing release.

Roan's hand slid down her stomach and dipped between us, and parted her folds so he could circle her clit. His mouth dropped from her neck to the nipple that was closest to him. The pink, rosy bud disappeared into his mouth as Sorrell mimicked his action on the other side.

Cress's brows drew together and I felt the inner walls of her body tightening around my cock as we all pushed her over the edge. She screamed and her body clenched around my own, triggering my orgasm, my seed spilling into her heated core.

Except it wasn't her core at all, it was just my hand. I felt a faint buzz of magic in my veins and knew that this would only be the beginning if we wanted to move the castle again. I'd give myself a brief respite before round two, knowing that I'd do whatever I had to for us to get Cress back safely.

CHAPTER EIGHT

CRESS

My eyes cracked open, but for several long moments, all I saw was gray and blurs. My head felt like a weight had been pressing down on me for ages. My limbs felt the same. A groan bubbled up past my lips as I forced my body to the side, turning and leaning over the threadbare cot and dry heaving onto the ground. Nothing escaped my lips but spittle and gagging noises.

I closed my eyes and breathed through my nose, trying to repress the urge to heave again. There was nothing in my stomach. The only thing that came up was bile and I didn't feel like going through the burn of that. Keeping my eyes shut, I crawled off of the cot and pressed my cheek against the cool stone floor.

Sweat collected against my skin and dried there. I couldn't say how long I remained like that. It could've been minutes or hours. The sound of keys jangling in the locks of my prison roused me some time later and I peeked my eyes open, sitting up and leaning my back against the cot as an unfamiliar soldier walked in carrying a tray.

I eyed it with trepidation. *Were they really feeding a prisoner meant to die? Or were they trying to advance the process by poisoning me?* My stomach rumbled with hunger nonetheless. I looked up to the guard. He was clad in leather armor and cautious as he moved towards me with the tray.

"Here." He tossed the tray to the ground in front of me and I winced when the edge smacked into my toes. The bowl that'd been sitting on the top of it, trembled and tipped over, whatever gruel that they'd slopped into it spilling out onto the ground. I didn't care. My eyes weren't on the bowl. They were on the hunk of bread to the side. It looked a little stale, but there were no mold spots.

The guard, however, didn't turn around and walk out like I expected him to. I lifted my eyes back to his and only then did he speak. "You should be grateful," he spat at me. "His Majesty shouldn't even be feeding a vile creature such as you."

"Vile creature?" I repeated the words, confused, before I realized he meant a Fae. "I'm not a vile creature," I snapped. "I'm a person and I have a name. It's Cress."

He scoffed, his head rearing back, but his eyes stayed on me. It took a second for me to put together why he was still in the room. Despite his harsh words, he was curious. Growing up in the convent, I'd always been told similar things about Fae—that they were faithless, disloyal, and dangerous. I'd never really paid attention, but that was mostly because I'd seen, firsthand, how some of the nuns had gone against their very own teachings to display the same accusations they hurled at others.

"What makes me so bad?" I asked the man, reaching for the tipped bowl on the tray and setting it upright.

"You're Fae," he replied.

I waited a beat and when he didn't say anything more, I tipped my head at him. "And that makes me intrinsically bad?" I asked.

His eyes flashed with anger. "I know how the Faekind are," he gritted out, hanging over me with a malevolent appearance.

"Oh? If you're so knowledgeable about them," I snapped back, "then tell me what you know. What kind of Fae am I? I've never really been told—there's a lot of speculation, but no answers."

The guard crossed his arms over his chest. "I will not stand for your trickery."

"Trickery?" I shook my head. "I just asked you a question." I reached for the bread as my stomach rumbled again, the feeling of not having eaten in a long while finally clawing at my insides. "Don't blame me if you can't answer it."

"I will not fall for your spells!"

I rolled my eyes as I tore off a bite of the bread and sniffed it before popping it into my mouth. It wasn't nearly as good as the delicious rolls the pixies brought me. "If I was capable of casting a spell, don't you think

I'd use it to get myself out of here?" I asked, chewing loudly as I leveled him with one of my 'are you serious?' looks. "What's your name, anyway?" I couldn't really talk to this guy without knowing his name. I'd already introduced myself. It was a little rude that he hadn't reciprocated.

"I'm called Geoffrey."

"Well, Geoffrey," I tore off another piece as I finished swallowing the lump of soggy bread in my mouth. "Sorry to break it to you, but I'm innocent."

His arms unfolded to his sides and he stepped forward until his booted foot kicked at the edge of my tray. "Liar!" he exclaimed. "You are Fae. The King's advisor—"

"Whoa, whoa, whoa!" I said quickly. I reached back and heaved myself up onto the cot, but something about my legs felt funny—was I still weak from that dream I had of Orion?—I shook my head. I needed to worry about what was in front of me right now. Orion would inform the others of my predicament. They'd do something. Soon. I returned my attention to the man in front of me. "I never said I wasn't Fae." He stopped moving, and I continued. "I said I was innocent."

Geoffrey's eyes followed my movements as I finished eating the bread. "No Fae is truly innocent," he finally replied.

I frowned. I had yet to see them, but I had to assume there were Fae children. I'd been a child once, myself. "Of course there are innocent Fae," I told him. "Just like you, Fae have babies. There are those who hate this war just as much as we do."

"Fae hate war?" The sound that he made was decisively not amused. "Fae live for war." This time when he looked at me, it was less of a stare and more like he was seeing through me. Into another place. Into another time. And the expression on his face made my chest hurt.

"Have you ever seen a Fae spew fire?" he asked, but before I could answer, he continued talking. "I have seen the beasts that they are. They can turn an entire battlefield into ash in a second if they're so inclined. The only reason they even put up with this war is because it amuses them. They love it. They crave it."

"That's not true!" I burst out. "They hate war just as much as we do!" How could I make him understand? It's not humans or Fae. It's Tyr! "Your King has no idea what's happening!" I confessed in a rush of breath. "His advisor is a Fae. Tyr is—"

I didn't see the slap coming until it was too late, but I certainly felt it as the back of his gloved knuckles smacked into my cheek and sent me sprawling. My foot tripped over the wooden bowl still sitting upon the tray on the ground and the rest of the gruel went flying, chunks of it hitting my leg as I fell. Heat radiated from my cheek and for several long beats of silence, all I could do was sit there. Shocked … confused … angry.

A heat built within me, sliding through my limbs. It infused my very soul.

"You are nothing but a disgusting liar!" Geoffrey spat at me. A bit of his spittle landed on my cheek, and a sizzling sound reached my ears. I blinked and lifted my palm to my cheek—the same cheek he'd backhanded. My hand was glowing—it was dim, barely there, but visible. As if a light had been turned on beneath my skin. "Our King is great! He is going to be the one to save us! You and your kind should never have been brought into existence. I curse the Gods who created you for they are not the same who created man!"

Geoffrey's words flew out at a great speed. So loud that they echoed in my mind. I heard them but didn't comprehend each word until several seconds after it was spoken. I was still too shocked. I'd been raised by humans my whole life. Up until a few short months ago, I'd thought I was human, but never had I suffered this kind of hatred in another creature as he so obviously did.

Not even the nuns. Some had been cruel. Downright uncaring to an orphan with nowhere else to go, but never before had I hated another person. Ariana was the first—I hated her—but not in the same way this man hated Fae.

As I raised my head and slowly got off the floor, I listened to him spew his anger and all I saw in him was sadness. *Why was there so much sorrow emanating from him? Why did it pierce me so?*

The louder he screamed, the more I felt it. Until it was as if a thousand knives were stabbing into my skin. *Stop!* I wanted to cry out. *Please! It hurts!*

I didn't know what led me to reach for him, but it was intrinsic knowing—I had to touch him. Or else something bad would happen. He didn't even see it coming. One moment he was there, screaming his lungs out, and then my fingers had barely brushed the side of his arm.

Geoffrey froze, his lips parted, but no words came out. His eyes dropped down to where I touched him and they widened when he realized that my skin was illuminated. It wasn't enough. My arm rose, further and further, until I felt flesh against the inside of my palm. The side of his neck and then his cheek as I pulled it in my hand. All of the pain I felt in him was magnified at the very moment of contact. Tears sprang to my eyes as a vision appeared in my mind's eye.

A beautiful woman with a happy, smiling face. Long dark hair. Running away from me ... no, not me. Him. These were *his* memories I was seeing. And something awful was about to happen.

The memory changed, morphing into something darker. Clouds rolled into the sky of the image I was seeing. Lightning and fire. Brimstone and death. I could smell it as if it were actually there. That same woman's face appeared once more, only this time, she wasn't smiling. She was crying. Silent tears ran down her face, clearing it from the sudden grime and blood that appeared on her skin.

"Amelie..." Geoffrey's croak broke the spell that had woven itself over the two of us. He blinked and then I did as well. The memory was gone, but the sorrow remained. "How did you...?"

"I-I don't know," I answered him honestly.

He stumbled back, trembling even as I tried to reach for him again. I didn't know why I wanted to comfort him so, not when he was just saying such horrible things about Fae—about creatures like Orion and Roan and Sorrell. Perhaps it was a deeper part of my being, the part that understood loss and pain the same that he had experienced.

"Keep away from me!" he said as he hurried towards the door. He banged on it once and it opened.

There was no chance to go after him. And even if I'd managed to, what would I have done? The door banged shut behind him as he disappeared. I lowered my arm and sank back down onto the floor, drawing my dirty legs up and wrapping my arms around them as I let myself cry.

She must have been someone very important to him, I realized. And even if she'd died because of the war, that didn't mean that others hadn't suffered a similar loss.

A new memory arose in the back of my mind—both a recent and old one. My parents in the forest. Was it real? I wondered. Had they really left me to save my life?

I sniffed hard and pressed my forehead to the tops of my knees. Hopefully, their sacrifice hadn't been in vain because even if I wanted to save the Kingdom and the Fae from their own deep rooted hatred of each other, there was no way I could do it from a prison cell, and there was even less of a way for me to do it once I was dead.

CHAPTER NINE

CRESS

I stared at the gray stone of my cell wall. A bug crawled out of the cracks, skittered up the brick and into another one. My head thumped back against the wall at my back. How long had I been here? How much longer did I have to go?

Geoffrey hadn't returned, but I wasn't left alone. Other guards must've been assigned to me because they came in random intervals I could never time. Some dropped off buckets of water, and some had chucked crusts of bread at me. Others had just slid the metal covering over the window at the top of the door, far higher than I could reach, and spat at me before walking away. Time was growing shorter and shorter.

Even as my stomach grumbled and growled for food, I found myself curling in against it—cradling it and wondering ... had my mother been this afraid before she died? Had she known that I was safe when she was taken into the realm of the Gods? Had my father?

My hands tingled as I lifted my head and stared at the black marks against the stone. My fingers twitched, little sparks coming to life, but a split second later they dispersed. Magic wasn't as easy as I had expected it to be. Roan had made it seem so simple. When he got mad, flames had just erupted without any actual effort on his part. These last few days, I'd tried repeatedly to conjure the feeling of magic I'd experienced before. The only time I managed to make anything tangible was when I thought of Tyr. The anger pressed forward and shot out of my fingertips, leaving scorch marks on the walls of my cell, puny though they were. That, too, left me feeling exhausted, and I had to conserve my energy if I was going to try and escape this place. I was sure the guys had a plan, but unfortunately, with them out there and me in here, there was no real way for us to communicate or for them to let me know what it was that they were planning. As each day passed, my panic and fear only grew.

Each time I tried to summon my magic on purpose, it felt like I was simply trying to move something with my mind. *Could Fae do that?* I wondered. If they could, I hadn't figured out how to do that either.

There was no doubt that I had magic—Groffet's exercise had proven that weeks ago. But useable magic? Whatever magic I did have, wasn't enough to aid in any kind of escape attempt. My frustration mounted. What good was it being Fae if I couldn't *do* anything? I couldn't rescue myself. I couldn't protect myself from

Tyr. I couldn't even get Roan's mother to like me and I was going to be her daughter-in-law—that is if I found a way out of my current situation. I wondered if I could, if that would impress her. Probably not.

I closed my eyes and resolved to try conjuring another bright orb of light and fire. Just as I decided that I was ready to try it once more, the lock on my cell door clanged as a key was inserted. I jerked my head to the side and shoved my hand under my butt to stifle any lingering brightness as the door opened.

A guard appeared, followed by two more. My heart pounded as they looked down on me. The first stepped forward and gestured for me to stand. "You're being allowed to bathe before your execution tomorrow as a courtesy to the executioner. If you fight or try to escape, we are authorized to beat you into submission and bathe you ourselves." He gave me a dark look. "You will not like our method of bathing."

I had no doubt he was right. I nodded even as my stomach twisted into a knot and his words hit me a second time. *Tomorrow? I was going to be executed tomorrow?* Shock and horror wrapped around my heart, squeezing the organ in my chest so tightly that I feared it would burst.

A second guard strode forward, slipping a keyring from the belt at his hip. "Up," he commanded as he approached.

I stood and locked my knees to prevent myself from falling over as painful prickles assaulted my limbs. I'd been lying down for too long and my legs had gone numb.

The third guard remained silent, but I could feel his beady eyes watching my every movement. I wondered if they would try to fabricate an escape attempt on my part simply to be given the pleasure of beating me. "Follow me," the first guard ordered, turning back towards the door.

The second guard who had unlocked my shackles prodded me in the side roughly to get me moving. My knees felt like they would give way at any moment, but I took a wobbly step forward and then another and another. As soon as I got close enough to the wall to use it as a crutch, I did. My hands fell on the stone and then slipped alongside the rough surface as I followed behind the first guard, out of my cell.

My original hope when they had told me I'd be leaving my cell was that the bathing chambers would be somewhere else. Despite their threat to beat me if I attempted an escape, I was planning to try, but as soon as I realized that they weren't taking me out of the tower, my hopes plummeted. No, wherever they were taking me, it was clear that it was in the same tower—likely just a different room made for bathing.

I was led to a small chamber barely bigger than the cell I'd been in for the last week. The door slid open and I was shoved inside. There was nothing in it save for one barrel in the middle filled to the brim with water. I sighed. It was still better than nothing, I supposed. The fact was, being cooped up in the tower's cell for a week, I was starting to smell like the backside of a horse. My nose wrinkled as I leaned down and sniffed my shirt to confirm. Yup. Definitely needed this.

"Soap." One of the guards tapped a bar of soap on my shoulder, and I took it. "That's your tub, beast."

"Thanks," I said. Beast, indeed. I shook my head and reached a finger into the barrel. The water was cold. I shivered just as it reached up to my second knuckle. This would not be a long bath, that was for damn sure.

I waited for the sound of the door to close as they left, but when it never came, I turned back and my eyes widened. The three guards stood there, blocking the exit with their bodies as they glared at me. "Um … are you going to leave?" I prompted. "I can't get undressed and bathe with you in here."

"You cannot be trusted," the first and tallest one snapped. "Get on with it."

Horror sank into me. They were serious. "Can you at least turn around?" I replied. The Princes were one thing, but there was no way I'd feel comfortable letting just anyone see me naked!

The head guard narrowed his dark eyes on me before slowly turning to face the door. He then nudged the other two and they did the same. It wasn't much, but it was better than having their eyes watching me as I undressed. I reached up to my shoulders and grasped the fabric around my chest and began to tug upward until I stripped the dress off. After I was finished undressing, I realized that the chamber itself was just as cold as the water. Goosebumps broke out over my skin, and I couldn't stop shivers from stealing over my body.

"Hurry it up," one of the guards snapped.

I hooked my foot around the stool next to the barrel and dragged it forward, then using it as a step ladder, I climbed up and into the barrel. Water sloshed out over the sides and I gasped as the cold water sank into my skin. The guard on the farthest right turned and looked back.

I squeaked and sank into the barrel up to my shoulders until the majority of my body was covered. "Turn around!" I huffed.

He glared at me but turned back. There was no getting used to the cold water. It just wasn't possible, but just dipping myself into the barrel made me feel ten times better than I had the hour before. I turned my body so that even if they looked back at me, all they would see was my spine. With care, I lathered up the hard cake of soap and used it to try and scrub the worst of the grime and dirt off my skin.

The soap they'd given me wasn't great. It scraped across my skin, leaving light pink marks. Once I'd done my best with my body, I moved the lather up to my hair. My hair was normally a golden blonde but now was a dirty light brown. I stroked the soap down my scalp, trying to wash the strands from the roots to the ends.

Once I was done, I dropped the soap out of the side of the barrel, covered my mouth and nose, and dunked my whole head underwater, scratching furiously at my scalp until I was sure I'd done my best to get clean. I popped up out of the top of the barrel with a loud gasp and slicked my hair back over my shoulders.

My teeth were chattering as I began finger combing the tangles from my hair. I was so focused on my business that I didn't even notice when the door to the bathing chamber opened once more. I dunked a second time, and when I reemerged, a new—and unfortunately familiar—voice stood out among the rest.

Tyr. I looked down. Of course, he would come when I was most vulnerable. Naked and cold.

"You can wait outside," he said as I scrambled to think of a way to get out and get dressed without being seen. It was impossible with how small and barren this room actually was. Me and the three guards were far too many people inside of it as it was.

"Sir, we're supposed to keep the prisoner under guard at all times," the head guard replied.

"You think I can't handle a small Fae woman who doesn't even have any power to speak of?" Tyr demanded.

"Of course not, sir."

There was a moment of silence where I prayed to the Gods that the guards wouldn't leave, but then, "We'll be right outside, sir." I could have cried or thrown something at the head of the guard who'd answered. Number three. The dickbag.

"Of course," Tyr replied lightly.

I peeked over my shoulder and watched as he stepped aside and the guards moved into a single file line as they exited the room. The door closed behind them and I jumped when the sound of a key in the lock turned, leaving me alone. With a fucking monster.

Tyr pivoted and met my gaze. A smile came to his face. "I wanted to come and make sure you weren't planning any last minute escape attempts," he said as he rounded the barrel, moving steadily closer and closer as his footsteps echoed up the walls. I sank deep into the water and crossed my arms over my chest even as I glared at him. "Your execution is currently set for tomorrow morning, just as the sun rises over the mountains. It's quite kind of His Majesty, don't you think?" he asked. "You'll be able to feel the sun on your face one last time before you die."

"How would I even begin to escape?" I asked. "I'm just one person. And as you so kindly said yourself, I'm not even powerful." His eyes dipped down to where my arms crossed over my front and I wanted to let go for just a moment—not caring if I flashed him everything— if only I could hit him. Give him a nice, clean throat punch right to his stupid neck. You know, now that I was close to him—he wasn't nearly as handsome as Orion. His neck was too long. His face too angular. His eyes too evil.

Slowly, as if he relished in making me feel uncomfortable, his eyes traveled up from my naked chest to my neck to my face. His smile was smug. "I also came because I heard you've been telling stories, Cressida." He tsked at me. "Naughty. Naughty. Telling all of those fine guards out there that I'm a disgusting Fae."

"How can you say that?" I demanded. "You are. I told them the truth. You don't truly believe that Fae are disgusting—you're just using them. The truth is that you're a monster and when I get out of here, I'm going to make sure everyone knows it."

He shrugged. "Silly girl. The truth is whatever I say it is," he replied. He stepped right in front of my barrel and leaned close. "And darling..." Tyr bent closer until I could see the darkness in his eyes, the way his pupils had all but swallowed the color of his irises, "the only way you're getting out of here is when you're being led to your death. That, I can assure you, is a kinder fate than any I would've given you. You should be grateful, really. I don't hate you—I just find you a nuisance. You're in my way. Nothing more. If I truly despised you, little Changeling, you would have no barrel to hide behind."

My eyes darted to the side as a chill went down my spine. He had a point. We were alone—the two of us. He could do unimaginable things to me if he so chose. No one would stop him—no one *could* stop him. As small as it was, this barrel was the only barrier I had from him right now. He could dump me out of it if he wanted. Kick me to the floor and beat me. He had magic—magic that was far more powerful than mine. I shivered as he stared at me, his eyes somehow seeming even darker in the dim light of the bathing chambers. The singular torch on the wall flickered, growing weaker as if he willed it to do so. I shrank down even more as his hand cupped the top of the barrel. If I let him, he could snuff out all of the hope I had placed in the guys. I swallowed roughly.

"Someone will figure out what you've done and you'll be punished for it," I said. I wanted to sound strong and intimidating, but even to my own ears, my voice didn't hold the same strength his had.

"That day will never come," he said as he finally released the top of the barrel and stepped back. "For now, I'm the King's advisor. He listens to me above all others. As for the Fae, I am untouchable. The first heir to the Court of Midnight. I will have my war, little Changeling, and when it is over—the ruins of this world will be mine. I intend to build my people up from the graves I save them from. This ridiculous charade won't be needed much longer, especially after your death tomorrow. Roan and Orion will be devastated. The Crimson Prince will lose himself and my brother, my dear, sweet, weak brother will go mad—it's in the family, after all. Everything is going perfectly." Tyr circled the barrel and moved back towards the door and as he did, I turned, following him with my gaze.

"You're wrong," I said. "They will stop you—even if I die." Though I knew they wouldn't let that happen.

Tyr paused and glanced back. "Oh darling, they won't even have a chance. You are simply the match that will light the flame that will set fire to this world. Without you, those two will fall apart."

"What about Sorrell?" I demanded.

Tyr shook his head. "You should know by now," he said. "All I need to do to ruin the Prince of Frost is tear apart his friends. Your death will kill them and killing them will kill him. Now, be a good girl and die prettily tomorrow."

He banged on the door and it opened a second later, allowing for his graceful exit, but even as he stepped from the room a dark laugh echoed back to me. After his departure, I didn't even care if the guards saw me anymore. It was far too damn cold. As they stepped inside, I hurried to scramble out of the barrel. One of the guards tossed something my way—a threadbare towel. I snatched it up from the ground where it had landed and used it to quickly dry myself off.

No sooner had I yanked my dirty dress up from the floor and slipped it over my head, and one of the guards stepped forward and grasped my upper arm. "Time to go back to your cell," he said.

I didn't make another sound; I didn't even ask another question as they led me back to my original cell and shoved me inside. They shackled me back the same way I had been and as soon as the door locked behind me, I collapsed onto my cot. I clasped my hands together and prayed that the guys wouldn't be too late. I'd given Orion all the information I could. They had to be on their way by now.

The light in the room waned over the next few hours and as it did, night fell. Each minute, I realized was yet another closer to my potential death. I trusted the Princes of the Crimson Court. That was all I could do now—give them my trust and hope that they would come through.

Death wasn't something I'd ever spent much time thinking about before now. I always assumed that I could survive whatever life threw at me. I had survived the nuns. I'd survived nearly dying after Ariana had shoved me off of a wall. I'd even survived the Court of Frost. I needed to believe I would survive this as well, so I closed my eyes and conjured the happiest memories I could. It wasn't any surprise to me that they all revolved around three stubborn Fae—one masked in darkness, one in fire, and one in ice.

Yes, even Sorrell. My cold hands reached up and

touched my lips—recalling the kiss we'd shared in my bed in the Court of Frost. I knew what I wanted the rest of my life to look like, and it didn't involve me dying or us fighting a never ending war because Tyr wanted to burn it all down.

I had to believe that there was more to my existence than being used for another's gain. I would not let myself be a pawn. Be that as it may, though, the second I saw the guys again, they were going to know the meaning of pain. I was going to kick the absolute shit out of their shins. Just because I trusted those assholes didn't mean they had to leave my rescue to the last minute like this.

I settled into my cot and curled my knees up against my chest. Even with my irritation making me grumble to myself about stupid Princes and their need for perfection and leaving me in a crummy tower like this, I hoped … more than anything that even if I did die tomorrow, I'd at least be able to see them one last time.

CHAPTER TEN

ROAN

The darkness of night encroached. Muted sounds echoed from the forest at my back as I stared up at the massive structure that was the capital castle of Amnestia. Cress was there just beyond our reach. After tomorrow, though, she would be back where she belonged. With me—with *us*.

"Roan." Sorrell's quiet voice called to me from the campfire side.

I didn't respond for a moment, choosing instead to let my eyes rest upon the outside of the castle a moment longer. My eyes slid shut and an image of Cress's face came to mind. Her beautiful smile— dangerously deceptive. If she never opened her mouth, she could've masqueraded as a high born lady of any Court. It was her personality that separated her from the others. Her laughter—loud and boisterous. She was so unapologetic in her excitement and adventurous nature. Knowing she was locked away in the darkness left a pang in my heart. Her kind of light should never have to suffer this kind of atrocity, and after tomorrow, I would ensure she never would again.

"Roan." Sorrell's voice grew nearer until I could sense him standing alongside me. I opened my eyes. "Come. You need to eat and then sleep. I'll take the first watch."

I nodded and as the two of us turned back to the fires, Orion stepped out of the darkness of the trees and into our little clearing. We lifted our heads to look at him. "The Court is secured," he announced before striding forward and lowering himself into a cross-legged position next to the fire.

Fatigue pulled at my bones. I knew they could feel it too. It had been exhausting to move the castle, not only from Alfheim to the human realm but to do so once more. The three of us were drained and I knew the only surefire way to increase our energy and replenish our magic was to fuck. Too bad none of us seemed all that interested in doing so unless it was with one golden-haired, smart-mouthed Changeling.

Orion withdrew a flint stone and one of his blades, then began sharpening the end. A battle was coming and on the break of morning, it would arrive. I could feel the clinging vines of bloodshed already weaving through my body. My blood boiled. My senses—though drained—were still as sharp as ever. We were so close to her. I wanted to feel her in my arms. I wanted to press her beneath me and pound my cock into her.

"Do you think the illusion will hold?" Sorrell inquired, directing his question to Orion.

Orion's hands paused their consistent up and down movements against the blade. "Groffet has everything under control," he said. "Ash will be helping, and for our purposes, the illusion will hold for as long as it needs to."

I knew what that meant. There was no way humans wouldn't see a Fae castle so close to the human King's and not attack it. We'd had to leave it several miles behind, but that also had been far too close for comfort. The spell that Groffet had concocted to shroud our Court in a repellant illusion would do its job, though. It'd make anyone who approached it confused and lost and the closer to the castle they got, the more their minds would weave shadows and disorientation over their memories. It would, however, likely only last for the next day or so.

That wouldn't be a problem since by this time tomorrow I expected Cress to be back in our arms or the human race would go up in flames. If she were hurt in this process, I would ensure it. Their lives meant nothing in the way of my devotion to her.

"Shall we go over the plan once more?" Sorrell asked. I grunted in response, which he took as an affirmative. Lifting a slender branch in his grip, he began drawing images in the dirt. "The execution is scheduled to happen at daybreak," he began, "when the sun reaches the horizon. As soon as the sky begins to lighten on the morrow, Roan and I will head into the crowd drawn by the announcements of a Fae execution."

I scowled at that. *Yes, we had heard*. King Felix had not made the news of the capture and soon to be murder of Cress secret. Tomorrow, amidst the upheaval, there would be onlookers ready and willing to watch her die.

And none of us would let them get their wish.

"As we wait for the King to arrive and oversee the proceedings," Sorrell continued, striking a line from two x's to a circle, "Orion—you'll enter the castle while everyone is preoccupied with the execution set up."

He had to find her before she was taken to the public, I thought, feeling my muscles tense. If he didn't ... I didn't want to think of what might happen if we messed this up. We couldn't. There was too much at stake. I took a deep breath and reminded myself—that was the very reason Sorrell and I would be in the crowd. We hoped to get in and get out without a huge battle, but if things were to go awry, we would be prepared to do anything —sacrifice anyone—to get to her.

"I should be able to sense her presence with the lingering effects of the dream magic," Orion said. "I will ensure that I am not seen."

Sorrell nodded and turned his eyes back to the drawings he'd sketched out. I could only imagine what he was thinking. Considering every angle of the strategy was his specialty. Orion's was stealth. But mine ... mine was fire. Mine was only necessary if all else went wrong and for both their sake and Cress's, I hoped tomorrow would go as planned.

"Sleep, Brothers," Orion muttered a moment later. "I will take the first watch."

"I've already told Roan that I would," Sorrell replied.

Orion shook his head. "No need."

"Yes, there is," he argued. "You need sleep as much as any of us."

I snorted. "We don't need sleep," I said. "We need *her*."

Silence echoed around me in the wake of that statement. Neither of them denied the claim. I groaned and rolled to my feet. "But if you two want to argue over who'll watch first, then I suppose I'll just take the first shift of sleeping. Better make up your mind sooner or later. Wake me when it's my time."

They nodded in unison and watched me with knowing eyes as I slipped behind the next copse of trees. I strode into the forest, unconcerned by the sounds of small wild creatures skittering around in the underbrush or the little insects that crawled across my boots. They were a part of nature and no threat to me.

When I guessed I'd gone far enough, I turned my back to a large oak and sank down until my ass touched the ground. I had a violent need inside of me and as I closed my eyes and returned to the image of Cress, it surged forth.

At the camp, she'd been so soft and smooth beneath Orion and me. Her little hands had touched with an innocence but a curiosity that was natural to all Fae. Though I had once doubted her heritage, there was none now. My cock practically pulsed behind the placket of my trousers and without thought, I reached down, undoing the laces as I freed myself to the cool night air.

I gripped my stalk and pictured Cress—my Crimson

Princess—on her knees before me. Her plump pink lips circling the head of my cock as she bobbed over me. The creaminess of her skin sliding against the roughness of mine. Magic power rose within me as I pumped my cock. I trembled as I squeezed and fisted myself.

It wasn't good enough. Nothing would be until she was with me again. Under me. All over me.

And it wasn't just me, I knew. No. Orion and I would have her again together. I'd come to accept that. She'd enjoyed his touch as much as she'd enjoyed mine and it was all I wanted in this world: to see her happy. Sorrell —the provoking bastard that he was—would fall as well if he hadn't already. That, most of all, was the ultimate fantasy.

Cress between not just Orion and me, but the three of us. Her mouth stretched around my cock as Orion pushed into her lower depths and Sorrell … a grin formed across my face. The icy prick would likely want the one place she'd be most hesitant to give. Even experienced female Fae had shied away from *that* particular act, no matter how desirable their partner.

My balls pulled tight against my inner thighs as my release grew closer and closer. My fantasies shifted and suddenly, it wasn't Sorrell laying across her back and spreading those hind cheeks of her hide. It was me. Oh, what it would feel like to press into that small, forbidden little chamber of hers. I'd press my cock head to her pussy first, circle it in her juices. There would be no denying her there. I'd have to fuck her if only to keep my sanity before I pulled back and ran the hot, wet, head up to her dark place.

The sound of her gasp filled my ears. It wasn't real, but Gods, I could practically fucking taste her anticipation. She would be so needy for me, so ready. Perhaps she wouldn't even deny me that place. I would be gentle with her, of course. At first, anyway. I would slip my cock into her backside and push until all of the breath had escaped her lungs. Then, once she'd gotten used to me filling her hole, I'd show her the true meaning of magic and release.

The muscles in my legs jumped as I tightened my grip around my shaft and pounded my fist in quick movements. One knee came up as I bent slightly towards the ground. I squeezed the palm of my hand over the head of my cock and groaned as spurt after spurt of cum came rushing up and out.

After several moments, I dropped my leg and leaned back. I'd have to clean myself eventually, but for the moment—despite the rush of euphoria and magic energy that had suffused my system—I was depleted. I looked up through the clear patches between the tree-tops and stared at the glittering night sky.

Tomorrow.

Tomorrow, we would find and rescue Cress. Only then could my fantasies finally come true.

CHAPTER ELEVEN

CRESS

Footsteps sounded on the stone floor outside my cell and my stomach dropped. *It couldn't be time yet, could it?* The Princes hadn't come for me yet. There had to be a mistake, right?

The keys clanked in the lock on my door and I knew that whatever time I had was up. A guard walked in and sneered at me, and as though that wasn't enough, Tyr appeared right behind him. The man was like a fly, just when I thought I'd gotten rid of him, there he was again, buzzing around and annoying the hell out of me.

"Ah, isn't it a glorious day, little Changeling? Just smell the fresh air. The weather is taking a turn for the better I believe, and I'm sure your life ending will only please the Gods even more. What do you think? Should we get on with it? Or maybe we should sit and chat a while more, let you hang in suspense." He laughed.

Was that a hint? I wondered. *Hanging? Was that how I was going to die today if I didn't get out of here?*

The guard cleared his throat.

Tyr nodded. "Yes, you have a point, Samson," he said, taking a step further into the room.

I watched him, feeling my heart start to beat faster. I felt stalked—like prey cornered by a much bigger predator. When it came down to it, that was exactly what I was. Prey to his predator.

"We should get this over with," Tyr continued. "After all, we don't want to keep the crowd that's come to watch the festivities waiting." Tyr grinned at me as I stared back at him. "Your death will be our entertainment for the day," he said. "It will be only one of many to befall Faekind and soon, all that will be left is a memory of what you once were."

His words were merely for the benefit of the guards surrounding us. There was no possible way he could want his own race to be killed. That was … genocide. As Tyr approached and bent down, and I gazed up into his eyes, I had to wonder … maybe he really didn't give a fuck who won this war after all. Because in the end—no matter who was left to claim victory—both sides would lose. That was how war went.

Clamping my lips shut, I glared up at him. It was difficult not to show my fear.

"So quiet now," Tyr commented. "What's wrong, little Changeling? Cat got your tongue?" He grinned as he reached for my wrist and yanked me up to my feet.

My lips parted, but before I could utter a word in

response, he reached out and grabbed my face, pinching my chin in his tight grip and squishing my cheeks. "You're very pretty for one, you know," he commented. "A Changeling, that is. What a pity."

I gasped as quick and sharp as a whip, he tilted my head to the side and then dragged his tongue up my cheek, from the bottom of my jaw straight to my temple. A shudder of disgust ran through me.

"I expected salt," he said, "from last night's tears. Did you not cry, little Changeling? Attempting to be brave?" He used his grasp on my face to shake me back and forth. "You taste delicious, nonetheless. There's something to be said about the fear of a young woman about to die. I can never quite get enough of it," he whispered just as he flipped my head to the other side and licked my other cheek in the same manner.

My muscles tensed as he chuckled against my temple. More disgust whipped through me. I shuddered with revulsion even as my gaze darted to the guard standing by, silently pleading with him to stop this. When our eyes clashed, however, he merely curled his upper lip back and looked away.

Why? I thought. *Even if I was a prisoner, why in the world would anyone treat another person like this? Why would he just stand there and let it happen?*

"Keys," Tyr said abruptly, holding out the hand that wasn't clamped onto my face to the guard. I heard the jangle of metal as the keys landed in his palm, and he finally released me so he could undo the chains that had been anchoring me to the wall. The second the weight of the fetters was gone I wanted to sigh in relief, even if they were just replaced with a set of new manacles that would lead me out of this hole and into something far worse—death.

The metal was cold on my wrists. Tyr's hands found my shoulders and turned me around, shoving me forward until I stumbled towards the door and I took solace in the fact that he hadn't chained my feet. "Let's get moving," the guard said, turning and allowing me out into the corridor.

I shuffled along, darting my eyes from one side to the next. There was no opportunity in sight, though. No spare moment where I wasn't surrounded by human guards with swords and dark looks. They would no doubt be more than willing to kill me before I even got to wherever it was this execution would take place.

They led me down a winding staircase and out of the prison tower—past silent cells where eyes gleamed in the quiet darkness. The silence was far more insidious knowing what was to come. Then finally, I was led out into the morning light. I halted just as fresh air— and the sunlight—hit my face. After being locked up for so long, the brightness of the sun was overwhelming and my vision was overcome with intense pain as I squinted to try and see my surroundings.

Slowly but surely, my eyes began to adjust. The guards, however, paid no heed as they shoved me along. I stumbled, nearly falling several times, as I was marched out into what seemed to be a courtyard. When I spotted the stage they had set for my execution my feet froze and refused to move again no matter how many times the guard behind me pushed against my back. My knees almost gave way several times, but all I could do was stand there and stare up into the unrelenting sun at the wooden stage—a beacon of my doom.

Finally, the guard huffed out a breath and picked me up, lifting me off my bare feet, and half carried, half dragged me towards the instrument of my demise. As he marched me up the stairs, I turned and looked out and realized that Tyr hadn't been lying; there was, in fact, a crowd. My stomach sank as I stared back at the onlookers who had all come to watch me die. My lashes flickered.

Where the fuck were the guys? Even as I tried to tell myself not to panic, panic was all I could feel. That was normal, I guessed, considering I was about to be horrifically murdered in front of so many witnesses. Oh, they could call it execution and justice all they wanted—the fact remained, I was innocent and they were going to kill me. It was murder in my book.

How could so many people want to watch someone else die? I asked myself. *Did the hatred between our people really run that deep?* Who was I kidding? I knew it did. Even if they'd taught me nothing else, the nuns had taught me that.

My fingers flexed inside my manacles. The desire to use my powers—the ones I'd been so desperately working on this entire week—rose, but I was unpredictable. My powers came and went. Even if my death was the end, I couldn't bring myself to unleash an unknown violence on people who didn't know any better. I needed another option, but as I tried to think of one, I was positioned into place and the King took to the stage, stepping in front of me to command everyone's attention. As soon as he was in my sights, all thoughts except rage vanished from my mind.

King Felix stepped before me and raised his hands to his audience. "Ladies and gentlemen," he announced. "You have come here to bear witness to a most auspicious event. This," he exclaimed, "is a traitorous Fae!" He turned and pointed my way just as one of my old guards stepped up and placed a noose around my neck before tightening it. I gasped, fear overtaking my anger for a brief moment.

There were several jeers from the crowd. Slurs. Curses. Blind hatred. I didn't understand it, and yet at the same time, how could I not? They were afraid. They were seeking out someone to blame for all they had lost in this Gods forsaken war that had gone on for too long.

"She infiltrated our country," the King went on, "learned of our ways and weaknesses, and then she went back to her Fae Kings and Queens and gave them the information."

"That's not true!" I cried.

"Silence!" he shouted back.

I tried to shake my head, but as I did, the rope dug into my throat, making it hard to breathe, and they hadn't even done anything yet. One of the guards stepped forward and lifted me off my feet as another placed a stool beneath me.

No! my mind screamed in rebellion. *No! Where were*

they? They had to be here. The guys would never let me die like this, not even Sorrell, despite the fact that I irritated him. My eyes sought out the crowd once more, but instead of looking at the people who had chosen to come to this horrible event, I looked for a familiar head of red hair, of ice white hair, of hair so black it resembled a raven's wing.

Tears began to prick at my eyes, and my throat tightened as I fought not to cry. Especially when the crowd began to steadily agree with the horrible things the King was saying. They began yelling at me, spitting terrible words that the nuns would have lashed me for even whispering. I gritted my teeth and bore it.

Yes, I was terrified, but the longer it went on, the less fear I felt and the more my anger grew. I refused to turn my gaze away. Not after everything I'd been through. I raised my head and looked out at the crowd.

"The Fae are dying in droves. Their poor weakling soldiers are unable to stand up to our men. Mark my words, before the year is over we will have a victory over the Fae and they will be eradicated from our lands. It will be the greatest victory our people have ever seen," The King shouted.

"That is not the truth," I said defiantly. "The truth is that *you* are the one killing innocents and you're killing Fae for simply existing. Whether it's Fae killing human or human killing Fae, it's wrong. You're wrong and the Fae are wrong. But you won't see that." I turned and glared at where Tyr stood by, smiling at me. "Not so long as you have a traitor in your Court."

There was a moment of silence that drifted over the

crowd at my words, and a few even hesitantly looked at each other as if they weren't sure how to react. Finally, the King stepped forward and brought his hand down in a sweeping gesture. "Enough!" he called. "It's time."

Hands landed on my shoulders and I was forced to my knees. It wasn't going to be a hanging after all, I realized as my eyes widened when a man stopped before me and set a stained block of wood before me. It was to be a beheading. My gaze jerked up and met Tyr's. His smile widened and he waved. Then, as if he didn't even care to stay, he turned and walked away.

Orion, Roan, and Sorrell's faces all danced in front of my eyes as the hands pushed me over the block of wood, my chin resting in the notch that had been carved out.

Just as the King raised his hand once more to signal the executioner, the ground rumbled beneath us. My chin was jarred as it smacked into the side of the block of wood. I lifted my head and when no one forced me back down, I realized something much larger had happened. The Earth was shaking. It went on for several long minutes and I felt the collective shock and breath that everyone in the crowd held. They were waiting for it to stop, I realized.

Instead, the shaking got worse. There were several gasps and before I understood what was happening, screams split the air. Several members of the crowd moved back, falling as they tried to get away. I turned, noting that my guards were all fixated on the tower above us as long tendrils of cracks began to form from the ground up.

This was my chance! I pushed to my feet, the mana-cles around my wrists clanging, and then just as black smoke began to pour out of the tower and a great explosion wracked its frame, I leapt to my hopeful freedom—off the platform and into the crowd.

CHAPTER TWELVE

ORION

The capital of Amnestia was a bustling place, and in the early morning hours, when children should have been just waking and marketplaces should have been preparing to open for the day, there was, instead, a lingering sense of excitement. A curiousness to the crowd as they ambled over the cobblestoned streets to the opened doors of the castle courtyard.

My brothers and I mingled in with the humans, casting magic over ourselves to keep our slightly otherworldly looks hidden. The slightly pointed ears. The vibrant hair colors. The sense of strangeness we exuded to these people. As much as we could disguise our looks, we could not hide our dispositions.

Anger. Concern. Fear. It hovered over each of us—that heavy sense of dread.

"Alright," Roan said, quietly turning away from me as he and Sorrell slipped further into the amassing crowd as more and more people came from the city to witness the event that would take place this sunrise.

An execution.

"It's time," Roan continued. "Go."

I nodded and, without another word, I called upon my magic—the very same I had been born with. The darkness of midnight. The ability to seep into the shadows and find the isolating darkness that dwelled within the corners. It was everywhere at all times because without darkness—*without me*—there could be no light.

Shooting forward between people gliding through the open gates, I wove through the lines—bypassing the guards. There was a reason we had waited so long to do this. Not only would the defenses of the castle be down as they prepared for the execution this morning, but it was an old human custom to invite onlookers to watch as the King killed a criminal. Only this time, it wasn't a criminal. It was Cress, my Cress.

When I glanced at small children, some barely old enough to toddle next to their parents as they entered through the gates, I felt a sickness pour into my stomach. Fae could be cruel, that much was true, but where, I asked myself, were there differences between our species? Humans, too, it seemed, could be bloodthirsty.

Shaking my head and dismissing that thought, I hurried to do my duty. Halfway into the main courtyard that all onlookers were led to, I separated myself and found an open alcove. Dipping into it, I hunted through the open corridors until I found a door leading inside.

The castle was well underway in preparation for the

morning's activities. Deeper I sank, into the shadows, avoiding all detection as servants bustled about and guards patrolled.

Closing my eyes, I sought out a hint of Cress. It was there, in the recesses of my mind, a lingering effect of the dream magic I had used mere nights ago. A vibrant glow of her energy. I grabbed onto it and followed the feeling of it, letting the trail of her power lead me. It was faint, muddled, and faded. Lack of sleep and high levels of stress would do that to a spirit. I only hoped that that was all that she had suffered. I didn't want to consider what the King might have done to what he thought was a traitorous Fae in his Kingdom. He was executing her now, but he'd had her for a week. In that time...

No! I couldn't stop to think of it. I needed to focus. Stopping inside an empty stairwell, I rasped out a breath, shaking my head and shoving my concerns back. It was my duty to find her, here and now, and retrieve her before anything more happened.

When I reopened my eyes, however, I froze. Dark wisps of power drifted towards me, rolling over the stairs before me, and these were not mine. The curling tendrils snapped at my ankles, wrapping quickly and jerking until my whole body was yanked into the air and held suspended.

Years of training—years of war—were finally found to be good for some things. It took no thought at all for me to retaliate. A knife flew from my grasp, yanked from my boot, and sliced through the shadows. A shrieking wail of agony pierced my skull and I was abruptly dropped. I lifted my arm and captured the knife before it fell.

"That's no normal blade, Brother."

Violence seeped into my bones as I lifted my head and caught sight of the man responsible for my presence in the human King's castle today. He came around the corner slowly, grinning as he clapped his hands.

"Iron," I stated solemnly as I stood and met his amused gaze with a wrathful glare.

His eyebrows rose. "And yet you wield it with no pain."

Of course I did—I'd wrapped the Iron blade, one of the few things that could cut through a Fae's manifestation of magic, in a protective handle covering. The blade, itself, was free, and it was what I would use to gut him where he stood. I took a step forward and Tyr lifted his hand, stopping me with a wall of black fire that erupted between us. I debated my chances of stabbing my way through it, but even with an Iron blade, I would still receive wounds from such a large manifestation.

The walls and stairs, however, remained unscorched. "Tut. Tut. Dear Brother," Tyr said. "You come to me with a look of such hatred in your eyes."

"You've taken something that belongs to me," I snapped. "And we are no longer brothers!"

Tyr's hand touched his breastbone. "That hurts, you know," he said mournfully. "Especially when I went through all of this trouble to find you. After all, as soon as you stepped foot within the castle, I knew you were here. I'm surprised it took you this long to come for your Changeling."

"Where is she?" I demanded.

A sigh left his mouth. "Gods, look at you. So consumed with lust for the poor thing. She's rather scrawny, if I may say so, especially after her days in here. The guards didn't much care to feed the thing."

I didn't even think. I simply let the second blade in my hand fly. Tyr stumbled as it slammed into his shoulder and just as quickly, the fire he'd conjured dispersed as his concentration was broken. My booted feet flew up the short steps between us and I slammed my hand into his throat, gripping and lifting him until his back crashed against the stone wall. Little bits of rock and dust floated down as I crushed his throat in my grip and leaned in close.

"Where. Is. She?" I demanded once more.

The fading light of her magic in my mind was growing fainter and fainter. It was more difficult than before to summon it back. Soon it would be gone. It would be far easier to get the information I needed from Tyr and then slay him here and now.

A hoarse, rough laugh left Tyr's lips. "You think killing me will save her?" he asked. "No, join me, Brother."

My mouth parted in shock. *Join him?* I reared back and simply stared at him—at the face of the man I'd grown up alongside, but also at the face of a brother who'd time and time again left me in battle to fend for myself. Simply out of boredom or amusement.

"Blood brothers should remain together, Orion," Tyr continued. "Though you may not like it, though you may hide from the truth, the fact remains, you and

I"—he grins and leans into my grip—"we are Midnight Fae and the Midnight Court is the most powerful of all."

I could feel a fire of rage welling up inside of me. "I may be a Midnight Fae." I said the words slowly, carefully as I watched every detail of his expression. "But I will never be one with you." With that, I reached up with my other hand and ripped the iron blade out of his shoulder.

Tyr grunted as it left his body. "More is the pity," he whispered.

My hand flew down, the blade in my grasp aiming directly for his heart. Murder, even among Fae, was blasphemous, but in this, I knew I was right. Tyr was a monster. He had betrayed not only me but the entirety of Faekind. He could not be allowed to live.

Yet, even as my dagger flashed, pain shot through me, starting in my stomach and spreading. My arm grew weak and dots flickered in front of my vision. *Wait* ... My eyes shot downward. No. How had I not...

Another blade, almost exactly like my own, stuck out of my abdomen. My head lifted and my eyes met Tyr's. My hand fell away from his throat as I stumbled back, reaching down to rip the thing free.

"You're not the only one who learned a few things in war, Orion." Tyr's words reached me just as I yanked the new blade from my skin. Blood soaked across my shirt. "You should've poisoned your first blade." The tone of his voice was smooth, unbothered, as if he was merely talking to me about the weather rather than the fact that he'd poisoned the blade that he used to kill me—

because I was dying. I knew it. I could feel it in my veins.

My vision wavered again and the next step I took, a last ditch effort to strike at him, fell short. Both daggers fell from my grasp and my head smacked into the wall as my body tumbled to the ground and then further, rolling down the stairs until I hit the bottom. Breath wheezed out of my chest, aching and sharp, and bringing me absolute agony.

In my ears, the ringing clomps of Tyr's steps grew ever closer until a shadow passed over my face. I opened my eyes, not realizing that I'd closed them, and stared up as he bent low over me, brushing my hair back away from my face as he smiled.

"I'll let you in on a little secret, Brother," he spoke slowly—or perhaps it was merely my mind slowing everything down. It felt like each second lasted an eternity. The pumping of my poison drenched blood through my veins made everything seem so painfully never ending. Tyr reached into his shirt and produced something.

My eyes widened as a globe illuminated in his palm. Barely the size of a small animal's head, I knew what it was right away. Though it was an impossible feat— though it shouldn't have existed—there, in his palm, was a Lanuaet. A miniature version. The Midnight Court's version.

"This is going to bring me everything I've ever wanted," he explained.

Lifting up as much as my body would allow, I tried to reach for it. Something inside of me told me to rip it away and destroy it before it was too late. Tyr pulled it back with a laugh. "Ah, ah, ah. Can't have you messing this up for me," he chuckled before putting it back into his shirt.

"What ... do ... you ... want?" I asked, panting through the anguish—both the mental fear and the physical suffering.

Tyr looked down at me as he rose back to his full height, and this time, when he answered, there was no amusement in his expression. No laughter in his eyes. This was the true him. The cruel brother I had known. The monster underneath the veneer of pseudo-friendliness he always put off.

"Power," he said. Tyr took a step back and lifted his arms, pointing them both to the ceiling.

An explosion rocked through the building and with wide, horrified eyes, I realized the truth. The ceiling cracked—spiderweb like fissures crawling across the surface before me. Finally, when it became too much, the whole thing buckled inward and came crashing down upon me and the world became nothing more than a gaping hole of true pain as flames burned across my chest.

Just before I descended into that darkness, the sound of Tyr's voice filtered back. "Until next time, dear Brother."

CHAPTER THIRTEEN

CRESS

Screams filled the air as the crowd realized what was happening. I dove off the platform, wincing as I prepared to hit the ground with jarring pain. The second my legs flew off the dais, however, warm arms closed around me. I flailed, panic taking over my mind. I didn't know how the guards had realized what I was planning, but I couldn't let myself give this chance up. I needed to escape.

My captor fell against the ground with a grunt and as I scrambled away, kicking up dirt in my haste—his hands fell on my waist and yanked me back. "Cressida!" Sorrell's deep, irritated tone reached me a split second later and I froze, only then realizing that it wasn't a guard but he who held me in his arms. "Stop fighting me," he ordered. "I need to conceal you."

The moment I stopped moving, something cold washed over my skin, making me shiver. The bindings holding my wrists together broke and fell away, and finally, I was able to move my arms. My head tilted back and met the cool, icy gaze of Sorrell. Never in my life had I been so overwhelmed and relieved to see such an expression of utter irritation.

"Are you harmed?" he asked.

I shook my head and then proceeded to throw my arms around him. I burrowed into his chest, tears pricking at my eyelids. They'd come. I knew they would, but they had sure let the clock tick down to the last fucking second. Recalling that, I pulled away and punched him.

"What took you so long!" I snapped.

Sorrell's gaze was an arrested one. He blinked down at me, his lips twisted into a grimace of shock. Then with slow deliberate movements, he took me by the shoulders and moved me back. "Don't ever do that again," he ordered.

Cue the eye roll. I snorted and would've said something had it not been for a screaming woman in a large peasant dress who ran between us, not paying any mind to the escaped prisoner—the one who'd almost been executed as well as the giant frost Fae at her side.

"What's going on?" I asked, turning my attention to the crumbling remains of the King's tower. "Was that part of the plan?" Small flames flickered in the near distance, but more worrisome than that were the plumes of black smoke that rose into the sky.

"No," Sorrell said haltingly. "It was not." My gaze returned to him and I noticed the deep set of his brow as he, too, tilted his head back and stared up at the tower. He appeared to shake himself out of whatever dark thoughts consumed him a moment later as he returned his attention to me. "We must go," he said, taking my arm and dragging me after him.

The urgency of his movements had me following after him. My feet stumbled along as we tried to avoid the leftovers from the crowd, many of whom were scrambling over one another trying to escape the falling debris.

"Where are we going?" I tried to ask above the noise, but it was either swallowed by it all or Sorrell simply ignored it in favor of yanking me further and further away from the castle. My money would be on the 'ignore Cress' option, and I wouldn't have minded so much, especially since he was here—rescuing me— except after several more steps something brought me to a sharp halt.

"What are you doing?" Sorrell snapped, whirling around as he tried to pull me forward again.

Against my will, my head turned back the way we'd come. "Something's wrong," I said. My chest felt tight, a darkness creeping into my soul. The trees were within sight, our escape right there, but a small voice inside was telling me to turn back. The wind pushed against my face, whipping my hair in tangles around my face. The effect of whatever force was driving me rippled out through the rest of my body.

"Cressida," he growled, nearly yanking me off my feet with his next tug. "We have to go. *Now.*"

"No." I turned and stared at him. Something was really wrong. My limbs felt like they weighed hundreds of pounds as I took a single step towards him—away from the castle. "Something's happened."

Sorrell stared down at me as though I were crazy. Maybe I was. Maybe this was a trick—magic put on me by Tyr—but I couldn't deny that every single drop of blood in my body was vibrating with anxiety. My hands tingled with awareness, sparks dancing at the edges of my fingers, my magic making itself known.

"What are you—"

"I think we have to go back," I said, cutting him off.

"Are you insane?" He gaped at me.

"I'm sorry, Sorrell..." No matter what he thought, I was. I truly was. He had come all this way to rescue me, but I couldn't leave. Not just yet. I had to follow whatever this feeling was. I didn't want to think of what would happen if I didn't.

His brows crashed down over his eyes and he reached for me intending, I suspected, to simply lift me up and toss me over his shoulders to force me along, but I couldn't let that happen. I didn't let him get the chance. Without a second thought, I turned and dove back into the crowd—fighting against the stream as I moved through people running in the opposite direction. Whatever spell he had put on me appeared to still be working because as I made my way back across the courtyard, towards the burning tower, and into the first entrance I could see, no one stopped me or even seemed to notice my presence.

I hadn't made it up a handful of stairs before a large body crashed into me, slamming me into the stone wall. With a gasp, I fought back, bringing my elbow back and smashing it into the sternum of the man behind me.

"Gods damn it," Sorrell's deep curse stopped me. "I will knock you the fuck out and toss you over my shoulder, Changeling."

"No, you can't," I insisted. "There's something really wrong. Please." I turned and looked up at him, beseeching him with my eyes. "*Please*."

He regarded me with a scowl for several seemingly eternal seconds before he pushed me forward with a curse. "Be swift," he ordered.

Thank the Gods, I thought as I pivoted back the way I'd been going and raced up the stairs, taking them two at a time. There was a string in my chest—a beacon that I followed, letting it lead me to whatever was waiting for me. The stairs grew more and more difficult to climb as the destruction of the tower was revealed. Several parts were completely covered by pieces of wall and roof and I had to crawl my way over them as Sorrell stomped behind me.

I didn't notice it until I nearly stumbled over the body in my path. My ankles slammed into something and I went down, falling hard and slamming my knees into the stairs. "What—" My words fell to silence as I realized who I was looking at. "Orion!"

He was half covered in rubble, several large chunks of the wall and wooden beams over his legs. I turned back, ready to beg Sorrell for assistance, but he was already there, his face sallow with horror as he lifted and tossed the beams to the side. I blinked when he took a large chunk of stone and threw it and, as it crashed into the wall opposite of us, it broke into several pieces, leaving a rain of dust and gravel falling from the crater-like hole he left behind.

"Orion?" He hefted Orion's completely limp body into his arms. I reached forward, running my fingers over his dirt streaked face, but as I wiped the worst of it away, I finally saw the truth. "Gods..." Sorrell's voice was horrified.

Dark, black lines were drawn across his body. Up his neck and over his arms—they covered every inch of his skin. My eyes rose to Sorrell's. "What does this mean?" I asked, shakily.

Sorrell's expression was pale and concerned. "Nothing good," he replied as he tapped Orion's cheek. "It's poison," he cursed a moment later.

Fear swelled in my chest. "What do we do?" I demanded. "We have to do something."

Sorrell cursed again as he stared down at Orion's slack face. Through clenched teeth, he took the front of Orion's shirt and ripped it open to reveal his chest. More black spiderweb veins traced down and collected over where his heart was.

"See how his veins are black?" Sorrell asked. I nodded. "There are only a few things that can do that to Fae, and humans don't know about them, which can only mean this was done by another Fae."

"Tyr," I breathed.

The dark look that crossed his expression would have fucking terrified me had it been turned my way. As it was, I knew the cause was the name I'd just uttered.

"Yes," he said through gritted teeth. "That would be my guess."

"So, what do we do?" I asked. "How do we help him?"

He bared his teeth as his eyes settled on Orion's chest, glaring down at the lines in his skin. The longer he went without saying anything the faster my heart raced. "Sorrell?" I tried again. "We have to try."

Finally, he hissed out a breath and shut his eyes, shaking his head. "We can try to boost his magical energy so that his body can fight off the poison on its own," he said.

"Okay, how do we do that?"

"It's dangerous," he replied. "That's the issue. For a poison this concentrated, it'll take an enormous amount of magical energy. More than either of us have. And even if we're successful, I can't very well carry both of you out of here."

"Then let me do it," I suggested. "Just to get him up and moving."

"It won't get him up and moving," Sorrell replied. "It would take both of our energies and some just to wake him, much less get him on his feet."

"Well, we have to try!" I snapped. "Just tell me how to do it. If we just leave him like this ... he'll die, won't he?"

After a brief, tense moment Sorrell cursed again and nodded. "Fine. Fuck. Okay. It's—difficult to explain. It's usually something a Fae learns as they grow up and master their magic, but you haven't."

As if I needed another reason to feel sorry for myself. I shook that thought off and pressed my hands down on Orion's chest. "Just tell me what to do," I ordered.

"Keep your hands there," he said, watching me. His gaze flickered from where my fingers rested, pushing harder into the black veins spreading over Orion's body to his face. "Close your eyes and reach for the power you have inside—every Fae in existence has a well of it. It's inside. For me, it's like a long dark lake of water and ice. To pull power from it, I need to focus on moving it with my mind. Lifting it and breaking the glaciers over it as they sink further and push my power back up with it. For each Fae, though, it's different. It may bring to your mind a different image, but start there."

I closed my eyes and tried to picture what he was describing. Try as I might, though, the image of a lake of ice and water never came. Instead, I found a glowing sun, burning bright and hot in the center of my core. I waved my imaginary fingers over it and though it felt warm to the touch, it didn't hurt me. The darkness around it pressed against the sun, making it smaller and smaller—pulling it away from me. I knew I couldn't let that happen. If I did, my magic would never come and Orion would die here in this crumbling stairwell of a prison tower.

Shoving myself forward, in my mind, I fought my way back towards the sun, and just as my fingers reached out and grasped it—the darkness gave way to a blinding light. "Yes." I heard Sorrell's voice in the back of my mind. "Just like that."

I felt my whole body grow warm as I brought the sun closer and cradled it to my breast. "Now, will it into

Orion's body," he said. "Let it fill you and then push it outward, through your palms."

I did as he said, letting the warmth of the sunlight fill my body—letting it overpower me and grow even stronger until it became too much. Then I began to push it. I shoved it forward, feeling the tingle of awareness move down my limbs—down my arms—as I let it release from my palms and fingertips. More and more, I pulled the light from my sun and pushed it outward.

Sweat collected at my temples. Pain began to radiate up my spine. I ignored it and kept going. "Cress..." Sorrell's voice was far away. "Roan's on his way—I sent out—"

Whatever he was saying was cut off as I shook my head and forced myself to concentrate on the task at hand. More light poured from me. My head began to ache. The warmth was dying down. It wasn't enough. Tears pricked behind my closed eyes. No, I had to give him more.

"Cressida," Sorrell's voice came from miles away. As if he were yelling over a vast amount of space. "You have to stop."

Stop? I thought. No I couldn't do that. Not until Orion was safe.

"Now, Cress!" Sorrell sounded angry. Had he ever called me Cress before instead of Changeling or Cressida? It seemed like such a stupid thought to have in the moment, but I couldn't help the wandering of my mind as I felt my body sag.

My eyes opened, but it felt as though I was lifting rocks off of them just to crack them. Beneath me, I saw that the black lines marring Orion's flesh had receded. Sorrell's ice cold gaze stared at me. "Stop," he ordered.

My head swam, and I had to put my hands on the stone floor to prevent myself from falling over. I was so dizzy that I didn't even notice that Sorrell had already stood and picked up Orion, slinging him over one shoulder like a sack of potatoes.

"Roan's coming," he stated. "He'll be here soon."

I would never know, I thought in the next instant because, as I tried to stand back up, the whole world grew distant and I felt myself falling back into oblivion.

CHAPTER FOURTEEN

CRESS

The first thing I heard when the world slowly came back to me was someone talking—a female. Whoever she was, she was really close. Practically right next to me, and she was nervous. Was she crying? The sound of sniffles reached my ears and I couldn't keep my eyes shut anymore.

Before I could seek out the girl, my eyes settled on my surroundings. Familiar stone walls that didn't have bugs crawling out of the cracks. No cobwebs either. But what told me that I was truly, finally back in the Court of Crimson was the little buzzing noise and then a flit of wings above my head as a pixie carried a big, fat, delicious looking bread roll. My mouth watered. My stomach rumbled.

"Cress?" The sound of my name being called in that familiar voice had my eyes seeking the girl out.

"Nellie." Her name came out on a croak. Gods, my

throat was parched, but I'd never been happier to see my best friend in my life.

Nellie flung herself at me, her arms going around my neck as I placed my elbows on the bed and tried to leverage myself up. The pixie above me jumped and the roll slipped from his tiny little hands and dropped on my head before rolling onto the mattress beneath me.

"I'm so glad you're awake," Nellie said. "We didn't know what to think. You collapsed on the way back and—"

"I'm fine," I assured her as the fingers of my free hand sought out the roll the pixie had dropped. I hoped he hadn't been carrying it anywhere to go to anyone else because I was famished. I shoved the whole thing into my mouth until my cheeks bulged and then quickly hugged my best friend back. Sweet, delicious yeast—my Gods this was the best thing I'd ever eaten in my life.

Even as dry as my throat was, it went down easily and already I wanted more. Maybe being cooped up in a tower and fed mystery soup and moldy bread for days on end would do that to a girl, but right then, I could've eaten a whole mountain of these things.

I coughed and sat up even more as Nellie pulled back and wiped quickly beneath her eyes. "You have no idea how worried I've been," she said, reaching for something on the table alongside the bed. I sighed in relief as she lifted a mug of water towards me.

Without even hesitating, I took it from her and downed what was in the cup. "I think I have some idea," I told her as I finished the drink and handed the empty mug back to her.

She set it on the table and turned back towards me, but before she could get another word out, the door opened and in walked Roan. He came to an abrupt halt when he saw me and then he jerked as someone behind him slammed straight into his back.

"Roan, what is—" Sorrell's irritated voice cut off as Roan stepped to the side and he realized the reason for Roan's sudden stop. "Cressida..." My full name sounded so strange to my ears, but sweet at the same time. It didn't matter that he was kind of an asshole. I was just so happy to be home that I didn't even think; I flung back the covers and dove out of the bed and straight into his arms.

Nellie squeaked as she, too, was thrown from the bed and onto the floor. Sorrell caught me readily enough and I looked down. "Sorry," I said quickly.

With an exasperated look, Nellie got up from the floor and rubbed her rear. "Well, good to know you're still the same as ever after being captured and almost killed," she said sardonically.

"Did you really think it would change me?" I shot back.

Her lips parted, but once again, before she could give out a reply, she was interrupted. "Nellie, could you give Cress and us a few minutes alone?" Roan asked.

Her lips pressed together and I could tell she wanted to argue. Instead of doing so, however, she sighed and nodded. Her hand gently touched my arm as she headed out the door. "I missed you, Cress," she said quietly. "I'm glad you're back. There's so much I have to tell you."

I reached out and snagged her fingers with my own

before she could let go. "And I want to hear it all," I replied. "Soon." Nellie looked up at me, her pale face tilting up as she smiled, and then she pulled her hand away and was gone, letting the door close behind her on the way out.

Sorrell released me and let my legs slide to the floor. Yet, when I moved to pull back, his arms encircled me, halting the movement. "Do you know how dangerous that stunt you pulled was?" he demanded, shaking me slightly.

My head jerked back as I looked up into cool, ice blue eyes full of such fury and something else ... that wasn't. No. It couldn't be. "Were you ... afraid for me?" I asked cautiously.

"Was I—" Sorrell's hands disappeared from my sides as he yanked himself away, turning as he stomped several paces away before turning back just as quickly and pointing a finger my way. "You are a menace!" he accused.

I blinked. "Yes? And?" *Did he think I would be shocked by that little proclamation?* The nuns had called me that more than once or twice. Coming from him, I wasn't surprised.

Sorrell's face registered an expression of shock and then more fury and then...

"Are you turning purple?" I asked before looking at Roan. "Roan, I think he's turning purple. Is he breathing? Make sure he's breathing."

"I'm breathing just fine!" Sorrell snapped, dropping his arm. "You, on the other hand, are lucky to be breathing at all! You could have died."

I knew that and perhaps it said something about me as a person that upon waking that wasn't my first concern. "Where's Orion?" I asked.

Sorrell frowned. "He's resting in his chambers," he said.

"What happened to the poison?" I took a step towards him. "Is it all out? Is he okay? Is he recovering? Can I see him?" With every question I asked, I took another step in his direction until I was right before him.

Roan huffed out a breath. "He's out of the initial danger," he answered, drawing my attention. "But he is severely depleted of his magic reserves. Groffet made a potion that will keep the poison at bay, but we need to get his magic back at full strength—Gods, we all do." At that last statement, he put a hand to his neck and cracked it. "It's been a few days since we rescued you from the Amnestia capital. There's more at play here and we don't know how much time we have left before we can expect another onslaught. Whatever happened at the King's castle—"

"Tyr," I said suddenly, cutting him off. "Tyr is planning something horrible. We have to stop him."

Sorrell and Roan exchanged a look. "What do you know, Cressida?" Sorrell demanded.

"Tyr is using King Felix for his own gain. He plans to have the races wipe each other out and when the King is killed and the leaders of the Fae are gone, he plans to take over and rule over what's left." My hands found the front of his shirt and clutched it for dear life. "We can't let that happen," I beseeched him. "So many people will die."

Sorrell's hand curved over mine and gently—much more gently than I expected from him—pulled them away. "We will stop him," he said. "Make no mistake—Tyr will pay for his crimes against Faekind."

"And the humans," I reminded him.

"For now," Roan said, stepping forward as he tugged me away from Sorrell and wrapped me up in his arms, "we need to recuperate." His fingers sank into my hair as he dragged me close. His nose touched my scalp and he inhaled. "Gods, how we have missed you, Little Bird. The very thought of your life being snuffed out before it was time—even if it was your time … I couldn't allow it. I can hardly believe that you're here now, in my arms."

The tremble of his voice reached deep within me and I found my arms lifting to encircle him, to drag him even closer. "I'm here," I whispered back. "I'm alive."

"You almost weren't," he choked out. "Cress, Little Bird, you cannot do that again. Ever."

"I tried to fight him," I said. "I didn't go willingly."

Hot breath touched my neck and then my head was ripped back and Roan's mouth descended over mine, devouring me and scorching me all the way to my core. My pussy pulsed with a fiery need I hadn't felt in days. I moaned into his lips.

Fingers against my scalp. Heat beneath my skin. I pushed up against Roan's chest, practically climbing him and, when his hands went from my head to my ass as he lifted me ever closer, I completely forgot that someone else was in the room until a cool hand touched my arm and Sorrell's voice intruded. "Roan, that's enough," Sorrell snapped. "If anyone could use the replenishing, it's Orion."

My head pulled back and I blinked as the lust Roan had created in me died down once more. "Replenishing?" I repeated, dazed.

Roan's hands gripped me firmly and a growl rumbled up from his chest. Then his grasp softened and slowly but surely my feet made their way back to the floor. My thighs were shaking with need, though. Just because he'd stopped didn't make the feelings go away. I felt as though I were on the edge of a crash—as if I'd stayed awake for far too long and exhaustion was about to pull me under, and yet I needed something. Something far greater than anything I'd ever experienced before. Needed it—whatever it was—like I needed to breathe.

Roan cursed. "Sorrell's right. Orion needs you far more than I do right now," he said through gritted teeth.

"He needs me?" I asked. "Then why are we just standing here? Take me to him!" I wanted to see him, to assure myself he was all right. The image of those black veins working their way beneath his skin rose to the forefront of my mind. It made me sick with worry. I could feel sweat beads pop up along my skin. "Please, Roan. I have to see him."

"He's in bad shape, but he's going to be fine," he assured me. "We'll take you to see him, but Cress ... you need to understand what he needs."

"What does he need?" I demanded the answer from him. Whatever it was, I would fight tooth and nail to get it for him. I would go to the ends of the Kingdom. I needed him to be okay.

"You, Cress," he said. "He needs you."

⚜

Roan and Sorrell led me to the same chambers that I'd spent my first night in when I'd initially stumbled upon their magical castle. What I knew had only been a few short months ago felt like a lifetime. My hand hovered over the door's latch and I glanced back as they both stepped back.

"We'll let you have some alone time," Roan said. "We have to shore up the castle's defenses."

I gulped. "What about you two?" I asked. "Don't you need to replenish your magic as well?"

Sorrell's jaw hardened, but it was once again Roan who answered. "We will be fine for the time being." He nudged me with a small smile. "Take care of him and then you can take care of us."

My eyes flitted to Sorrell, waiting for a denial from him. I half expected him to tell me that he wouldn't require my help in that snotty, aristocratic tone of his, but when he looked back at me, all I could see was melting ice and the promise of something dark. I shuddered in response, quickly turning back to the door and lifting the latch as I pushed my way in and let it close behind me.

Inside of Orion's chambers, the room was dark, but I followed what I could remember. The stairs were to the side, and my hand curved around the banister as I climbed into the garden. The smell of flowers and wet leaves assaulted my nose and the glass that let in the light from the sun and moon—however fake it was since the windows didn't always ascertain the true time on the outside—illuminated the immediate area.

A dark shadow was cushioned on a mattress on the floor. "Orion!" I cried, hurrying towards him. My knees hit the ground at his side and my hands roved over his body. He'd been stripped from the abdomen up and there were still some fine gray markings under his skin. Tears assaulted my eyes. "Oh, Orion..." I sniffed as I closed my eyes. "I'm so sorry."

"Cress?" Orion's voice was quiet and his hand rose to touch my cheek. My eyes popped open and I jerked my gaze up to meet his. His eyes were cracked, though just barely, but his face was pale and his lips were practically as gray as his veins.

"What has this done to you?" I asked him.

"Nothing you can't help me with," he said. Orion's hand caressed my cheek, his thumb stroking slowly over my skin. I raked my teeth over my bottom lip and leaned into that touch.

"They told me what you need," I said. Sex, I thought. Fae needed touch to survive—they needed it to replenish their magic. And all three of them had refused to take a lover since I'd been gone. My heart was both full and broken at the same time. *What must that have cost them?*

"We don't have to do it now, sweetheart." His words drew me out of my haze of guilt.

"What?" I jerked back. "Of course, we have to do it now. Look at you! We're doing this."

I reached for the blanket over his lower half and pulled it down, stopping when I realized he wasn't naked from the waist up, but completely and utterly naked all the way down. My eyes bulged. "Uhhh..."

"I'm surprised you didn't notice before," he chuckled as I stared at the hardened shaft jerking against his belly.

"I was a little distracted," I muttered as I pulled back and reached for the fabric of the gown I'd woken up in. Lifting it, I tossed a leg over both of his and lowered myself down until I was straddling him. "But it's good, I can work with this. You're going to be fine."

"Cress—" His hands moved up my arms as he struggled to sit up.

"No!" I pushed my palms against his chest and tried to shove him back down. "I got this!"

"Cress, you don't have to—"

"Yes, I do," I snapped, pushing harder. *Damn it, why was he so much stronger than me even when he was ill? It just wasn't fair!*

"Cress, I will be fine. Groffet has a potion—"

I let my head thump against his chest even as his cock pressed against my slit. "I want to," I whispered, stopping him. "Please, Orion. I want to." I needed to assure myself that he was truly here, alive and well. I didn't need anything else but that.

A large palm landed on the back of my head and I felt his lips press against my scalp. "You know that I cannot resist you when you're like this," he whispered.

"Does that mean you're going to give me what I want?" I asked, gently lifting my hips and rubbing against him.

A groan left his chest and that was all the answer he gave before his other hand went beneath the folds of my gown to grasp his shaft and guide it towards my opening. A soft gasp escaped my lips as he sank inside. It'd been so long—forever, it felt—since we'd done this. My hands arched up to wrap around his back and in movements as old as time, I began to ride him.

Up and down, up and down, I lifted myself and fell back over his shaft. His clenched teeth did nothing to hide his grunts of pleasure. My vision swam as I held onto him. Heat poured from me into him and then from him into me. *Magic*, I realized. *Fae magic.*

Orion's fingers stole beneath my gown and found the little bundle of nerves above where we were connected. I gasped and arched up as his hips lifted and pounded against me with more force even as his fingers pinched and rolled that bundle. Stars danced before my eyes—little flashes of light. My air sawed in and out of my throat as my nails sank into the skin of his back and dragged downward.

He groaned and fucked into me even harder. Our heads tilted and our lips connected. Tongues tangled. Breaths mixed. And on the next shift of his cock into me, he pinched my clit again and I exploded. Fire raced through my mind, burning away all clear or logical thought until there was nothing but him. Nothing but us. Nothing but the magic.

CHAPTER FIFTEEN

SORRELL

"What do you think you're doing?" Roan's quiet but firm question made me turn back towards him as the door to the library closed behind us. Across the room, Groffet bustled between rows and stacks of books, seeking an answer to all of our problems—as if it could be found in a mere dusty volume.

"What do you mean?" I inquired absently, wiping a bit of dust from my shirt as I brushed against one of the towers of books Groffet refused to find a new place for. The crazy, old man.

"Cress," Roan stated, catching me off guard.

I paused and looked back. "I will repeat," I said slowly. "What do you mean?"

His fiery gaze locked onto my face. Then he shook his head. "I've seen the way you look at her, Sorrell," he said. "You pretend like you don't feel it, like you don't see how you feel—but it's obvious."

With careful movements, I pivoted my body so that instead of looking at him from over my shoulder, I was facing him fully. "I don't know what you're talking about," I stated.

"That," he snapped, gesturing towards me. "It's that right there—you're refusal to admit it. Willful ignorance. You know, but you don't want to know. You feel it, but you don't want to feel it. You're drawn to her."

"I am not drawn to the Changeling," I sneered, working to put a little disgust into my tone.

Roan's gaze, however, remained steady—unimpressed and no doubt, unconvinced. "Why do you fight it?" he asked.

"There's nothing to fight." I sniffed and turned away, moving across the room until I reached the platform that held Groffet's workspace. I sought him out, but the damn troll had disappeared on us. I growled in irritation. "Where is that old man?" I snapped.

"You can't walk away from this." Roan's voice lifted and floated to me from across the room.

I sighed and spun to face him once more as he approached at a much slower pace. "I'm not walking away from anything," I said. "I do not feel the same way that you feel towards your little Changeling."

"You were worried for her," he pointed out.

I gritted my teeth and cursed my powers as ice began to form along my fingertips. Anger always came out as cold—always cold. Whereas she was anything but. The Changeling—Cressida—she was like a ray of sunshine, warm, life giving, beautiful. I shook my head, warding away those unwelcome thoughts.

"What do you want from me?" I asked, fixing Roan with a dark glare. "What is it that you hope to get from me by trying to convince me that I care for the Changeling the same way you and Orion do? I'll allow that the two of you care for her. I'll even step back and let the two of you keep her. You still plan to marry her; I'm no idiot. You meant every word you said at the Court of Frost. You intend to make her your Crimson Princess."

"She could be yours as well."

Shock ricocheted through me. *Was he ... offering the girl to me?* A deep yearning awoke within me. The desire to feel her golden locks across my chest, stroking down my abdomen. Her mouth around my cock. Her body in my bed.

With a croak, I responded. "She wouldn't want me." I meant it. She was smart enough to realize that I was no good for her. I had been nothing but cruel to her since the moment she'd fallen into our laps and there was nothing in me that wanted to stop now. She responded so beautifully to my icy rage. She didn't shrink away in fear. Wasn't deterred by it. She rose to my challenges and made me want to pin her down and show her just what I could do to her to make her submit to my will.

"Sorrell," Roan barked.

I blinked and realized the ice had reached up to my forearms and small dustings of snow were falling from the edges of my hair. With a jerk, I reached up and shoved my fingers through the strands, stripping away the snow and letting the ice fall to the floor and melt beneath my boots.

"You want her," Roan said. "Admit it."

I stiffened. "Why is this so Gods damned important to you?" I growled.

"Because hiding from your feelings will only serve to destroy you later," he answered. "Of anyone in this world, the three of us should know that best, don't you think?"

Words escaped me. I could not tell him he was wrong. It would be a lie, and yet, I wasn't ready to admit to anything that had to do with the Changeling. The longer Roan waited, the more frustrated he became until small little tendrils of smoke began to seep from his hair. He huffed out a breath and turned away just as a small flame erupted.

He didn't appear to even be aware of his movements as he reached up and patted it out. "You'll regret your obstinance, Brother," he snapped. "Gods help you, but I hope you cave soon. Don't think I haven't noticed how you haven't touched another Fae female since she arrived. We need to be restored and if the only one you're willing to let help you is her, then I truly hope you pull your head out of your ass soon and realize what she means to you, or risk her hatred. The choice is yours." With that, he stormed for the exit, opened the door, and left.

I sank into a nearby chair as the library doors clanged shut behind him. My head sank back and I found myself staring up into the ceiling. *Was he right?* I wondered. *Of course, he was.* The Changeling had altered everything. She'd fallen into our world and had wrecked all of our well laid plans to master each of our magics, end the war, and take our places as Kings.

Maybe it appeared that I hated her now, but my feelings were as far from hatred as they could possibly be. Anger— yes, I felt anger. At myself. For wanting her. For desiring her. And then I felt it towards them. That was what made me feel the deepest guilt. I was angry at my friends, my throne brothers—the only men who had ever gained my trust and kept it—because they wanted her, they felt no need to hide it or fight it, and because of that, they had her.

Right now, I had no doubt that Orion was fucking the Changeling. Bringing her to orgasm over and over again. Giving her the very same pleasure I wanted to pull from that fragile looking body of hers. I was in trouble. She had wormed her little self between the three of us, but I wondered ... briefly ... if maybe it wasn't to pull us apart, but to seal us even closer together. With her between the three of us, there would be no power in the world that could separate us.

An idea popped into my head, and as I sat there, my mind gave it life. We Fae were weakened when sepa- rated. In our individual Courts meant to give power to no one great entity, but what if the Courts were brought together? What if all of Faekind could be ruled under one entity. Not a King, but perhaps a Court of Kings?

I sighed and I shifted back, my hand falling over the side of the chair to bang into something beneath the table at my side. I jerked and looked down, finding a familiar instrument. With a frown, I reached beneath the table and sought out what I'd seen, and when I pulled my hand free, in it was an old violin I hadn't seen in ages.

"What the—"

"I see you've finally found it." Groffet's words made me jump from my chair and whirl around.

"Groffet," I gritted his name out through clenched teeth. "Do not sneak up on me, you insolent troll!"

He stared back at me over the wide bridge of his nose and huffed. "Do not be angry at me, young Prince, for your own absence of mind."

"I wasn't—" The denial died on my lips. I had been absentminded, too focused on her. I shook my head and turned away, only belatedly realizing the instrument I clutched in my hand until it banged loudly against the table. "Shit!" I cursed, pulling the violin up and inspecting it to see if it was damaged.

Groffet tsked, the sound an irritating judgment in an otherwise silent room. I lifted my gaze and offered him a dark look. "If you have something to say, old man, say it."

Groffet waddled across the floor until he stood just on the other side of the table and then shuffled around it until he was at my side. His fat troll fingers reached for the violin, and though I narrowed my eyes, I released it to his grip.

"You have not played her in a long time," he said quietly, as he moved his hand down her neck and over her body. Several strings were missing, as was the bow. "But I believe you have found her again for a reason."

"There's no time for music lessons, Groffet," I said. "What have you found?"

Groffet didn't answer me right away, but as much as I hated it, I'd grown accustomed to his impertinence. He would speak when he was ready to and no sooner. "There is something in the works," he finally said after several long moments. He handed the violin back to me and took a step back. "But it will not be ready for a night or two. I must make the necessary preparations. I recommend you and the other majesties take this opportunity to heal. You will need it for what is coming."

Although his words were serious, my mind stuck on the word majesties. I snorted. "Since when do you refer to us by our titles?" I asked with a shake of my head.

Groffet smiled, revealing crooked, yellowed teeth and a small dimple set into the side of his face that I'd never seen nor noticed before. "The time is coming where all will know you only by those titles," he said cryptically, but before I could ask what he meant, he shuffled away and left me standing there holding an old violin.

I sighed. I would need something to keep my mind off of Cress and the others, something, perhaps that could distract me long enough for me to finally make a decision.

About her. About our Court. And about Faekind as we knew it.

CHAPTER SIXTEEN

CRESS

My body ached in the most delicious way when I awoke the next morning. The warmth of a masculine body was pressed to my back. Real sunlight— at least, I was pretty sure it was real—streamed in overhead.

It was by far the most peaceful way I'd woken up since being captured. So, instead of ruining it by turning and waking up my bed partner, I exhaled and snuggled back into Orion's embrace. His arms tightened around me, pulling me back against him even more. A low growly noise sounded behind my ear as he released a breath.

"Cress." My name was a sigh on his lips and it made me smile even as my chest tightened.

We stayed like that for a long moment. His hands clenched and unclenched around my stomach and his heart beat faster against my back, letting me know that he was awake. As my sleepiness faded, too, I wriggled around until I was facing him, earning a deep, throaty chuckle from his lips. His dark eyes gazed intently into mine while his hand came up and brushed a lock of hair from my face. While his expression started off amused and pleased, it slowly morphed. His brows drew down low over his eyes and his lips pinched

"Cress, I—" he began

"What's wrong?" I cut him off, reaching for him. My hands moved over his naked chest and abdomen. "Is it the poison?"

"No, Cress." His hands captured mine, stilling their frantic movements. "It's nothing to do with that. The poison is receding. I'll be completely healed before the end of the day." His dark eyes met mine. "Thanks to you."

"Are you sure?" I pressed.

"Yes." He nodded and then lifted his hand to slowly stroke a knuckle lightly down the side of my face.

"Then what's wrong?" I asked insistently, worry creasing my brow.

His pinched lips curled down into a deep grimace. "I…" Orion sucked in a breath and only when it shuddered back out did he continue. "You were taken because of me," he said. "For that, I'm sorry. If Tyr hadn't known of my interest in you then you wouldn't have been in danger. I put you in that position."

"Orion." I reached up between us and touched his face, securing my gaze to his and staring into his eyes for a second longer before I continued—just to make sure he was paying attention. "You are *not* responsible for your brother's actions. You are not Tyr." His lips parted and before he could get out another word to oppose what I was saying, I reached up and silenced him by holding one of my hands over his mouth. "In fact," I said, glaring at him meaningfully. "I'd say you're about as opposite from your brother as you could get. You care about others, you care about me, you care about how this war is affecting Fae kind. The only thing Tyr cares about is power. Nothing else."

I took a breath, trying to calm the riotous anger that was blisteringly hot inside of me. "Do not equate yourself to him," I ordered, "because you are so far above him, there's no competition. You are brave and amazing and you mean more to me than you could possibly understand..." My words trailed off, and as they did, he reached up and gently tugged my hand away from his mouth before turning to place a kiss against my palm.

"Do you understand?" I wondered aloud.

He frowned but didn't say anything for a long moment. Then, still holding my hand, he reached forward and pulled me onto his lap. "Understand what, Cress?" he whispered as I settled over him.

"How much I love you?" I asked. His brows shot up and his lips parted in surprise. I hadn't exactly intended to blurt out the question, but there was no taking it back. So, I shored up my courage and sucked in a breath. I straightened my spine and met his gaze head on. "I do," I stated. "I love you—and Roan." When he didn't immediately respond, I harrumphed and glared at him. "Well?" I pressed. "Are you going to say anything?"

He coughed out a laugh, shaking his head—the dark

locks of his hair swiping back and forth with the movement. When Orion lifted his head once more to look at me, though, and I saw the blossoming smile spread across his face, my nerves settled. I breathed out a sigh of relief and loosened my hold that had dropped to his shoulders. I hadn't even realized I'd been squeezing so tight.

"I love you, too," he said. "More than life itself—I would die for you."

My heart felt like it could soar right out of my chest. I swallowed roughly, blinking back tears. *Why in the name of Coreliath was I on the verge of crying? What was wrong with me?* I sniffed hard and forced them away. Happy. I was happy. This feeling was so incredibly intense that it swept through me and I found that my lips were twitching, a smile forming that could have rivaled Orion's.

Orion's hands moved down and around my body until he pressed them against my spine, pulling me closer so that my breasts were smashed against his hard chest. His head came down and mine lifted. I knew what he wanted. His lips met mine and I shuddered as he consumed me. It wasn't the starving ravenous hunger we had for one another last night, but a reassurance that the bond between us was solid and unshakable. This kiss was a slow, leisurely exploration of each other, but at its core was a new tenderness, one that came from the depth of our bond.

The door down on the lower floor of Orion's chambers rattled and was thrown open and Orion and I broke off the kiss. "Good morning!" Roan's voice sounded from down below, followed by the thumping of his footsteps as he ascended the stairs and his head popped up over the garden's railing before the rest of him followed. "Good to see you're both still alive. I brought breakfast."

He waved his hand as a contingent of pixies floated forward, carrying a couple of trays laden down with fruits and breads and cheese. "How's the patient?" Roan asked, nodding between us as he swiped up a fruit and pulled a knife from his pocket, slicing it into chunks that he popped between his lips.

"Much better," Orion grunted as he gently settled me off of his lap and to the side. I reached across him and grabbed what looked like a shirt that had been tossed aside. He'd been naked when I'd come in last night, but this area was a mess of clothes strewn about. It was sort of amusing—all these plants surrounding a dark, messy figure. I pulled the fabric over my head and reached for one of the trays, snatching up a bun and shoving it into my mouth.

The warm and yeasty goodness practically melted on my tongue.

"You look well, Brother," Roan said, moving over as he watched the two of us.

"Cress worked her magic on me," Orion said as a wicked grin curved his lips.

The back of my hand slapped his chest before I'd even realized I'd moved. "I—uh…" I stuttered as they both shot me knowing looks. "Can you pass me more bread?" I asked.

As Orion did, he turned and faced Roan. "Where are we with a strategy?" he asked.

Roan popped another piece of fruit into his mouth and swallowed before responding. "I've got a meeting scheduled with the guards. Before we came back, I sent a few men to scout the area and follow the King's supply chain."

I shoved another one of the delicious rolls into my mouth and groaned as I chewed it slowly before a thought occurred to me. "Where's Sorrell?" I asked, tilting my head so that I could see around Roan's form against the railing, but there was no sign of anyone else but the three of us in the room.

Roan pursed his lips and tossed the core of his fruit at the pixie flitting above his head. The pixie snatched it out of thin air and my eyes widened as I watched the little creature unhinge its jaw to a disproportionate size compared to its small body. It bit into the dead core and swallowed the thing into two bites. It was kind of gross, but when the pixie finished its impromptu meal, it sighed and its wings fluttered as if it were happy.

"Sorrell is concerned," he said.

I eyed him. "Regular stick up the ass concerned..." I prompted. "Or..."

Roan didn't even crack a smile at that and instead, merely shook his head. Shit. That meant it was a serious type of concerned—one he likely agreed with. "The human King—"

"King Felix," I said, cutting him off briefly.

He shot me a look that made me suspect he didn't

appreciate the interruption. I merely shoved another roll into my mouth and tilted my head back, batting my eyelashes—the picture of complete and utter innocence … because, you know, that's totally what I was. Innocent.

"King Felix," Roan restated, narrowing his gaze on my upturned face as he did so, "has gotten far too brave. His colluding with Tyr is evidence of that."

"He doesn't know that Tyr's a Fae, though," I said, swallowing my mouthful quickly.

"Regardless," Roan said as Orion put a hand on my arm when I moved to get up, "the fact that he even considered kidnapping a Fae and executing her—never mind that we were able to stop it—proves that this war is far from over. I have no doubt that he's gearing up for an attack on our countrymen."

"And Sorrell?" Orion questioned.

Roan sighed. "He's overthinking our options. We have Cress back, and we know at least some of what Tyr is planning, but we don't have any definite steps forward and Sorrell seems to think that something big is on the horizon. I, unfortunately, can't disagree with him. If King Felix is willing to go to such lengths just to kill one Fae." He paused and gestured to me before continuing. "There's no telling what else he's willing to do or already planning. And Sorrell…"

I frowned, leaning forward, across Orion's chest as I waited, impatiently, for Roan to finish his last thought. When he didn't, I raised my brows. "Sorrell *what?*" I demanded.

"He's lacking in magical energy," Roan replied with a glance to his boots. He closed the pocket knife he'd been holding, shoving it along with his hands into the pockets of his dark trousers as he leaned against the railing. His brows furrowed in concentrated thought. "He hasn't replenished in well over a month, and I worry that he's going to insist on risking his life for the cause—No." Roan shook his head, the red locks of his hair sliding across his forehead as he did so. "I *know* he will.

"So, we can talk to him," I said, looking to Orion. "Right?"

"It's not going to be that simple, Little Bird," Roan answered and when Orion shook his head at my hopeful expression, I feared they were both right.

"It's not just him, it's also about the coming battle," Roan said thoughtfully. "We need to figure out what to do with the humans. We can shepherd our own people, but if we want to have any chance of peace, we need the humans to stop fighting us, and they don't seem likely to do so, especially after years of the King's propaganda against us."

I sank against Orion's chest, my own squeezing tight. The odds were stacked against us. What could we do? They were Royals, yes, but to face the facts—they only had so many men and King Felix had an entire Kingdom.

"Can Groffet do anything?" I asked, an idea popping into my mind. He was old, wise, and had hundreds of books in that library of his. He was the only one I knew of that the Princes looked to for guidance. "Couldn't he help us come up with a plan?"

Roan and Orion each looked at me with sad frowns.

I hated it—that expression on their faces. It was as if they were thinking that the war was already lost. It wasn't.

"We have to do *something*," I insisted.

Orion calmed me as he stroked my arm and pressed a chaste kiss against my forehead. "We will," he assured me.

Roan gestured absently to the room. "This is what it's like, Cress," he said, his voice growing grave. "This is what it means to be a Royal. We have to make the decisions that will affect the entirety of our people—and if we choose wrong…"

He let the statement hang, but I only shook my head. "Then we won't choose wrong," I said. "We *will* figure this out."

They were both quiet for a long moment, Orion's fingers smoothing up and down the outside of my arm. "There will be panic," he finally said. "We have to keep things under wraps for now. Only people we can be sure to trust must know of everything that's happened."

Roan nodded and so did I. I was fine with that. I even agreed with it, as long as they didn't give up hope. Because in the darkness of war and all that we were bound to lose, hope was the one thing that, if taken from us, would truly result in the loss of everything we held dear. When I took Orion's hand in mine and looked at Roan as he met my eyes from across the room, I realized I had finally found where I belonged, and I wasn't giving that up, not without a fight.

CHAPTER SEVENTEEN

CRESS

After Roan's less than ideal news and the conversation we'd had over breakfast, I'd left Orion to recover in his chambers and had gone in search of Sorrell myself. While Roan was at a strategy meeting, I planned on finding Sorrell and finding out if there was something he knew that the rest of us didn't.

My search, however, had reached a dead end halfway through the day. He was nowhere to be found. Not outside where new guards were patrolling the wall. Not in his chambers—which had been difficult enough to find on my own, even with a few pixies along to guide me. Not even in the library—and that had been my most hopeful place to find him. Wherever he was, it was apparent that he didn't want to be found. It almost made me want to find him just to spite him and his annoying ability to hide from me.

I moved along the corridors slowly, thinking, trying

to figure out any of the other places that I knew he could be. Every so often, I'd see one of the other Fae nobles who lived in the Court. Some would pause when they saw me, seeming unsure of what to do. A few bowed. A few ignored my presence and kept walking as if they didn't see me. It didn't bother me much; if I was going to sneak up on Sorrell, I'd need all the invisibility I could get. He probably knew I was hunting for him and had hidden away on purpose. The asshole.

After several more hours of searching, I finally gave up and headed for the throne room where I knew Roan would be. I paused on the threshold of the room. The doors had been closed, but it appeared that whoever had come in or left last had accidentally left one of them cracked. I peeked in, listening to the sound of Roan's commanding and authoritative voice as I did.

Set in the middle of the room was a long wooden table. From where I stood, I could only make out papers and small figurines on top of it. Around it though, there were plenty of massive Fae—all clothed in the same leather coverings I knew soldiers wore beneath their armor.

I stepped closer to the door, placing my palm against the surface and leaning my ear into it. The second I did so, however, the door creaked open and several heads lifted and turned my way. Heat rose to my face as Roan turned and caught me standing there.

Whelp, I'd never been much for stealth anyway, I thought, deciding to push forward. I crept into the room, shifting the door open even further to allow me access. I lifted a hand and waved.

The corner of Roan's lips twitched and he shook his head at me before waving me forward and continuing on with his speech to the soldiers. As I moved forward, heading for the outstretched hand he offered me, my mind was catapulted back to a time not that long ago, when I'd snuck in here and been caught just like I had moments before. Though I knew it wasn't, it felt as if that event that had happened so long ago. As if it had been a different life, like it had happened to a different person.

"I want three on this wall, two on this one, and at least one lookout," Roan was saying when I finally made it to his side. "Are you okay? What's wrong?" Roan asked as soon as I was close enough for us to have a private conversation and not have to shout over the soldiers.

"It will be done, Your Highness," an older Fae with a silvery beard said.

"See to it," Roan said before glancing down to me. "And give me a moment. I'll be back."

"You don't have to stop for me," I protested as Roan's hand touched my side, rounding it as he led me several paces away from the table.

"It's fine," he said. "The men needed the mental break anyway. Is everything okay?"

"I'm fine, just taking a walk," I reassured him. "I was trying to find Sorrell, but he's—"

"Don't worry about Sorrell right now, Cress," Roan said, cutting me off. "You need to rest and recover from what happened to you."

I frowned up at him. "What happened to me?" I repeated, confused.

Roan's eyes darkened. "What you experienced at the hands of the human King—"

"King Felix," I corrected him again.

He glared at me, and I shrugged. "I'm fine," I assured him. "Really. Now that I'm back, I feel better than ever. I'm golden, really."

"You're sure you don't need anything?" Roan pressed, his hand tightening on my side.

I liked the hot pulse of his palm against me even if it was over fabric, and if he'd meant in any other way, I would've said I needed him to take me to his chambers and fuck me until I couldn't see straight. But I knew his intentions and they had nothing to do with anything other than my wellbeing. "No, Roan," I said on a sigh. "I don't need anything. I was just searching for Sorrell"—I eyed him with a glare, wondering if he knew where he could be and was keeping it from me—"and I got curious as to what you were strategizing in here."

He sighed, sounding exhausted. "I'm just concerned," he said, finally. "Word of your almost execution has reached the other Courts and we've received communications from them indicating their concern."

I arched a brow. "Really?" I deadpanned. "Your mother is concerned for me?" If that wasn't a bald faced lie, I'd eat my left shoe—and though I could pack in the rolls, shoes … not so much.

Roan's lips twitched for a brief moment. "Fair," he said. "Perhaps she doesn't much care for you, but she and the Frost Queen are concerned. You may not have been my mother's choice for me, but you will be the future Crimson Princess and eventual Crimson Queen.

You were abducted and almost executed by the human—"

I eyed him and he sighed.

"By King Felix," he said, correcting himself before he even finished. "Our race was betrayed by one of our own. This showcases that it's no longer our guards or our soldiers that are very much in danger; we all are. King Felix is no longer happy to just sit back and murder our brethren on the field of battle, where we might expect. He no longer seems to care about honor or dignity. He and Tyr have threatened you, which means they have threatened us all—including royalty."

"What do you mean?" I couldn't quite wrap my head around his words. If royalty was threatened then that meant both he and Orion—even Sorrell—were in more danger than I'd originally believed. "You're not planning on going out to the battlefield are you?" I demanded.

Roan frowned. "Of course we are," he said.

"You can't!"

"Cress." When I would have moved away from him, Roan's hands found my upper arms and held me still in front of him as his head dipped and his eyes met mine, colliding with what I was sure was a show of fear and panic in my own expression. "We are used to this. Sorrell, Orion, and I—we've all been on the battlefield before. We can handle ourselves."

"That was before I knew you," I said. It was before I had come to care for them, to love them.

Roan's hands tightened on my arms, squeezing roughly. "Our race was betrayed by one of our own," he stated. "You, as my fiancée, are by extension considered part of the Royal Court families. Tyr went after you. It's only a matter of time before they come after all of us. We have to hit them before they hit us." I gulped at his words, but I didn't say anything. His hold loosened until finally he released me and took a step back. The second his skin left mine, I felt bereft, but I couldn't make myself reach out to touch him. I was in too much shock, trying to process his words, and think of something —*anything*—that I could do to fix it. "The Court of Frost is talking about coming to Amnestia. They want to provide more soldiers and support to us when we retaliate for your abduction."

"What? I didn't think they had that kind of power anymore. I thought they remained in Alfheim because they couldn't move to the human realm?"

Roan blew out a breath. "The Queens are determined. They know that if we were to attack the King on our own, we'd be weak. They are also very angry over Tyr's deception and betrayal. They've contacted the Court of Midnight to determine whether or not Tyr was acting on his own, but the Midnight Royals aren't responding to the messengers."

"What have the messengers said?" I asked. Surely, whoever had gone had gotten the information about the Court of Midnight would know something we didn't. "I'm pretty sure that Tyr is working alone," I said. "He didn't speak as if he had partners—at least any that knew of his plan."

"The Queens have sent messengers, but when I say there's been no response," Roan replied, "I mean that there's been absolutely nothing. The messengers haven't returned. If what you told us is true and Tyr is expecting to rule what's left after this war—the Queens would rather die in battle than live to see that happen."

I bit my lip in frustration, but before I could say anything, the older guard from before stepped around the table and called out. "Your Highness?"

Roan huffed out a breath, turning towards him. "One moment, I'll be right there," he called out before pivoting back to me. "I have to go, Cress."

I crossed my arms over my chest and stared up at him.

"Don't be upset," he said.

"I'm not upset," I said. Upset was far too tame a word for what I was feeling. "I'm scared. I'm worried. I'm frustrated."

Roan lifted a hand and cupped the back of my head, bringing me towards him as he leaned closer. "I know," he whispered. "But I promise you, this will all be over soon."

I shook my head. I couldn't see how that was possible. Though I knew the war had been going on for decades now, it felt as if recent events had made it all new again. It felt as if it had just begun. "I'm going to head to the library to see Groffet and Nellie," I tell him.

"Okay, have fun. Don't harass Groffet too much," Roan said. His fingers slipped out of my hair and he sighed, turning away. I watched him take several steps back towards the table and just as I was about to leave, he jerked to a halt, flipping back around and moving faster than before until he reached me.

My eyes widened as Roan grabbed me around my

waist. My hands lifted and flattened against his chest as he crushed me against him and his head descended. I moaned involuntarily as his lips took mine in a bruising kiss.

Desire whipped through my body like a sudden wildfire. His tongue delved into my mouth as one hand splayed against my back and the other rose to cup the nape of my neck, positioning me just where he wanted me. His lips were hard and demanding against mine.

By the time he was done, my lips felt swollen and I was light-headed. He pulled away, just far enough that we could make eye contact, and whispered, "Tonight, you're mine."

His lips landed on mine once more, but only for a brief second, and then he was gone. When I opened my eyes, I saw him moving back to his soldiers, his head held high and his shoulders pushed back. He appeared every single inch the Royal Fae Prince. The commander and the protector.

I stumbled away, my hand grasping at the wall the second I grew close. Once I was out of the throne room, I leaned against the cool stone wall of the empty corridor for a moment, letting my heart calm itself.

Nellie, I reminded myself. I had to go and see Nellie. She'd said we needed to talk the last time I'd seen her. Hopefully she would be enough of a distraction to keep me from turning back and dragging Roan back to his chambers when I knew he had work to do.

CHAPTER EIGHTEEN

ROAN

C ress's departure brought me back to where I needed to be—strategy and planning. War. Even though humans and Fae had been at war for two decades, in the last several months, things had changed. A Changeling had been found—the last of her kind. I wondered if Cress even realized how special she was.

Changelings were creatures born of Fae and yet raised among humans. A tradition that had been popular when the coexistence of each race had been symbiotic. Now, all I could see lying in wait for us was extinction. This war would end, but the cost ... the cost, I worried, might be too great.

I didn't enjoy the idea of killing off the humans. There was something intrinsically wrong about eradicating an entire species. And if it came down to it, I knew Cress would fight against it. My head lifted and I stared through the entryway where she'd gone. Then there was the matter of her little human friend. A dull pounding ache began in my head.

"Your Highness?" the sound of one of my soldier's voices brought me back to the present.

I gave him my full attention. "Where were we?" I demanded.

He straightened at my tone and then gestured to the table before us. "We were discussing entry points into Norune Castle."

"How many are there?" I asked, looking down.

The map before me was hand drawn—but applied with magic, bringing the etchings to life. The mountains and castle stood upright as well as the little village that surrounded our target. We were given a bird's eye view of the place that would be our next objective.

"Three main gates, Your Highness," the man stated, pointing to each of them in turn as he continued talking. "The main entrance at the front between the village and the main road. A side entrance to receive supplies for the main hub, and a back entrance that appears to be sealed to make people think it's unusable."

"Is it?" I inquired, narrowing my eyes on the placement of that entrance—with its main wall facing a forest that would be easy to conceal ourselves in.

"No sir. We believe it's fully functional and merely 'sealed off' to present the idea of inoperational. From what our scout managed to gather, the entrance is an emergency one to be used in the event of crisis. It was likely built for the Duke and his family to escape if they were under siege."

I shook my head. They would be under siege soon, but there would be no using that entrance. That entrance was about to be one of our operating bases. I pointed to it on the map. "I want two men stationed inside the forest," I ordered. "We're not going to let anyone leave with the supplies they have in there." I lifted my head and looked across the table to the Fae who'd brought me this information—Xantho. "You're sure they have a hidden cache of supplies in here for the King?"

This information needed to be good. The war had slowly descended into mere tensions, but after Cress's abduction and Tyr's betrayal, a new phase of this long suffering conflict had finally hit. Now it was our turn to hit the human King where it hurt—his supply train.

"Yes, sir." Xantho nodded. "I seduced a young human who works within the castle and made some inquiries. She said that the Duke Everett is a close personal friend of the King's; he's been storing the King's extra supplies there for years."

If we did this—no, I shook my head, *when* we did this—an entire castle would be out of food. It was distasteful but such was the product of war. Hard choices that harmed innocents in the effort to stamp out the evil of hatred. I closed my eyes and reached up, pinching the bridge of my nose.

"Your Highness," Xantho said, leaning forward. I opened my eyes and fixed him with a look. "This is the right decision," he said. "Once the human King has no extra supplies, nor anywhere to store them, we'll be able to lay siege to his castle. If he decides to retreat and block us off—he'll receive no aid, no food, and no medicines until he surrenders."

"He won't surrender," I replied. That much I knew for sure. I'd seen his conviction at Cress's intended execution. The rage in his voice, the hatred he had spewed into the crowd of onlookers had been melodramatic and over staged. Yet, I had seen the honesty in his face. With each and every word, he truly believed in his right to kill as many Fae as he could until we were all wiped out. As it was, our race was not thriving. We couldn't in Alfheim now. It was a barren wasteland just waiting to perish. It was ruthless and dangerous. Soon enough, even the Frost Queen and my mother would have to come to grips with the fact that they resided in a dying world. I sighed. "King Felix would rather die than surrender to us," I finished.

The first guard slammed his fist on the table. "Then he dies," he said harshly. "That man has taken numerous lives of our loved ones. Even if he does surrender, we will show no mercy." The others surrounding the table shifted and grew restless. A few even voiced their agreement.

No. I wouldn't ask them to show mercy to a man such as him. My upper lip curled back. "He will be tried and executed for the crimes he's committed in this war," I assured my men. "But the villagers..." I gesture to the surrounding area of Norune Castle. "Like this one, the King's palace is surrounded by a capital city. There are people who live there—women and children. We kill the fighters," I stated. "The soldiers and the men, but we leave the innocents aside."

"Children grow into adults," an older guard, Leif, with a long scar torn down the side of his face spoke up. "We leave the seeds to grow and they will plant more destruction in the end."

No. This was where I drew the line. I let anger darken my voice. Fire erupted at my scalp and I did nothing to tamp it down. "We leave the children," I repeated. "Regardless of your convictions or beliefs, I am your Prince and you will follow my commands." I took a moment to glare around the table as silence descended. Several of my men frowned. They were confused by my statement—they agreed with Leif that to let the children of the soldiers who had killed their friends and family live made no sense.

I had to make it make sense, I realized. I pointed to the map and conjured magic, slowly—one by one—little figures began to draw themselves and then lift off of the parchment. Small figures. Pregnant figures and little ones who ran around the larger, slender frames of the others like darting little animals.

"If we eradicate the possibility of another generation of humans," I began, "we become the very monsters they believe us to be."

"Who cares what the humans think?" one brave soldier erupted. "We know the truth."

I lifted my gaze to the man and stared him down until he grew uncomfortable, shuffling back away from the table a few steps before lowering his eyes. Only then did I continue. "If we do this," I said. "Kill the children— the seeds—we will no longer simply be suspected evil, but we will be true evil." I shake my head. "No. Our main objective is the King and the former heir of Midnight, Tyr Evenfall. You may not like it, but you will obey. Any man seen killing unjustly will be reported to me and tried for the same war crimes as our counterparts." I searched the room, meeting the eyes of every Fae brave enough to raise his head. "We are not monsters," I told them. "We are Fae. We are warriors."

Silence echoed in the wake of my announcement and one by one, each Fae stood back and brought their right fist up, clenching and slamming it against their chest as a sign of respect. I nodded to them, an acknowledgment of their bravery, of their sacrifice thus far and future sacrifice if our war should need it, though I prayed to the Gods, we wouldn't.

"Go," I ordered. "Replenish your magic. Train and rest. We will leave for Norune Castle within the next two days. You have until then to prepare."

The men dispersed and I sighed, already feeling as if I were another hundred years older. "You spoke well," a familiar and welcomed voice said.

Turning, I offered Orion a small smile as he approached. "How is your recovery?" I asked.

He nodded. "I'll be well enough to travel with you when you go to this castle," he stated, stepping up to the table alongside me. He remained quiet for a moment and then he spoke again. "This is the beginning of the end," he said. "When the King is dead, and my brother, we will have won the war that has plagued us for decades."

"We should feel celebratory, shouldn't we?" I asked sardonically.

Orion's dark eyes rise to meet mine. "No," he replied. "It's understandable why you wouldn't. In war, there are no true winners. Only victors. We'll attain our victory."

I watched him curiously and sympathetically. Of all of us, he had given the most in this war. Few people truly knew of the horrors he had endured on the battle-fields. The scars that coated his body were messages—remembrances of what he had suffered. Lifting a palm, I grasped the shoulder closest to me.

"When Tyr is executed," I let the words linger on the edge of a whisper as I spoke them. He and I both knew that there would be no other outcome. When Tyr was captured, regardless of whether or not the Queens would demand a trial, he would die. We couldn't allow any other conclusion, not after all Tyr had done. "We will be here for you—Sorrell and I—as we have always been."

Orion stiffened under my hand and moved so that he shifted out from beneath it. "I will kill him myself," he said suddenly.

"No, Orion." I began to shake my head, but before I could utter another word, a blast of darkness rushed out from beneath the cuffs of his shirt, startling me back. I reared away as smoke darker than the inky blackness of night seeped from beneath his clothing. His neckline, his pants legs. Soon enough, he was shrouded in it. Covered completely as the smoky dark-ness clung to his frame, wrapping it's disturbingly life-like tendrils around his body until he appeared to be drenched in a cloak of his own making.

Darkness.

Shadow.

Cold, quiet, fury.

"I will end this," Orion announced. "Once and for all."

My lips parted, but no words emerged. It was all I could do to stare back at him, watching as the magic he usually kept contained was unleashed. A lesser man might have run. Perhaps it made me the same as a lesser man to admit that, in that moment, I feared him. I feared the ferocity in his tone, the wildness in his eyes that I hadn't seen since he'd first arrived at the Court of Crimson—silent, cold, and seemingly unfeeling. He'd been nothing more than a boy, afraid to love, afraid to care for anything, and far too broken.

He didn't need me to fear him now. He needed me to be with him. To help him. To center him. Mindful of the pain the shadows could cause, I stepped closer rather than away. I reached into it, grasping at his shoulders and shaking him slightly to get him to look at me.

"Together," I rasped as the skin over my knuckles and hands began to prickle. It was as though a thousand tiny needles were being driven into my flesh over and over again. I gritted my teeth and bore the pain. He had endured far worse. "We will get him and the King," I said. "And we will do it together."

CHAPTER NINETEEN

CRESS

W hen the library doors were finally in front of me, I hesitated. It wasn't that I didn't want to see my best friend, but so much had happened in such a short time that I wasn't sure what she would want to know and what I could divulge. The guys hadn't said anything about keeping what happened a secret, but wasn't it illegal to tell humans certain things about Fae Court? I sucked in a breath and decided that it didn't really matter. Nellie was my best friend. She was exempt from such laws … hopefully.

I pushed open the heavy wood door and saw Groffet sitting at his workstation. He gave me a nod of greeting and said, "Your human friend is in the back stacks on the left."

"Thank you," I said, flashing him a quick smile.

I wound my way through the aisles of books and

other items, most of which looked like scrolls and leather bound volumes of ancient texts, but other items didn't look like anything I'd seen before—jars of weird looking animal body parts, herbs-like branches that looked more humanoid than tree-like. My steps slowed as I passed them, but I kept walking until finally, I saw Nellie sitting in the furthest corner, surrounded by cushions and books, with a heavy tome open on her lap. Despite the open book, however, her eyes were closed. I got closer, only realizing when I was a step or two away that she'd fallen asleep. Soft snores were emitting from her half open mouth.

"Nellie," I whispered, trying not to laugh as I sat down on the cushion next to her.

When nothing happened, I shook my head and reached out—patting her arm and then pushing it gently until her lashes fluttered. Nellie jerked up and blinked, looking around. It only took her a moment to realize I was the reason for her sudden awakening. As soon as she saw me, her face broke out into a wide smile. She shoved her book aside and flung herself forward, her arms wrapping around me. "You came," she said as she pulled away. "I was worried you'd get side-tracked again."

"Well, better late than never, right?" I said with a wince. I wasn't surprised by her assumption. The Princes had taken up pretty much all of my thoughts recently. A result, I assumed, of all that we'd been through together, and okay, maybe the fact that I was, kind of, stupidly falling for them.

"I know, but those Princes keep you pretty occupied," Nellie replied with pursed lips as if she'd been reading my mind.

I narrowed my gaze on her. "You haven't picked anything magical up since you've been here, have you?" I asked suspiciously.

She smacked my arm. "I am not the one who goes running into any castle they find," she replied tersely.

There was a brief moment where I widened my eyes at her innocence and she stared at me with a reproachful look that I knew so well. Then, all at once, the two of us burst out laughing. I doubled over, clutching my stomach as my laughter ricocheted up to the rafters of the library and Nellie shook her head at me.

When the giggles died down, she sighed and then touched my arm, reaching down to take my hand and pulling it into her lap. "I want to know everything that's happened," she said seriously. "I was so worried for you, especially when they came back from that other Court without you."

I took a breath. "It's a lot," I admitted. "I don't even know where to start."

"At the beginning," Nel suggested, her fingers tightening on mine.

"Just the trip to the Court of Frost was intense," I told her. "Then when we got there—I met the Fae Queens."

Her eyes widened. "What were they like?" she asked, her voice dipping to a whisper as if they were watching.

It wouldn't surprise me, though, if those two rotten, old hags were spying on me—especially the Crimson Queen.

"They were perfectly horrid," I snapped. "They hated me—that much was clear. And Roan…" I stopped and groaned. "He didn't help matters when he just suddenly announced me as his fiancée."

"He did what?" Her jaw dropped, her mouth gaping open.

I nodded and pulled one of my hands out to pat the top of hers gently in understanding. "Oh yeah," I said. "Didn't ask, just announced it. To be fair, he did it thinking that it would act as a protection against anyone who tried to hurt me."

Her expression turned worrisome—her brows drawing together and forming a little wrinkled V in the middle of her forehead. "That obviously didn't work," she said quietly.

I winced. "No," I said. "But I can understand the attempt. Do you know exactly what happened?" I inquired.

She shook her head. "Just that you'd been kidnapped and taken to the King's castle. No one would tell me anything, but I had a feeling it was bad. After you were back, that's when I found out about the execution." Her hands began to tremble against mine. "I was so scared."

Yeah, I understood that. Had our roles been reversed, I would have been terrified out of my mind. "I'm okay now," I assure her quickly, squeezing her fingers roughly. I bit down on my lip, considering what to tell her. "There were courtship events," I said. "Special ceremonies that happen when a Royal gets engaged. In the middle of the last one, it was Tyr—Orion's brother—who disrupted it. He kidnapped me and opened some portal to the Kingdom of Amnestia." I swallowed against a dry throat as I recalled the Run of the Gods and how it had started so differently than how it had ended.

"Why?" Nel frowned at me. "Why would he do such a thing?"

"Because he's helping the human Kingdom," I confessed. "His plan is to force the Fae and humans into a battle that will wipe out all of the major players."

"Even his own brother?" Her lips parted in shock. "How could he do that?"

"Because he's evil," I said. "Because he doesn't care who gets hurt as long as, in the end, he's the one left with power. He wants to rule over the ruins of what's left after the war and he doesn't care what he has to do to make that happen. When the Princes came to rescue me, he even…" I trailed off, remembering how Sorrell and I had found Orion with his veins turning black with poison. "He tried to kill his own brother," I finished.

Nellie and I sat in silence for a moment. Neither of us spoke and yet so much connection filtered between us. The fear. The relief. The worry over what the future would bring.

Finally, she spoke. "So, what happens now?"

I shrugged. "We come up with a plan and we take him down, I suppose," I said.

The corner of her mouth curled up in a rueful grin. "You make it sound so easy."

"Psh." I lifted one of my hands away from hers and waved it through the air. "We can do it. We've faced much worse. Remember that one time when Sister Madeline tried to cook the Winter's feast?"

Nellie's face blanched and she shuddered. "Cook was furious," she said. "She burned the whole hog."

I wrinkled my nose. "It smelled horrible," I agreed.

"Not that you would've eaten it," she replied, eyeing me. "I've noticed, though, that you seem to eat well here."

"The food here tastes good," I said.

"Do you think it has anything to do with it being Fae food?" she inquired, leaning forward as she reached for the book she'd laid aside. "I think I figured out why you had such a hard time eating at the convent. Fae are supposed to eat only things that come from nature. Wheat and fruits and nuts and—"

"Well, I do eat a lot of bread," I supplied, cutting her off. "Does that count?"

She rolled her eyes, snapping the book shut once more. "Yes," she huffed. "It counts." The two of us lapsed into another moment of quiet, and then, she grinned at me. "So…" she began. "You and the Crimson Prince?"

My eyes shifted away as I reached up and gently scratched the underside of my jaw. "He was just trying to protect me," I said.

"But … you're engaged?"

I winced. We hadn't really talked about it since I'd been back. "Sort of?"

"Either you are or you aren't," Nellie said with a raised brow.

"We are?"

"Are you telling me or asking?"

I blew out a breath and dropped my hand back to my lap. "Oh, I don't know." I released a groan. "When he did it, it was because of the Court of Frost and his mother—it was like a vow of protection. Not really an engagement."

"That's not how he acted when he returned without you," she replied with a mischievous grin.

I narrowed my eyes on her face. "What do you know?"

"Clearly he still doesn't realize how much trouble you attract."

"I do not attract trouble!" I reached over and smacked her arm. Both of her brows rose as she pursed her lips at me. "Not much," I amended in a quieter tone.

A bubble of laughter left her, bringing a smile to my face. It was nice to see her laugh again after all we'd been through in the last few weeks. "Okay. I'll stop pressuring you," she said, then after a beat, she added, "about him—you will, however, have to tell me about the dark Fae. What was his name?"

"Orion?" I guessed.

"Yes." She nodded. "He seems quite taken with you as well. How does that work?"

"We … uh … share?" I said, feeling my cheeks heat. Nellie and I had never had the opportunity or a reason to talk about things like this before. We'd been raised around mostly women and young boys our whole lives. The only boys we'd ever known had come from the village and they'd been nothing like the Fae I knew now.

163

Roan, Orion, and even Sorrell were warriors. Their shoulders were twice the width of an average boy's. They were men—Royals—and far more than I'd ever anticipated.

Nellie's mouth had dropped open and she just stared at me in shock for a moment before asking, "Does that make you a Princess then?"

I snorted in response to that. "I'm being called the Crimson Princess, but that doesn't make me a real Princess," I told her.

"You're a Gods damned Princess," Nellie suddenly burst out.

I blinked, staring at her in shock. "Did you just curse?"

"Hey, I have the right to be shocked by everything that's happened," she said, pointing a finger in my face. "It's not every day that I find out my best friend is a Fae Changeling and then, a Princess!" Nel shook her head again. "No wonder that cold one was concerned—he was a bit frightening when they returned without you." Her eyes turned to her lap and she shivered as if recalling something particularly unwelcome. "You're royalty."

"Wait." My mind wasn't catching up as fast as I thought it was. I pushed a finger into my ear and wiggled it around before turning my head and leaning closer. "Can you repeat that? Who was worried?"

"The cold one," Nel repeated. "You know the one with the longer pale hair?"

"*Sorrell* was worried?" My brows shot up towards my hairline. "Are you sure?"

She nodded, looking at me as if I was acting odd. I couldn't be acting any more odd than the Frost Prince of assholes actually giving a horse's ass about me. Then again ... he had been there to rescue me with the others. I thought that had just been because of the others, but what if it was more?

"I know you know that Roan and Orion both care about you, but he does as well. It's pretty clear that they all feel something for you," Nellie said with a sigh.

I was quiet for a moment before I replied. "I care about each of them as well," I admitted quietly. "I never expected this ... any of it really. I think that night I came here, it was the castle calling me. The horrible noise." I shuddered at the memory of how it had pierced my skull and rendered me unconscious. "I think ... maybe it was fate. That we were meant to meet. I'm grateful to the Gods—because without what happened, without finding this castle and meeting the Princes, I would have never known what I was. It's bizarre to think about, but they each..." I sighed. "They each complete me in a way I never expected. I didn't even think something like this was possible, let alone with multiple people."

"It's certainly different from the abbey," Nellie said, sounding slightly wistful.

A thought occurred to me. Nellie hadn't asked for this. I'd uprooted her from her life and forced her into this world with me. Guilt blossomed sharp and ugly in my stomach. "Would you want to go back there?" I asked quietly, curious

"No, not at all," she replied. "Even though I was terrified out of my mind to begin with, you're my best friend." Her eyes met mine and a smile formed. "Wherever you go, I want to be there for you. It's just … I do sometimes wonder what's happened to them, you know?"

"I know what you mean." I scooted over and slung my arm around her shoulders. "I bet Sister Madeline is dancing with joy that neither of us have returned to corrupt any of the younger children."

"Sister Ermine is probably feeding them something foul to help cleanse the evil from their souls," Nellie added with a chuckle.

"Sometimes I wonder how I survived that place at all," I said. "But then I think about everything I've gone through since and wonder if the sisters being the way they were really did prepare me for what the world was like."

Nellie was quiet for a long moment before she leaned her head against my shoulder and said, "Maybe. It wasn't like they knew what you were, though. Both of our lives have changed. In fact, they both changed the night the castle showed up. Yours may have changed faster, but I think I'm catching up." I squeezed her shoulder. "Both of our lives have morphed into something terrifying and dangerous, but it's an adventure I don't think either of us would change. What the nuns did for us was prepare us for change. Each day is something new, something that tests us and who we are at the core of our beings. Something that helps shape us into who we are going to be. We can let it grind us down or we can rise up and fight against it.

"It doesn't matter if it's something to do with the

Fae or with the humans, we have to treat it all the same so we can show them that they are equals. You and I might understand how similar Fae and humans are, but from their perspectives, they are polar opposites. If we lead by example then maybe they will catch on. It means we can't let any of it break us, though. We have to be strong for each other and for the people we represent."

"That was quite the speech, young lady," I said, nudging her with my elbow. "Sister Eleanor would be proud. She always knew you were smarter than me, which is completely unfair, I might add," I teased. "I'm the older one here. I should be the wise one."

Nellie pulled away from me and turned to face me. "It's not just you and me, Cress."

"What do you mean?"

"There's ... someone I've come to care for." Her words were quiet but said with conviction. There's a sharpness, a force in her tone I've never really heard before. "He's been my rock through everything. As much as the Princes care for you, they don't really think about me, and when they told me that you'd been taken, I fell apart. If Ash hadn't been there, I don't know what would have happened. As much as I wanted to believe them, to have faith that they would get you back, the three of them against the King and his army seemed impossible.

"I've never been so scared, but Ash was there through all of it. He helped me stay strong. He's so sweet and caring and smart. Not to mention he has a wicked sense of humor. The best part, though?" She sighed and seemed to prepare herself for something. "Cress, he knows I'm human, but he doesn't care."

"Wait, he's Fae?" Of course he was Fae, I already knew exactly who she was talking about. I recalled seeing him in Groffet's library. I shook my head.

Nellie licked her bottom lip before continuing. "He's kind and understanding and strong, Cress. I thought he would be like all of the humans are towards Fae—angry and scared and hateful, but he's not. I think … I think I love him and that he returns my feelings."

My heart squeezed tight inside my chest. "Wow." It was all I could manage. The only word that I was able to slip out because I was still frozen in a state of pure surprise.

"Are you upset?" she asked hesitantly.

"What? No!" I jumped forward and snatched her hands up once more. "No, of course not, I'm glad you've found someone. I'm happy for you, really. I'm—okay, truthfully. I'm a little jealous that this has been going on, but I've been so mixed up with the Princes and the Court of Frost and then the near execution—"

"It's not your fault," she said, stopping me with a laugh. "I understand why you haven't been around."

"What I'm trying to say," I began again, feeling a burn at the back of my eyes, "is that if you love him then I'm happy and he's stupid if he doesn't love you back."

"Are you tearing up?" she asked.

"Me? No," I lied. I cleared my throat. "You'll have to officially introduce me to him so I can give him the appropriate warnings and whatnot."

"Warnings?" Nellie's eyebrows rose.

"You know, just the general 'hurt my best friend, and I'll break your kneecaps' or 'if you don't treat her right, I'll have Roan set you on fire'—nothing too horrifying," I said with a grin.

"Threatening to break someone's knees or burn them alive should not make you so happy." Nellie frowned as she pulled her hands back and crossed her arms over her chest.

"It's not the threat that makes me happy but the fact that it's needed. You have someone for me to threaten. That's a fabulous thing."

"You don't need to threaten him. He won't tell anyone anything, he's very discreet, and he's promised to protect me for the rest of my life should I need it." A blush rose to her face, staining her cheeks bright pink.

"It's going to happen, so you may as well get used to it. He needs to know where I stand on the matter. Besides, if I can scare him that easily I'll be surprised. Roan and Orion certainly don't find my threats very menacing." I sighed and had to stop myself from pouting. Just once it would be nice to threaten them and have them take it seriously.

"You're a Princess now though, that in itself might scare him," Nellie reminded me.

"Meh, not really a Princess. Roan and I are engaged, but we're not married yet—if we ever will be." I grew somber. "The war needs to end before anything else happens."

Nellie's gaze softened. "It will," she said. "I truly believe that people—of all races—don't want to live in such fear and hatred."

I forced a smile as I leaned forward and hugged her to me. I hoped she was right. I prayed to the Gods she was. Tyr was my biggest concern, though. Something told me he would not be defeated easily. The future was unclear and it was that more than anything else that scared me.

CHAPTER TWENTY

Cress

Roan's chambers were well warmed. Someone had stopped by several hours before to light a fire in the hearth, for which I was grateful. It seemed as though eons had passed since we were in the Court of Frost, but honestly, I was glad to be back here. Where there was warmth in more ways than just the temperature.

The door creaked open well after night had fallen and dinner had been brought and taken away. Roan appeared in the doorway, his head down. In his hands, he carried something I couldn't quite see. He stepped into the room and let the chamber doors shut behind him before he looked up and noticed my presence.

"Cress..." He seemed surprised to see me there.

I floundered for a moment. Hadn't he said that he would see me later tonight? Was I mistaken? I didn't think so. Maybe he'd forgotten. I shuffled forward, pausing several feet away before I reached him, unsure if my presence was welcome.

"Hey," I said. "I thought—do you want me to go?" I asked, gesturing to the door at his back.

"What?" He blinked. "No. Of course not." Roan's head jerked down to the satchel I now saw he was carrying and then back to me. He sighed and tossed it on a lounge nearby before striding forward. "I'm sorry," he said as he approached me. "I didn't expect to see you here."

"But you said..." I didn't get a moment to finish reminding him about his earlier words before his hands were on my shoulders and his mouth was on mine.

I sighed and sank into him. My arms came up to wrap around his neck as I arched up onto my tippy toes and kissed him back. He tasted of fire and ash and heat. When Roan finally pulled back, I was gasping for air.

"I forgot that I'd asked you to come to me tonight," he whispered, panting. "Forgive me?" I was happy to know I wasn't the only one left affected by the burn of that kiss.

My chest felt tight as I dragged more air in. I felt light-headed. "There's nothing to forgive," I replied.

He smiled and brushed his full, masculine lips over my mouth once more before leaning away. "Give me a moment," he said. "I've been in the war room all fucking day. I'm tired and I would really like a bath before we do anything else."

Feeling brave and more than a little unwilling to let him go, when Roan released me, I reached up and snagged his arm—holding him by the wrist with both of my hands. His eyebrows rose.

"Maybe I could join you?" I offered.

There was a brief moment of silence and then a beaming smile overtook his face—he looked so boyish like that. Almost nothing like the hardened, mistrustful Fae he'd been when I first met him. But then again, I had seen that Fae again in a smaller way when I'd spied on him during his strategy meeting.

Unlike me, who'd grown up in isolation far from the majority of the war, I had to remember that Roan and the others ... they'd grown up in the middle of it all. They had seen battle and bloodshed and the front lines. My hand tightened on his wrist.

Roan stepped forward and brushed my cheek as he grinned down at me. "I would love that," he admitted. "Give me a few moments to get ready?" he asked. "You go ahead to the bathing chambers, I'll make sure no one disturbs us."

"Don't be long," I said, firming up my voice even as the corners of my mouth twitched.

He chuckled. "I wouldn't dream of keeping you waiting," he replied.

I released his wrist and stepped back. "You better not," I warned him playfully before I turned and headed for the door.

The corridors were quiet as I headed towards the bathing chamber, recalling how—not so long ago—I'd been overwhelmed by this castle. Now, it seemed like the only home I'd ever known. The convent hadn't been a home; just a roof over my head with lots of strings attached. My mind wandered as I roamed the hallways. Every once in a while, I'd run into another Fae. Some of them turned their noses up at me still and kept walking, but a few—far more than I expected—paused and nodded their heads in greeting.

By the time I made it to the bathing chambers, there were fewer people. No one hovered outside the bathing chambers and when I peeked inside, there was no one present either. Stepping into the warmed room, I spotted a pale skinned little pixie fixing a pile of bottles and vials along one of the large bath's shelves. Its little oblong shaped head popped up and its beady black eyes widened upon seeing me.

One moment, the creature was focused on its task, and the next, it was flying at me. Chirping and waving its hands around as if it was trying to communicate. I grimaced and shook my head before putting my hands up.

"It's okay," I said, thinking the pixie was trying to get me to leave. "Prince Roan sent me."

That seemed to calm the pixie. It stopped waving its arms and stared at me for a long moment before huffing out a breath and flitting away—back to its duties. I'd guessed right, I assumed. It had been trying to get me to leave, obviously preparing for Roan's bath. I turned away from the creature and began to undress. I removed my dress and underclothes, laying them across a nearby half wall. Despite the steam wafting up from the waters in the bath, once I was naked, a chill swept over me.

I decided I wouldn't be waiting for Roan after all.

Without a second thought, I rushed into the bath, diving into the heated, swirling milky white liquid and sighing as warmth began to seep back into my skin. Leaning back, I dunked my head and ignored the high pitched chirping of the pixie as I accidentally flicked water his way.

This is so much better than that stupid barrel, I thought as I swam halfway across the bathing pool. The water rippled around me as I spun in a circle before squeezing my eyes shut and taking a huge breath and sinking deep into the center of the bath.

I hovered like that for so long, so focused on just feeling the clean and heated water around me, that at first, I didn't notice new ripples moving within the bath until a wide male arm wrapped around my waist and pulled me up to the surface.

I gasped as Roan pressed his mouth to my ear. "What are you doing, Little Bird?" he asked, the deep timbre of his vibrato sliding through me, heading straight to my core. "Hiding from me?"

My chest squeezed tight as I tried to capture my breath. "No," I said, but with the way my voice came out all breathy and airless, I didn't sound too confident.

Roan chuckled, the sound of his amusement vibrating against my back, making me close my eyes as I rested against him. He was naked. So was I. I could feel the hard length of him at my back, his cock pressing against my ass. When I felt his other arm lift, I opened my eyes and saw that the pixie had stopped its work and was staring at us expectantly—as if waiting for a command.

"Go," Roan ordered, swiping a hand through the air.

The pixie nodded once and then flitted up and away, disappearing as it slipped from the room, and then I was left alone with a mountain of a Fae at my back— hot, horny, and feeling very playful. I liked that, too, I admitted to myself. We hadn't had much time to play. There hadn't been a true moment of leisure in a long while.

As soon as the pixie was gone, Roan spun me around and I found myself chest to chest with him—my breasts brushing against the top of his abdomen as I stared up into his fiery gaze. "Now that we're alone..." he said, his eyes trailing over my face and lowering until his attention landed on my breasts. A low groan left him. "By the Gods," he whispered. "Little Bird..."

Roan's head dipped down as the arm encircling my waist lifted me up against him just enough that he could kiss the top of one breast and then move even lower until his mouth closed over one stiffened nipple. I gasped as my hands shot into his hair. Fire licked against my fingertips, hot and dangerous, but I didn't care.

Desire flamed my belly, opened me up as I arched into his mouth. Roan's tongue flicked over the hardened bud before he switched and lavished attention on the other one. All the while, my thighs began to rub together. Wetness sticking to my skin that had nothing to do with the waters surrounding us.

When he lifted his head once more, his lips rising to take mine in a fast movement, I jumped, wrapping my legs around his waist and clinging to his frame with all the strength left in my thighs. He chuckled against my mouth, reaching beneath me to capture my buttocks in his grip and heft me further against his chest. I shivered as air rushed over my wet skin, but I couldn't help myself.

I kissed him violently, passionately—eminently aware that I had nearly died a handful of days ago. I needed this. I needed him.

"Roan." His name was a rasp pulled from my throat when we broke off to take a breath of air. He strode forward, wading through the pool of water until we were at the shelves alongside the bathing chamber's center. He settled me there, freeing his hands to rove over the rest of me. Despite the low station of the shelves, my lower half was still surrounded by water and the higher shelves with the bottles and vials the pixie had been fussing with earlier clanged as Roan pushed against me even harder.

I could feel him, the hot, hard length of him pushing against me. "Cress," he whispered back. "Cress, Little Bird, I need you."

My back arched as he reached between us, down into the water, and stroked his fingers down my entrance. He slipped back up and circled the bundle of nerves there and my head went back, the ceiling taking over the entirety of my vision as I shook against him. It was there—the peak of my pleasure—just out of my reach.

"Roan," I croaked, reaching up and grasping his shoulders. I stared up into his eyes, seeking, begging silently. "Please."

It was all I needed to do. Roan reared back, his palms going to my inner thighs as he shoved them apart to make room for his wide hips. He pushed forward, sinking into the water as he pushed the head of his cock into my entrance. Then as his fingers circled around, gripping into my asscheeks, he pulled me forward and straight onto his shaft until he'd plunged in to the hilt.

A shocked gasp left my lips just as a low groan left his. I could feel my skin tingling. My heart racing. Everything in the room narrowed to him and me. Magic sizzled along my nerve endings, heating me from the inside out. Roan's head lifted and his eyes met mine as he pulled out and then in a slow, torturous move, sank back into my pussy.

Pleasure filled me as my nails sank into the skin on his upper arms. I moaned as he began to pound me, his hips pulling out and thrusting back in until my ass scraped the shelf he'd set me on and my head grew faint from the movement and steam. I held onto him for dear life, and I could feel it when he grew close to his own release—knew it was upon him when he reached between us and stroked that bundle of nerves once more. I started shaking before it even came, but the second he pinched me, I lost it.

I opened my mouth on a silent scream that was swallowed by him as his lips descended and he shoved himself forward into my pussy one last time, holding me tight as he came apart under my hands and lips.

This, I realized, was everything. This was what I was fighting for.

Roan pulled his mouth away and dropped so that his

forehead was pressed against mine. "You fucking wreck me, Little Bird," he admitted through panting breaths.

I stroked my fingers up and down along his spine as I turned my head and pressed my cheek to his chest. "The feeling," I admitted into the quiet of the bathing chamber, "is entirely mutual."

CHAPTER TWENTY-ONE

CRESS

I stared at the closed throne room doors and counted down the number of seconds that ticked by. I'd lost count ten times, and each time I restarted, I always hesitated—hoping the doors would open and I'd be allowed entry. As it stood, however, the Princes had been locked inside with some of their top soldiers for a while now. Days, it felt like—but hours was probably more accurate.

Finally, after what felt like forever, my eleventh countdown was cut short as the doors were thrown open. I scrambled back and jerked to the side, out of the way, as Sorrell stormed into the corridor, a layer of ice trailing beneath his booted feet as he moved. The second he saw me, his eyes sparked and snow began to fall from the ends of his hair.

Instead of unleashing whatever fury he was so obviously feeling—a strange occurrence for sure since I was accustomed to seeing him act stoic and unreadable—he whipped around and pointed a finger back towards the entryway. I peeked around and saw that Orion and Roan stood there, both of their arms crossed and severe expressions on their face.

"I am not staying behind!" Sorrel shouted, the echo of his deep voice making one of the chandeliers within the throne room shudder in the background.

My eyes widened. Several soldiers stood around a table towards the center of the room, but each one of them was turned away.

"Calm yourself, Sorrell," Orion said as he and Roan stepped further into the corridor. The doors closed behind them, leaving the four of us in relative privacy, though I had a feeling Sorrell hadn't expected me to be out here, waiting for them. And now I was privy to whatever was going on and my presence only seemed to irritate him further.

"This is ridiculous," Sorrell hissed. "I'm perfectly capable of riding and fighting." A wave of cold air slapped me in the face and I shivered involuntarily. Roan noticed and moved closer, unhooking the cloak at his back and wrapping it around my shoulders.

"We're not questioning your ability to ride and fight," Roan said as he stroked a warm finger down my cheek before returning his attention to his throne brother.

"Then you'll be taking me with you," Sorrell commanded, his tone leaving no room for argument. But an argument there still was because neither Roan nor Orion appeared to be caving in to him.

"You're wasting the precious little magic you do have by throwing a tantrum!" Roan turned and shouted back.

"When was the last time you replenished your magic supply?" Orion's voice was calmer but no less intense. His dark eyes fixated on Sorrell and refused to deviate.

"I have plenty," Sorrell replied.

"That wasn't an answer," Roan pointed out with a dark huff. "Just tell us the truth."

"I am the Prince of Frost and one of the rulers of this Court," Sorrell's voice lowered and ice began to form along the wall around us. I drew Roan's cloak even closer.

"Cut the Gods damned theatrics, Sorrell," Roan snapped, his voice lowering. "You're exhausted and it's starting to show. Orion isn't even shivering—" He paused and gestured to where Orion stood, completely unfazed by Sorrel's magic ice.

In the blink of an eye, the cold air receded. The frost that had been spreading over the door and floors and walls thawed, leaving behind nothing but the residual moisture. "We're doing this because we are concerned," Orion said. "We understand you're frustrated, but until you replenish your magic, you need to rest."

"Yes," Roan agreed with a nod. "And even if that wasn't the case, one of us would have had to stay back anyway. What if something were to happen to the two of us out there? You would need to remain behind to lead."

"We have our seconds," Sorrell said. "You know I do not *need* to be here. I should be out there—fighting for our people."

"Not until you're rested," Orion repeated.

"And what, pray tell," Sorrell bit out, glaring at the two of them and completely ignoring my presence, "am I supposed to do *here*?"

Both Orion and Roan exchanged a look. "Have you considered training Cress?" Roan asked. "You were quite adept at it in the field."

"As I can attest," Orion agreed.

Sorrell's face went slack and then, slowly, he pivoted and stared at me. I blinked at the ferocity in his glare. I put my hands up. "I didn't suggest it!" I said quickly.

He shook his head, but instead of responding, he turned and faced Roan and Orion once more. His hands curled into fists at his sides and it looked as if he wanted to slam one of them into their faces. Finally, his fingers relaxed and he stepped away, turning and pushing out a deep, unsatisfied breath.

"Do not get yourselves killed," he said quietly, so quietly that I wasn't even sure if he had meant for the three of us to hear. Roan and Orion's stern faces softened, and then together, they stepped forward, and each of them clapped a hand on an opposite shoulder.

"We wouldn't dare," Roan said. "Only you have the right to kill us."

"You're Gods damned right I do," Sorrell replied, sounding mulish.

Orion said something I couldn't hear and Sorrell turned, glancing over his shoulder at my wide-eyed expression. He scowled but nodded at whatever his friend had said. Roan let his hand slide off his shoulder and he, too, turned and faced me.

I glanced down quickly at the cloak he'd draped over my shoulders, wondering if he was about to request it back now that it appeared that Sorrell's anger had calmed enough that I didn't feel as though we were back in Alfheim. He stepped closer, completely eclipsing my vision of Sorrell and Orion as his hands fell on me. He gripped my waist and hoisted me against him.

"You're leaving," I said, realizing what was happening. "When?"

Roan buried his face into my neck as I wrapped my arms around him. "Soon," he said. "Sorrell will be remaining behind."

Yeah, I wasn't the brightest, but I'd caught that much. I sighed, scraping my teeth over my bottom lip. When I pulled back I barely had a chance to look at him before his lips were on mine, hot and demanding. He kissed me like I was the sun and he'd been in the dark his whole life. He devoured me, his tongue sinking into my mouth and twining with my own. The kiss continued until I was left panting and weak at the knees as he unwrapped the legs that he'd urged around his sides not moments before and set me back down on the ground.

"You'll be safe," Orion promised, startling me as he appeared at our sides.

I jumped slightly, but before I could say anything Orion was pulling me into his embrace as well. His head dipped and his lips were on mine just as fast as Roan's had been. While Roan's kiss had been all fiery passion, Orion's was a slow, sensual seduction that had me aching for more than just a kiss by the time he was done.

"We'll be back soon, Little Bird," Roan said, dropping another kiss—a much more chaste one—on my fore-head before touching my cheek with his fingertips and then turning to look at where Sorrell stood with his arms crossed over his chest.

"We'll be back as soon as we can," Orion said, mirroring Roan's actions.

"You both better come back safe and sound or Core-liath help me..." I rasped.

I heard them both chuckle just before the doors to the throne room opened. It was as if their soldiers had been eavesdropping or perhaps had known to wait a specific amount of time before exiting. Roan and Orion nodded to them and as a unit, the men all headed off, leaving me staring after them with dread forming a pit in my gut.

Sorrell's head pivoted back from where he'd watched them go until his cool, blue eyes settled on me.

"They'll be okay, right?" I asked, needing the reas-surance.

"They are warriors, Changeling. Each of us has fought in the war for years. This is not an excessively dangerous mission. The likelihood of them not returning is low. I have no doubt they will return to us unharmed."

I nodded, but inside, I couldn't help the worry that had yet to disperse and it became too much for me to hold inside. My gaze trailed back the way they'd gone. "It doesn't matter," I found myself saying, "if they've been warriors since the beginning of time. I don't care if they've never fallen in battle. Until I see them again, I won't be able to think of anything but them." I curled my hands into fists, feeling Roan's cloak warm against my sides. "I hate that I can't go—that I have nothing to give them on the battlefield. No skills of my own. That I can't protect them."

Sorrell sighed out a long breath. "Then I suppose I will be training you," he said. "For a Fae, the first step in entering the battlefield is learning how to control your magic."

"I'm not much of a fighter," I said with a wince. "But I hate seeing them go alone. Not knowing whether or not they are okay, or even alive—it's worse when I can't see them. It makes me feel sick." My fingers clenched against the outside of my stomach.

"They aren't alone," Sorrell replied, though I noticed that his gaze had returned to where they'd gone as he spoke. "They have each other as well as our soldiers."

"And what if the King expected us to attack his pantry? What if there is a whole battalion waiting there for them?" I shot back.

"What if the sky turns purple?" he countered.

"Don't," I warned as I knew the logical lesson he was preparing to give me.

"You can't focus on the what ifs, Cressida. It does nothing for you. Focus on the now, on what you can do in this moment to make it better, to prevent yourself from feeling this way again."

"You don't get it, do you? The only thing my mind will focus on is them, on how my heart feels like it's out there with them." I threw my hand up toward the window. "Riding around with them, getting ready to fight. It doesn't feel like it's in my chest anymore. It's like I can almost see them in my mind, but I don't know what's happening. The mere thought of them dying without someone there—without me there—it breaks me. It scares me."

Silence descended between the two of us and I knew I'd probably insulted him. I couldn't find it in myself to care, though. Everything I'd said was true. When I looked up, I found Sorrell's eyes on me. We stared at each other for a long moment as I waited for him to say something, until I couldn't stand it anymore. "What?" I blurted.

He stared for another moment before shaking his head and turning away. "Nothing," he said.

He began to walk away, only to stop and turn back. He moved with such strength and purpose. Had Roan said he looked exhausted? I couldn't see it in him now. Only intensity. I backed up as he towered over me, his icy gaze glaring into the depths of my soul. "If that's how you really feel—like you want to join them on the battlefield—then I will train you," he said. "Some Fae are more powerful than they appear and, with the right training, you might, *might*, be able to ride with them someday."

"Really?" I asked. "You think so?"

"I never say anything I don't mean," he replied coolly.

"Thank you, Sorrell. Truly."

When he turned and started to walk away again, he looked over his shoulder and arched a brow. "Are you coming?"

I blinked. "Oh, you mean now?"

"Yes. Now," he growled at me as his gaze dipped to the cloak around my shoulders. "And get rid of that thing. It'll get in the way."

With that, the Prince of Frost stormed off and I slipped Roan's cloak off my shoulders as I trailed after him, preparing to figure out if he was right and maybe I was one of those Fae who was more powerful than I appeared. I prayed to the Gods he was right.

CHAPTER TWENTY-TWO

CRESS

Sorrell's anger was visible—actually tangible. A layer of ice coated the ground beneath his feet as he led me out into what appeared to be a courtyard made for training. There were no bushes or shrubbery, just an empty space with bales of hay and blocks of wood.

He didn't even seem to be aware that he was oozing frost. I bit my lip and considered telling him, but when he stopped suddenly and whirled around, nearly causing me to collide into his back, I decided against it. I wanted to live and he looked mad enough to cut me down without batting an eye.

"Training," he spat the word as if it were vile and offensive. To him, I supposed it was. He'd been ordered to stand down by Roan and Orion and even as little as I knew about Sorrell, I knew that orders were not something he took easily. "Here is where we'll train until they get back," he stated.

"Okay," I said easily.

"You managed to do well enough in the heat of the moment," he continued. "But healing and sharing energy to restore life is not the same as being able to actively use your magic defensively."

"What about offensive?" I inquired. "Won't I need to know that?"

His anger melted a bit, but his facial expression remained cold. "No."

I frowned. "Why not?"

"You simply won't need to use your magic offensively," he said.

I huffed out a breath and crossed my arms over my chest. "I'm not stupid," I snapped.

One light colored brow rose. "I never said you were," he replied.

"We're in the middle of a war," I said. "Of course I'll have to use my magic offensively. Hell, I could've used it in that damned tower. I tried—" My voice cut out as I recalled my absolute failure. In the face of my capture, imprisonment, and escape, I had been utterly useless. I'd had to rely on others for assistance and things were only going to get worse. "I practiced in my cell," I admitted to Sorrell. "But even with a week of practice, all I managed to conjure were a few orbs of light and heat."

I waited a beat after those words left my lips. I half expected that Sorrell would scoff at me and tell me he wasn't surprised that a Changeling like me was incompetent. Even the physicians at the Court of Frost had said that my magic was weak, but any magic was better than none, right? When he still hadn't said anything after a long moment, I glanced up.

Sorrell was looking at me with a peculiar expression. One I hadn't seen on his face before. As if he were stunned by my mere presence and then also, at the same time, trying to dissect what I was.

"Do you believe yourself to be ... weak?" he asked hesitantly.

I shrugged. "Well, yeah." Wasn't that obvious? Ever since I'd found out I was, in fact, a Changeling and ever since my magic had first formed, I'd wondered why it came so much harder for me than it seemed to for everyone else.

"Why?" Sorrell commanded, his brows drawing down low over his eyes as he continued to stare at me.

"I can't *do* anything," I confessed, and despite my best efforts, I could tell my feelings of frustration and shame were heard as well. "I was trapped in a small room in the dark for a week with nothing else to do but practice and all I managed to do was shoot off a few sparks. My magic is worthless."

"No magic is worthless," he said sharply, stepping up to me so fast that I nearly stumbled as I tried to back away—so used to him trying to keep from touching me rather than seeking me out—but he captured me and held me with his hands on my elbows and his eyes on mine. "Say it," he ordered.

"W-what?" I stuttered. My mind had gone blank. The

only thing I could see or think of was the swirling mass of blue in his eyes.

"Repeat after me," he said. "No magic is worthless."

I frowned at him. "Mine is," I argued. "It doesn't do anything. I think I'm magic-incompetent."

"That is unacceptable," Sorrell said, shaking his head. He squeezed my elbows until I winced. "Say it."

I pressed my lips together out of rebellion for several long seconds, but Sorrell's gaze remained on mine, fixated on my face as if he was ready and willing to hold me in place until I caved to his demands. I shifted on my feet, and still, he kept his hold.

Huffing out a breath, I finally surrendered. "No magic is worthless," I grumbled under my breath, just loud enough for him to hear.

His cold, icy eyes narrowed on me for a moment and then he released me, nodding. "Good," he stated. "That's the first step in your training."

I gaped at him. "A sentence?" I blurted. "You've got to be joking."

"I do not joke," he replied.

That much was obvious, asshole, I thought, but once again I kept my mouth clamped shut so the words wouldn't accidentally slip out. That had earned me many nights of no food with the nuns.

Sorrell turned away from me and strode across the courtyard until he stopped several paces away from a large block of wood. He lifted his arm and pointed a finger. Immediately, the temperature in the area dropped and long spikes of ice formed in mid-air, hovering just behind where his finger was aimed.

Then, with a flick of his wrist, he sent the spikes shooting through the air and straight into the block of wood.

"Offensive magic can kill," he began, and I realized that this was part of my first lesson. I hurried to stand closer to see better. Sorrell didn't appear to realize until he moved to face me and found me right there. He froze for a split second and then continued, his body moving stiffly as he stomped past me to the hay bales, his words flying off his tongue.

"Defensive magic is meant to protect," he said. "While offensive magic is meant to attack. Neither of these is the core of what the purpose of magic truly is."

"Then what is it?" I piped up.

Sorrell paused as he hefted a hay bale off of its pile and dropped it in the middle of an open space. "Magic comes from the Gods," he stated, slamming the hay down. "And therefore, it comes from nature. Nature is neither defensive nor offensive—nature does not fight, it simply is."

I wrinkled my nose. "And that means..." I hedged, waiting for him to finish his explanation.

He rolled his eyes as he rounded the bale of hay and crossed his arms over his chest. "It means that magic is a part of nature. It is in how you use it that determines what it becomes."

"Yeah?" I crossed my arms over my chest as well, mirroring him. "Well, I'm terrible at using it."

Sorrell inhaled as if he were trying to contain a violent emotion. His chest expanded and his eyes closed briefly and when they reopened, they centered on me.

"If you say something like that again, you will regret it," he warned me.

I snorted. "What are you going to do?" I asked. "Spank me?" He arched a brow, but neither confirmed nor denied it. I frowned. "You can't."

"Oh?" He tilted his head to the side, a sinister grin appearing on his lips. I was so used to him frowning that seeing anything close to a smile on his face made my whole body respond. I stepped back and let my arms drop to my sides. "Try it," he offered.

And give him permission? I thought. *No, thank you.* Then again ... I remembered what it had felt like having him over me on the bed back in the Court of Frost. In that moment between sleep and wakefulness, he'd been all over me—hotter than I'd ever seen him. His mouth had devoured mine.

Instinctually, my thighs tightened and I bit down on my lower lip. Sorrell's gaze moved down to that lip, focusing on it for a long, silent moment, and then he straightened and turned away, the muscles in his shoulders pulled taut as he strode back to his place in front of the hay bale.

"Enough delaying," he snapped sharply. "I want you to practice on this." He kicked the bale.

I stepped forward, looking from him to the hay, "Practice on that?" I repeated. "What exactly am I supposed to do with it?"

"You're going to light it on fire," he stated.

I blinked. "I think I heard you wrong," I said. "It sounded like you said I was going to light it on fire."

"You did not hear me wrong," he replied. "You are."

"I can't!" I hissed at him. *How many times was I going to have to tell him before he got it through his thick skull? I couldn't use my magic like that!*

"Yes, you can," he said. "And you will." I shook my head. He was crazy. "At least give it a try, Cressida," he ordered. "How am I to train you if you don't even try?"

I grunted and grumbled under my breath. "You're going to regret this," I muttered as I turned and stomped a few feet away before whirling back.

This time, I mimicked what I'd seen him do earlier. I lifted my arm as he stepped to the side and watched. I inhaled and focused on the hay bale, concentrating all of my energy into the tips of my fingers. The heat began to build under my skin, all of it sliding forward as I worked to push it towards my hand.

"Come on," I hissed under my breath. "Do *something*." I shook my hand as if that would make the magic come.

A spark formed and then fizzled out. I stared at my hand in half horror and half humiliation before my gaze jumped to Sorrell. He didn't even blink as he said, "Again."

"But—"

"Again," he ordered.

I turned back and started all over again. The energy built. The heat built. I pushed it forward. It rushed beneath my skin, all of it sliding through until it reached the tips of my fingers. I closed my eyes and let out a breath.

Just let it go, I thought. Just release it. Let it out.

Almost as soon as those words had entered my mind and flitted back out, I felt something rush out of me. All of the heat and energy, and as my mind connected the dots, my eyes shot back open in time to see a puny little glowing orb slam into the bale of hay. Except instead of setting the thing on fire as we both expected, it merely sank into the hay and glowed for a moment as rays of golden light emitted from it. The thin ropes that bound the bale together snapped and the hay collapsed in a heap. I frowned down at the mess my magic had made.

"Interesting..." Sorrell said, sounding both confused and curious.

"Interesting?" I squawked, looking to him in horror before pointing to the hay. "Did you see that? It didn't do anything!"

"That's not exactly true," Sorrel said with a shake of his head.

"Well, snapping a few measly little ropes doesn't mean that my magic works," I huffed.

"Your magic works just fine, but I believe there's something we need to ask Groffet about it."

I scrubbed my hands down my face, hating the tears burning in the backs of my eyes. Sparks and light and no fire. That was it. I was the worst freaking Fae in the history of Fae.

"Cressida?" I barely heard Sorrell's voice as he approached. I was too caught up in my own self loathing.

Why was I even here? I wondered. *What was the point of my existence if I wasn't even good at anything? The nuns had been right. I was clumsy. Stupid. Too stubborn for my own good. I was absolutely unimpressive. A problem every-where I went.* I sniffed hard.

"Cressida!" Sorrell's shout finally caught my attention, but I just couldn't deal with his scolding right now. It was too much.

I spun to face him. "What!" I shouted back.

"Look," he snapped, pointing down at me.

I followed his gesture with my gaze and gasped at what I saw. My skin was glowing. It was as if every pore of my body was filled with a dull light. I was illuminated. Golden sparks danced along my skin. Across the courtyard, the protective magic vines that covered the stone wall began to slither against one another, vibrating as if they felt a strange presence.

"W-what...?" My gaze found Sorrell's again. "What does this mean?" I asked.

He shook his head as he stepped closer and then carefully, very carefully, he reached up and grasped my wrist. Together, the two of us watched as my skin very slowly, returned to its previous state. The glow faded until it was gone completely.

"Sorrell?" I prompted.

He shook his head, staring at me once more with that peculiar look. "I don't know, Cressida," he admitted. "I don't know."

My heart sank. If Sorrell didn't know, then this was definitely not a good thing.

CHAPTER TWENTY-THREE

CRESS

S weat slicked down my back. It soaked through my clothes and made the fabric stick to me. My skin felt overly warm, as if I was very close to a fire. I opened my eyes and looked down to see that it wasn't just warm, it was glowing. *I* was glowing. I gasped as the light emanating from beneath my skin grew brighter and hotter. I wasn't near a fire. I *was* the fire. Blazing hot light was pouring out of me. My sweat sizzled on my skin. I scrambled back, trying to get away, but there was no getting away. Whatever was making me feel this way was *inside* of me.

My body fell into the darkness and the second I hit something, my eyes slammed open and a scream lodged in my throat. It took me several seconds to realize that I wasn't burning alive. I was in Roan's chambers and I'd fallen right off his bed. My breath came in short eclipsed pants.

What in the name of Coreliath was that? A dream, I knew, was the answer, but it had been so real and so strange. There'd been no one there with me. It had all just been … me. I shook my head and slowly worked my way up the side of Roan's bed until my trembling feet were beneath me once more. There would be no more sleep after that nightmare.

A deep sigh left me as I looked up and scanned the room. No doubt the horrible illusion had been the result of all of my hard training. Sorrell had worked me over good and my limbs felt their exhaustion. Still, I wasn't able to do so much as light a bale of hay on fire. I was a terrible Fae. Useless.

The darkness of the room made me squint as I wavered forward, moving slowly through the rest of the room with my hands outstretched. My head pounded and my stomach rumbled. I stopped as I reached the chair next to the door. My feet paused there, and I wondered if it would even matter if I left the room now as I was. It wasn't like I was naked. Did I really need to change out of my nightgown to go grab a bite to eat in the middle of the night?

My hand fell to the door latch and I pulled it open with the decision—no, it didn't matter. I wasn't likely to run into anyone anyway. I meandered down the stone hallways and passed closed doors—likely chambers of the other Fae who lived here.

Down the corridor, several dull beams of moonlight poured in through open non-glassed windows. A soft melody caught my ear. Something soft, growing louder and louder. The closer I got, the more I realized it was coming from outside.

Someone was playing music.

I hadn't heard music like this before. It was enchanting. I stopped halfway down the corridor and simply closed my eyes for a moment, taking it in. Each note felt like a caress. It was sad—so sad. A wailing of a violin, singing into the night of things lost and never found. Of souls ripped apart and hearts broken. Then the tone lifted and it was as if the sun was rising to a new day. A beginning was forming and I realized it was the same melody played over and over again. It sounded like a whole life being lived and then the death of a loved one only to be reborn.

Finally, my curiosity got the better of me. My eyes opened and I continued forward. I felt compelled—dragged—towards whoever was playing this song. Heart in my chest, I moved towards the open windows, where I found a garden. Three small steps led into a grassy area very unlike the training courtyard from earlier. This garden had miniature stone statues and trees and rose bushes and the smell of night blooms that scented the air around me.

I kept my footsteps light as I strode through the small garden until I saw it—the stone table and alongside that, the musician. My eyes widened at who it was.

In the silver gleam of the moon's light, Sorrell held a black violin tucked beneath his chin. The melody he played captured my heart. It was one of lost loves. Of sorrow and an agony so great that I couldn't help but feel it deep down. He played without tears, though every note lingered—clinging ever desperately to the air surrounding him.

Somewhere in the back of my mind, I realized what I was doing. I was intruding on a very private moment. I shouldn't have been there. Yet, like the small beady pixie eyes I caught every so often as I glanced about the garden—hiding in the shrubbery as they, too, listened to the lonely Prince's song—I couldn't pull myself away.

The night air was fresh and chilly against my skin, but I paid it no mind. It was hard to notice anything but the man with the violin. His eyes were closed as he played. Mine couldn't help but follow him as he swayed to the music. It was odd seeing him like this—so unreserved, so open, so … soft. Gone was the usual bitter expression he usually wore. It almost appeared as if he was sleeping as he played. He was so relaxed, his fingers easing along the bow and neck of the instrument.

It was mesmerizing to watch.

Glints of silver moonlight touched the violin every so often as his bow drew across the strings and his fingers danced on the neck of the instrument. It didn't hold a candle to the beauty of his face though. As he worked towards the crescendo the earlier relaxation of his features turned pinched. The sharp planes began to contort with emotion and his pale skin and icy hair glowed in the moonlight as though that was where this ethereal being belonged.

Each sweep of the bow seemed to pull at my heart, the melancholy sounds only reaching further into my soul now that I was closer. The sorrow and pain that was being expressed through his music was unlike anything I'd heard before and it made me ache for him. It made me want to march forward into the garden, stop him, and pull him close. I wanted to hug him, hold him, to promise him that whatever made him play this heartbreaking music ... would be okay. That he would be okay.

It was too much. *I shouldn't be here!* My mind finally screamed at me. I'd known it, but it had been too exhilarating watching him as long as I had. Now, it was time to go.

When I turned to leave, my foot caught on the edge of one of the larger statue platforms—only instead of a statue sitting upon it, a potted plant was. A grunt flew out of my lips as I fell forward. My hands smacked outward, grabbing onto the platform. I tried to wrap my fingers around the pot, but the thing slipped away from me at the last moment—crashing to the ground and bringing the haunting music to a sudden halt.

I froze. My heartbeat froze. The breath in my lungs froze. Then, slowly, I lifted my head to meet Sorrell's gaze.

His eyes were sharp fragments of ice, shining wickedly without emotion. Though he was far slimmer than many men I'd come into contact with, there was still a strength in his gait. There was a calm, cool confidence in his usual demeanor that was gone now—no, not truly gone, just less prevalent. It was because he was open. His expression, usually so guarded, was vulnerable.

His gaze clashed with my own, and that vulnera-
bility faded. "What are you doing here, Cressida?" he
demanded.

CHAPTER TWENTY-FOUR

SORRELL

There were very few things in life that had surprised me as much as one little Changeling woman. Cressida was becoming far more than surprising though. She was a mystery. And the one question we should have been asking continuously until we'd gotten a satisfying answer repeated itself over and over in my mind:

Where had she come from?

Not the convent, obviously, but before she'd been dropped there. Who was she? Who were her parents? What Court would practice the Changeling tradition amid the beginning of a war with the very creatures they would be giving their child to? Were they still alive?

When we had first come upon the Changeling—Cressida—Groffet had devised the test. He was the one who had told us that she was of the Court of Crimson, but now I wasn't so sure. *Could it be?* I wondered absently as I strode through the empty and quiet corridors of the castle. Was she ... from *that* Court?

I almost dreaded the concept. The Court in question had been eradicated on what I suspected were my own mother's orders—hers and the Crimson Queen's. I had been too young to know much about the fourth Court of our lineage. The Brightling Court.

It was a sad story—the Brightling Court. I hoped I was wrong. The only way to know would be to ask Groffet. Something I would have to do later when the others had returned. An insidious feeling rose at the reminder that they were out there—Roan and Orion—doing what I, too, should be doing. Fighting alongside our soldiers. Infiltrating the castle of the King's ally. Destroying supplies. Weakening him. Wounding him as he had wounded us when he had taken Cressida and nearly killed her.

Anger rose up, fast and furious, inside me. My fists clenched at my side. The hard thumps of my booted feet sounded against stone as I stormed through the castle back to the library. I was in desperate need of a distraction. Moonlight streamed in through the windows—real moonlight. I slowed to a stop as I neared one of our inner gardens. There, resting against a stone table beneath the sky, was my violin.

With a frown, I stepped out into the night and moved toward it until I was standing in front of the table. I stared down at the instrument in confusion. I could have sworn that last I saw this piece, I'd left it in the ... *Groffet,* I realized. That meddling, old man. He was planning something. Teasing me as he always did—leaving out reminders, little mementos to tempt me.

My fingers moved to the neck of the instrument and slowly, I stroked my hand over its frame. I couldn't help but feel tempted by this old thing. It was certainly one of humanity's greatest accomplishments—the violin. Unlike its creators, the instrument was completely and wholly gentle. *Fragile, in a way,* I thought absently as I lifted it from the table's surface.

My eyes caught on the bow, just to the side. Groffet was smart. He knew I'd be up roaming the corridors—I could never sleep when Roan and Orion were out there. Not so long as they were not near me. Perhaps it was the pain each of us had suffered as children—the loneliness of being Royals that had driven us together, made us into what we were. True brothers of the throne. Whatever the reason, I was as bound to them as they were to me. I did not like the feeling of not seeing them, of not being there to fight alongside them.

But maybe this … this old memory could distract me, if only for a moment.

I lifted the violin and reached for the bow, lining up the instrument under my chin as I pressed down and then slowly dragged the bow across the strings. In the light of the moon, the music came to me. I needed no sheets, no instructor—only muscle memory. The music that rose from the strings was a pure cadence. It lifted into the air, a melody that I knew from the heart simply because that was where it came from.

It was no true song, not one with a name, only a collection of notes strung together that I had long thought of. I was its creator. Its master and slave as I played it until it was done and then started it all over again.

I couldn't say how many times I played it only to replay it, when the sound of something breaking startled me out of my reverie. My fingers froze along the bow and I quickly set it down, turning towards the noise, when I realized that the focus of my thoughts before I'd found the violin once more had appeared.

Cressida stood there, eyes wide, golden curls hanging around her face as she stood over a broken potted plant that had obviously been knocked over by her attempted exit.

I scowled. "What are you doing here, Cressida?"

"I-I-I … uh..." she stuttered, her gaze jerking from the plant to me and back again. "I'm sorry?"

I sighed, stepping away from the nostalgic instrument and towards her. "An apology does not answer my question," I stated.

She blushed, her eyes lowering to the floor as a delicate pink hue rose to her cheeks. I paused, frowning at her. *Why would she be blushing?* I wondered silently.

"I heard the music," she confessed quietly. "And I … I came to see who was playing it."

I stiffened. Shit. I hadn't even been thinking. Of course, I shouldn't have played that damned thing here. In the center of the castle. Anyone could have walked by —someone did walk by, I amended my thoughts, returning my attention to the Changeling.

"I apologize for disturbing you," I said.

"Oh no." Her head whipped up and she shook it

vehemently like an animal shaking off water—*how in the world could I find that so adorable?* I wondered. *No,* I mentally corrected myself. *I didn't. It was annoying. She was annoying. She was a danger.*

"I thought it was beautiful," she said. "You didn't disturb me."

Discomfort sidled beneath my skin. I coughed as I turned away. "It was nothing," I said, and then, "let me walk you back to your chambers."

Cressida tipped her head back and stared at me. "Why won't you let me compliment you?" she asked suddenly.

I froze, my lips parting in surprise. "What do you mean?"

"You don't let me compliment you," she repeated. "Do you let anyone?"

It took me a moment to gather an answer to such an absurd question. "Compliments are unnecessary," I told her, leading her back towards the inner corridor and away from the garden.

"No they're not," she replied. "They're very necessary."

"No, they're not," I corrected her.

She shot me a dark look. "Just because you don't see a point in them doesn't mean they're unnecessary."

"Then what, pray tell," I challenged her as we walked, "is the point in complimenting a person other than to gain their favor?"

Her pretty blue eyes rolled. *No, not pretty, damn it.* "True compliments are given without the expectation of anything—not even favors or good standing," she said.

"Complimenting someone with sincerity makes the other person feel good. It expresses a person's kind opinions. Like just now." She gestured between us. "I told you that I thought your music was beautiful, but you called it nothing. I'd think it was just because you didn't like me if I didn't know any better."

"Oh?" What a curious and obstinate little thing she was. "Then do you?"

"Do I what?" Her head tipped back once more as she looked up into my face. I was captured by her and for the first time, I realized that she and I were well and truly alone. Earlier, we had been alone in the courtyard for her training—but this was something entirely different.

We were in the dark—no Roan, no Orion. Just her and me. It was a unique thing, something I'd never expected to happen, and that was an error of my own design. I should've realized that there would come a time like this. She was here to stay. Cressida—Cress— was intertwined with Roan and Orion and … for the first time, I thought to myself how I might not quite hate the idea of her being the same way with me.

"Sorrell?" she called my name, recapturing my attention and pulling me from my thoughts as we moved through the darkened hallways.

"Hmmm?" I hummed back.

"Do I what?" she repeated.

Ah, yes, her question, I thought. "Do you know better?" I finished.

Her full lips split into a wide grin. "Normally, I'd say

absolutely not, but with you, I'm starting to understand."

"And what is it that you think you understand?" I questioned.

"You," she replied. "You're so cold and bossy, and you alienate yourself from nearly everything and everyone —save for two others. Roan and Orion." Her gaze fell away from my face as she turned back towards the corridor, walking forward. "You don't deny my compliment because you hate me—though..." She trailed off for a moment before looking back at me. "There was a time that I thought you truly did hate me."

"There was a time in which you were correct," I said. The words were out of my mouth before I could recall that they would be offensive, but to my utter shock, she didn't act insulted or even surprised. She simply nodded at me as if she had expected that answer.

"But you care about *them*," she continued as if I hadn't said a word. "I think if anyone else were to compliment you but those two, you would still say the same thing you said to me—that it was nothing."

I sighed. She was looking far too closely at something that didn't matter. "Roan and Orion are my brothers," I told her. "They do not compliment me. They give me their opinions."

"And if they gave you the opinion that your music was beautiful, what would you say?" she asked.

I gritted my teeth. "It's just music," I told her.

That brought forth a laugh, and Cressida laughed like she lived—fully and with no reserve. Her hair shook at the sides of her head as she tipped her chin up and released her laughter. It brightened her face and I was transfixed. My feet slowed to a stop.

She stopped, too, pulled to a halt by my inability to keep going. "What's wrong?" she asked, tilting her head curiously.

What was wrong? I repeated the question to myself. All of it was wrong—I had been wrong. About her. About myself. As I stood there in a corridor filled with shadows, she glowed like the only source of light. Brighter than any flame. More brilliant even than the Goddesses of old.

"Sorrell?" she frowned at me, stepping closer as her hands drifted up to my arms—as if touching me could ease the turmoil I didn't think she even realized was causing to riot inside of me. But as soon as her fingertips grazed my flesh, I was unleashed.

Grabbing her, I turned and slammed her back against the wall. A sharp gasp left her lips just before I dipped my head down and devoured them. It took a moment for the shock of the suddenness of my movements to reach her, but once they did—I half expected her to push me away or to fight me. She did neither.

Instead, Cressida's arms lifted even further, wrapping around my neck and pulling me against her body. I crushed her into the wall—her soft, small frame delicate and oh so breakable beneath me. I had always wondered how smaller people—humans and delicate females— could face the world as if they were not constantly on the verge of shattering. Cressida was one such female.

She took my fucking breath away. She feared very little and what she did fear, she still faced. It was time that I admitted that my so-called hatred for her had been born out of a place of fear—of what she could do to me. Of what she could do to my brothers. This little woman—although infinitely delicate in stature—had the heart of a warrior. And whether she realized it or not, she had completely overtaken the three of us.

Yes, the three of us. Not just Roan and Orion, but me as well. I was enraptured by her. I hated that fact, was terrified of it. *But what if,* I wondered idly, *what if I stopped pushing her away and just accepted it?* Accepted that she was undeniable to me now.

My mouth parted from hers as we both gasped for air, panting, our chests pushed tight against one another. "W-why would you..." Her words came with no small amount of confusion. "Sorrell ... do you ... want me?"

"Cressida," I whispered her name as I reached up and held her head in my hand. "Want is a pathetic word for what I feel for you." *Desire. Craving. Need.* Even those were not enough.

She shook her head as if trying to clear away her thoughts and yet, when she returned her gaze to mine, there was still clear bewilderment. "I-I thought you hated me," she said.

"Hate," I replied, "is a powerful emotion to cover up another powerful emotion."

"What—" I didn't let her finish asking the question. I couldn't. I wasn't ready to admit it yet. All I knew was that right here, right now, I needed her. My lips pushed hers apart and I let my tongue sneak forward. She rose to my bait, moaning into my mouth as I reached down and hefted her into my arms. The skirts of her night-gown pushed up her thighs all the way as her legs spread and she wrapped them around me.

"Cressida," I said, releasing her once more. "Tell me yes. Say yes."

Even after all that I had put her through—all that I didn't deserve, but would take anyway—she didn't hesitate. And in that darkened hallway, with her legs wrapped around my hips and my hand in her hair, she tipped her beautiful face back and gave me everything with one word.

"Yes, Sorrell. I'm saying yes."

CHAPTER TWENTY-FIVE

CRESS

My back slammed into the wooden frame of the door, but I didn't offer anything more than a light grunt as Sorrell's mouth came down on mine —*hard*. Everything about him was hard. He was massive and all over me. Inside of my mind, and soon, he'd be inside of my body too.

He fumbled for the door—it was almost cute how rushed he seemed. Almost as if he were afraid I would rescind my consent. I wouldn't dare, not now. The fact was, I wanted this as much as he did. Perhaps more. This, it seemed, was something we'd been slowly moving towards since we first met. Since the first time he'd looked at me with those cold, angry eyes.

There was nothing cold in his look now. He was all molten heat and sinful promise even as he pulled back and, instead of unlocking the door as a normal man might, he reared back and kicked it in. I gasped as my whole body jerked against him.

"Sorrell!" I snapped. "Don't destroy the castle."

"It's my castle," he replied. "I'll do whatever I damn well please."

I didn't have a response to that, not that he gave me time to think of one. As soon as the door was opened, he strode through and turned, slamming it shut—only this time, it didn't close all the way. Probably had something to do with the gaping broken side. Sorrell groaned and I knew it had nothing to do with how he was still carrying me.

I smirked down at him. "I told you so," I said.

His eyes flashed. "You enjoy testing me, don't you, Changeling?" Somehow, in the time between when we'd first met and now, that name had become more than an insult. He didn't say it with anger or disgust, but with a heated promise of something pleasurable that would soon come my way.

Sorrell turned and strode across the room, stopping before a large bed. He unwrapped my legs from around his waist and deposited me there. "Do not move," he warned.

"Or what?" I asked. "Are you going to punish me?"

One finger came up and curled under my chin to tip my head back. "Yes," he said. His head tilted down and then the tip of his nose touched my jawline. "I'm going to spend the rest of the night punishing you for all that you have put me through."

I shivered. Whatever punishment he wanted to

LUCINDA DARK & HELEN SCOTT

exact, I had a feeling I was going to like it. "Now stay," he ordered.

Sorrell stepped back, leaving me bereft of his presence—of his burning intensity. I was left to watch him stride back across the room to right the door. He shut it properly and then put his hand to the frame. Slowly, a blanket of ice began to form over the broken lock. It crept up and around the entirety of the door until the whole thing was sealed shut with a layer of frost. Only then did Sorrell pivot back and face me.

"Now you're mine," he said. "And no one will be disturbing us for the night."

I watched him as he moved back across the room, inching towards me. He paused halfway to me and my pulse began thumping faster as he reached for the hem of his shirt and ripped it over his head. The white, filmy fabric dropped to the floor, forgotten. My lips parted and my mouth watered. I'd always known that beneath the clothes, Sorrell was hiding the body of a warrior.

Strong lines were etched into either side of his abdomen and across. His shoulders were broad, but his eyes—they were the most formidable. He continued his path to me even as my eyes dipped to the pale blond happy trail that led from his belly button into the top of his black trousers.

When Sorrell once again stood before me, he stared into my eyes. His hand reached up and cupped my head, fingers sifting through my curls as he pushed lightly. "Get on your knees, Cressida."

Between my legs, my core throbbed. I was transfixed, completely at his mercy. It was heady, my desire for him. Unable to control my limbs—my knees bent and in small increments, I slid to the floor until I was on my knees before him, looking up at his massive frame. His hand remained in my hair, a comfort as he continued to stroke me—running his fingers through my blonde locks.

"You know what I want?" he asked.

"Yes," I whispered back.

He nodded to the front of his trousers and immediately, my hands lifted. I touched the front, feeling the ridge of his cock beneath the fabric. Within seconds, I had him freed from his pants. I gasped as I saw his cock for the first time. Long, thick, and pale, it made my mouth water.

"Cressida," he urged, grasping it by the base with his free hand. "Suck it."

My lips parted, my mouth opened, and I let him guide the head of his shaft between my lips. The pressure on the back of my head was warm, but the feeling of taking him into my mouth was hotter. I sucked him down, swallowing around his hardness—following the velvet covered vein with my tongue as I lapped at him.

A low moan escaped from above, sounding in my ears as I attended to him. I squeezed my thighs together —pressing them into one another as hard as I could. The sound of his pleasure in my head as I sucked his cock was pure ambrosia. A trickle of thrill shot up my spine. This was happening. I was really doing it.

Sorrell's cock pulsed in my mouth, against my tongue. Slowly, we began to work together in a rhythmic movement. I'd pull back, pushing against the hand holding my head, and then he'd push me forward once more—thrusting his dick to the back of my throat. My hands came up, clenching against his rock hard thighs.

He thrust into my mouth again and again, sometimes moving slow and sometimes moving fast. I relished in it all, feeling both submissive and powerful all at once. Until finally, he'd had enough. Sorrell's hand contracted at the back of my skull, his fingers sinking into my hair and then curling as he ripped me away.

"That's enough," he said through gritted teeth. A moment later, I found myself being lifted into his strong arms and thrown back onto the mattress. "Spread your legs," he ordered as he shucked his pants the rest of the way off and then toed off his boots.

I moved further up the bed, feeling the leaking wetness of my arousal on the inside of my thighs. I grinned back at him, feeling dangerous and playful.

"What if I don't?" I shot back.

Sorrell's eyes flashed—glowing in the dark room—a brilliant blue that was so light it was almost white. "You will regret not following my commands, Changeling." His voice lowered and that, too, left me feeling mischievous.

I walked backwards on my hands and feet until I reached the headboard.

"Spread your legs, Cressida," he repeated as he crawled onto the end of the bed. "Or I'll make you."

I grinned. "Then make me," I challenged.

No sooner had the words left my lips than a shriek followed it as Sorrell dove on top of me. His hands found my wrists and brought them together, pinning them in one of his palms. With his free hand, he reached down, finding the hem of my nightgown, and ripped it up my thighs.

"Tell me something, Changeling," he panted as he leaned close. I closed my eyes and arched into his touch as I felt his fingers slipping up my thighs. "Do you like pain?"

It took me a moment to fully comprehend his question. My eyes opened once more. "Pain?" I asked.

Sorrell released my hands and reached for the neckline of my nightgown, grabbing it and ripping it straight down the middle. The sound of tearing fabric reached me just before the feeling of the material pulling taut over my skin only to be released once more did. He quickly divested me and began tearing it even more— ripping it into strips.

"Yes," he said. "Pain. Specifically, the erotic kind."

I was too consumed by his actions—confused and also a little curious—as he used the torn strips of fabric to quickly bring my hands together and tie them. He then anchored them to the headboard, fitting my hands inside slots I hadn't seen before and then tying me there as well.

"I've never really experienced it, I guess..." I said absently.

"Would you like to?" he asked, trailing his hands down my now naked sides. I trembled beneath him as air washed over my skin.

"I-I don't know," I confessed.

Sorrell moved over me, his hands pushing between

my knees as he forced my legs up and out. "Do you trust me?" he asked, leaning close. His warm breath feathered over the skin of my stomach.

"Y-yes?"

"Are you asking or stating?" he clarified.

"Stating?"

"You don't sound sure," he said.

I huffed out a breath. "I'm not sure," I admitted testily. Here we were, naked and pressed against one another in his bed—not something I'd ever really seen happening—and I felt my pussy pulse, but all he was doing was asking me questions. Questions I didn't understand. "I don't know how pain can feel good," I told him.

Sorrell pressed down on top of me, his shaft lining up with my core, but instead of slipping it inside, he merely let the underside rub against me—between my folds and over my clit. I clenched, tightening, and felt empty inside. When he chuckled, the sound vibrated against my nipples, making me moan in humiliating wanton desire.

What the hell was he thinking? I wondered even as I shifted my hips to rub against him more insistently.

"Patience, Cressida," he said, kissing the tip of my nose. "If you say yes, I promise you won't regret it. Now, answer me correctly this time, *do you trust me?*"

I stared up into his ice blue eyes for a moment, biting down on my lower lip before I jerked my head in a nod. "Yes," I breathed.

He smiled, a radiant and also disturbingly evil look crossing his face. "Good," he said, slipping back until he was almost completely off of me. With his wide, strong hands, he grabbed me around my hips, lifted, and flipped me as if I were no more than a sack of laundry.

The bindings around my hands grew tight, but there was still enough elasticity that, even though my wrists jerked and remained bound, it didn't hurt. I felt Sorrell move in close, arranging me how he liked. I should've known it would be like this with him. With Roan and Orion, sex had always been out of control—fire, burning in the moment. Even in the tent in Alfheim, there'd been a point where we'd thrown all attempts to make it last out of the window.

But Sorrell—I really should have expected that he would be far too controlling to let that happen. Especially in this. His hands moved over my skin, touching my spine, trailing down it until his fingers sank down between my buttocks and even further until he touched my pussy. His thumb flicked over the bundle of nerves above it and I jerked, gasping as my bound hands smacked into the headboard.

I didn't feel it. I couldn't feel anything but what he was doing to me. All I could focus on was him. "I'm going to make you scream, Cressida," he whispered against my spine even as his fingers worked down below.

I believed. Gods, I was halfway to screaming right now and he hadn't even entered me.

"I want you to count them for me," he said.

"What?" I looked back just in time to see his free hand arch up and come down hard across my ass.

I gasped out, jerking forward once more. The burn

of pain spread across my butt. He waited a beat and then repeated himself. "Count, Cressida, or it will quickly turn less pleasurable."

Thoughtless. Confused. And embarrassingly … still very, very wet … I obeyed. "O-one," I stuttered out.

His hand came down again.

"Two."

Again.

"Three."

He spanked me with his palm, never hitting the exact place more than once. He peppered my ass with the smacks. I shuffled around on my knees, feeling uncomfortable. He said to trust him, but I didn't understand. *Why this? Why a spanking?*

The teasing, I realized a bit belatedly. I'd teased him. This was the punishment he'd been talking about.

Only, the more he continued, the less like a punishment it felt like. The pain spread and grew heated until I rested my head against my hands, mumbling the counts that my mind was somehow able to keep up with even though I didn't even hear the numbers as they slipped out of my mouth. I was so focused on how *good* it all felt and trying to figure out *why*.

Every spank sent tingles up my spine. My ass was growing sore, and when he paused to cup it, his hand felt cool against my heated skin. I moaned as he moved down to my thighs. Slapping each one in turn and then covering them in the same burning treatment as my butt. I couldn't stop myself even if I'd tried. I couldn't help it. I was growing restless with one hand spanking me and the other gently moving over my folds. I wanted more—I needed more.

"Want something, Changeling?" I'd never heard him sound so amused before. I might have appreciated it if I hadn't been so desperate.

"You know I do," I shot back, earning myself another harsh spank right in the crease between my ass and the back of my thigh that made me bite down hard on my lip to keep from crying out.

"Then maybe you should try being polite, Cressida, and ask for it," he suggested.

"Please," I hissed out.

"Please what?"

"Please fuck me," I begged.

"That'll do, Cressida," he said, pulling his hand from my pussy. Sorrell's hands found my hips and he knocked my knees apart, guiding the head of his cock to my core. As soon as he pushed inside, I moaned. My hips moved back on their own, wanting more.

He shushed me as I hissed and struggled to get more. I tried to shift backwards with my knees pressed to the bed, but he held me still. "Let me," he said. "Just stay still."

He thrust, stretching me inside as his cock powered forward. I whimpered. Fuck, he was big. Just as large as Orion and Roan, but perhaps longer. It felt like his thrust would never end and I was surprised when I finally felt his hips pressed against my thighs.

"There." Sorrell's voice was rough as he spoke. He reached up and stroked his fingers through my hair before grabbing hold of it and leaning in to my ear. "Now, comes the fun part," he said.

That hadn't been the fun part? I thought a split second before he pulled out and slammed the full length of his shaft back into me.

"Oh, fuck..." I breathed.

Sorrell chuckled but didn't say a word as he began his ride. He fucked into me, thrusting his cock back and forth into my pussy. Sometimes, he would move slowly, dragging it out and then inching it back into me in what felt like long increments. And then, he would fuck faster —driving my body forward until he was fucking me against the headboard with my breasts against my bound hands and his hands gripping my hips, using them as holds by which he could push me away and pull me back onto his cock.

He felt hot, almost as if he were on fire. His skin seemed to radiate the heat. *Magic?* I wondered. That was right—he needed this. The sex. The intimacy. He'd been denying himself, but now I could feel the surge of my magical energy replenishing itself. I wondered if he, too, could feel his.

I moaned and whimpered. Animal like sounds left my lips and I had no control. No. None of it was mine. All of the control belonged to him and he used it to drive me up and over the edge. When my orgasm hit me, I threw my head back and screamed as the pleasure slammed into me.

In the distance of my mind, I recognized that I wasn't the only one that had reached the peak. Sorrell's hands grew rougher against my sides. His head dipped down to kiss the space between my throat and shoulder and he groaned into my flesh as he released himself inside of me.

When the two of us came down from the high, I found myself clinging to the headboard for dear life. Panting. Soaked. Shaking.

"Let me help you," Sorrell rasped, reaching around me to quickly untie my bindings. I slumped over onto the mattress, exhausted and completely spent.

"I think you killed me," I said. "Roan and Orion are going to be pissed."

Sorrell paused as he got off of the bed, holding the remains of my nightgown and ties in his grasp. After a moment, he kept moving. "You think so?" he inquired. I could tell that he was forcing himself to appear unconcerned. His tone was light, but the stiffness of his shoulders suggested otherwise—especially after what we'd just experienced.

"Yeah, I'm pretty sure they wouldn't like it if I died," I replied.

Sorrell moved to a bowl in the corner of the chamber and filled it with water. Using the scraps of fabric torn from my dress he dipped it into the water and cleaned himself before using another to come over to me and do the same for me. My face flamed and grew heated as he spread my thighs and wiped along my core.

"You're not dead." He sighed.

"You tried though," I said. "You tried to kill me with sex."

The look he gave me when he straightened and tossed the rags to the side and climbed into bed with me was unamused. I pushed against his chest and smiled up at him. "What's wrong?" I demanded.

He looked down at me for a moment before rolling to the side. Sorrell, for all of his intelligence, was a warrior in body. He weighed a ton, and as such, the mattress sank under his superior weight and I was unintentionally rolled towards him. Once I was against his side though, he didn't seem inclined to push me away. Instead, an arm came around me and I was cuddled up to him in less than a heartbeat.

I liked this new version of Sorrell. Oh, he was still commanding. Constantly in control. This was the lover in him. The man who felt emotion and stopped hiding behind it but only in front of people he truly trusted. I was now one of those people and I'd never felt more honored.

My fingertips stroked against his chest. "Sorrell?" I prompted.

"Hmmmm?" He hummed in the back of his throat, sounding distracted.

"You're thinking of something," I said. "What is it?"

His jaw tightened and then slowly released after a moment. "Roan and Orion—they will return soon," he said.

"Are you worried they won't like this?" I asked, meaning us—what had happened between us tonight.

His lips pursed. "I'm not sure." His brows drew down low over his eyes as he seemed to contemplate something. "Roan said something not too long ago..."

"About me?" I asked.

"Yes, about you," he answered before looking at me. "I don't think they'll be upset."

"Then what's the problem?" I asked.

"I don't know why they wouldn't be," he said. "We have shared everything since the three of us embarked on our journey as future Kings. We saw our counterparts —the other Royals—all drowning beneath expectation and pressure from the old generation. Some perished in war and the three of us … we decided that we would not be like them. We separated. Roan managed to convince his mother to give up the Court of Crimson to him—a feat she regretted later on, especially after she learned that he planned to share leadership with Orion and I."

"They're not going to blame you," I assured him.

"I know," he said. "That's just it, though. Roan … he spoke as if he expected this to happen, and at the time, I still denied it."

"Denied what?" My nose twitched and I forced back a yawn.

He shot me a rueful grin, one of the first of its kind I'd ever seen from him. "My attraction to a stubborn little Changeling," he answered.

"I kind of like you, too, even if you act like a horse's ass sometimes," I said.

He shook his head and then curled his arm, pulling me so close that I felt as though I were half on top of him. I couldn't find the energy in myself to care. He was warm and so was this bed. My eyelids flickered and that yawn I'd forced back burst free.

"You should sleep," he suggested. "You're tired."

"But I want to make sure you're okay," I protested even as my eyelids drifted down.

A wide, masculine palm slid down my back, stroking slowly and lulling me deeper into oblivion as exhaustion overcame me. I felt a press of lips against my forehead and then Sorrell's voice rumbling beneath my ear. "Sleep, Cressida. I will wake you in the morning."

And as much as I wanted to stay awake, my body had other plans. Even as I drifted, falling deeper and deeper into the oblivion of sleep, I wondered if maybe he hadn't taught me in other ways tonight. Because when he commanded that I sleep, my body instinctually settled in against him and I found no will to fight against him or his orders. Like Roan and Orion, Sorrell had me completely captured now and I didn't want to ever get away.

CHAPTER TWENTY-SIX

ORION

Norune Castle stood before us like a mountain in the night. The weak illumination of moonlight cast the entirety of the structure in shadow, making it appear more ominous than I believed it would have seemed had the sun been shining down on it.

Roan motioned toward the first squad of soldiers and at his silent order, they separated from us and moved ahead and to the right of the wall that surrounded the castle. If we needed it, they would be our distraction. Our footsteps were silent as we made our way through the castle's outside grounds, an easy spell that muted any sounds we made. Added to the cloaking spell we were using, even the few guards stationed along the walls of the castle, marching slowly back and forth under the moonlight, wouldn't be able to detect us until it was too late.

"Go," Roan said to his second commander. "Quickly.

Be swift. Be silent. No casualties. This is not a killing mission."

"Understood, Your Highness," the commander replied with a nod.

I turned my attention back to the wall for a moment, scanning as Roan and I waited for the others to slip around to the door we had seen on the map. Only two lookouts would remain, but I still felt better knowing that there would be several guards missing from tonight's shift—all out on the town, drinking and whoring. Whores that a few of my men had assured would be well compensated for distracting the Duke's soldiers.

The map had made this door seem like an unusable entrance, but unusable it was not. It was overgrown and nailed shut with planks of wood crisscrossing over the surface of the entrance. Easy obstacles that we had quickly overcome.

"What are you thinking?" Roan inquired. "You're quiet. Are you sure you're up for this?"

"I'm fine," I replied. "Just being cautious."

He and I waited several moments, listening to the night and sounds of nature deep in the forest. "Come on," he said after a beat. "We're next."

Together, Roan and I slipped inside the 'unusable entrance' and found the darkened corridor that lay beyond. I could hear the sounds of our men several yards ahead, moving swiftly towards our target. As we moved towards the men, a soft noise had the two of us halting our footsteps. Conjuring a ball of fire, Roan turned back and froze, his eyes widening. I followed his gaze until my own landed on the small upturned face of a pale human child. Her hair hung in flat strands around her rounded cheeks, and in her left fist she held the paw of a stuffed animal creature—sewn together with what looked to be different colors of patchwork cloth.

Her little nightgown was at least a size or two too large for her tiny frame. Big blue eyes blinked up at us and she lifted her free hand to rub at her eyes as if trying to understand what she was seeing. A servant's child. That was the only thing that made sense. As far down in the castle as we were, the servants' quarters were likely not far from the storage chambers we were after.

Roan and I exchanged a look. "What are you doing?" the small child inquired, sounding both sleepy and confused.

"Orion," Roan hissed. I knew what he wanted, an illusion, but human children were far less susceptible to our powers than their elders—a fact I doubted any human realized.

I ground my teeth together. No, an illusion may not work, but there was no way we would kill this innocent child. It was the one sin none of us were willing to commit. Soldiers and adults were fair game, but children knew not of their parents' and elders' hatred. Children still had the opportunity to overcome that tainted bile.

It appeared that both of us were hesitating far too long for the child's attention because after a moment more, she toddled forward, eyes wide as she reached for the leather encasing the boots that reached up to my knees.

"Whoa," she muttered. "I can see myself." She turned her face upward—so trusting it made my chest ache. The child's golden hair reminded me of Cress and all at once, I wondered if this was how our Changeling had seemed as a child. Youthful. Vibrant. Innocent. Loving. I tried to picture it and the image that came to my mind was so very easy to form. "Who are you, sir?" the small girl inquired again.

Her little chin twitched and just before I was set to answer her, she reared back and sneezed. Roan grimaced, but I didn't mind. It was cute. I reached down and with gentle hands, I lifted the child into my arms. As she slipped her slender, frail hands around my neck, she released her grip on her stuffed toy. Without being asked, Roan dipped down and retrieved it, handing it back to the girl.

"Take care of her," he ordered quietly. "And meet us at the room."

I nodded my understanding and was relieved when he marched off, though he left a hovering orb of fire nearby so that the child and I weren't in complete darkness. "Where'd he go?" the girl asked.

"Never mind him, darling," I said. "You're lost, aren't you?"

Her blue eyes lifted and met mine and I stilled as I felt one of her tiny hands touch my chin, her soft fingers smoothing against the unshaven bits of my jawline. "You're prickly," she said with a high pitched giggle.

Holding her in my arms lit a craving within me. To

see Cress as a girl, or perhaps to see her hold her own child in her arms—*our child*.

"Are you lost, sweetheart?" I asked again.

The girl tilted her face up and nodded. "I had to go potty," she confessed quietly, her cheeks turning pink with embarrassment. Even as young as this child was, I understood. Such things were private, especially for little girls.

"That's alright," I told her. "I'm here to lead you back. If I take you to the main part of the castle, can you find your way back to your chambers on your own?" She considered my request for a moment before nodding. "Good, then let us be on our way. Can you tell me which way you came from?"

She pointed into the darkness and I began walking. As I strode down the corridor, I kept the cloaking spell up and lifted a palm to cup the back of her head. Though it would be far more difficult for a child to believe a full fledged illusion, it wouldn't be that hard to settle her into a light sleep and put the thought into her head that our meeting had been nothing but a strange dream.

The girl's head dipped and rested against my shoulder, her skin warm against my own as she nuzzled into my neck like a curious animal. Soon, the soft little snores began to drift up from her mouth. I shook my head.

"I'm sorry, little one," I whispered to her, though I knew she couldn't hear me. It felt only right to apologize for what I was going to do. "When you wake, all will be well, but for now, I must corrupt your dreams," I said quietly as I sent a tendril of my darkness into her through where my hand was connected to the back of her head. It delved into the sides of her head and in through her open nose and mouth.

Not once did she stir, and once I was satisfied, I quickly found my way up to the main hub of the Duke's castle. There, beneath a large open window, I found a small sitting area and laid the small child upon it, turning her face away from the light, hoping that soon, when she woke, she would only remember wandering the halls and falling asleep here with no one else the wiser.

I pulled myself away from her little by little, finding it far more difficult than I expected it to be. Any child, even human, was precious. It went against my instincts to leave her so out in the open even knowing she would be safer here—away from me and the other Fae that were hunting for our targets down below.

When I made it back to the tunnels, I saw Roan waiting out in the corridor for me. He lifted a hand and extinguished the flame that had followed me before turning towards the open door at his side.

"There's something you should see," he said.

I nodded, allowing him to lead me further into the room—a large open storage space filled to the brim with barrels and bags of food and wooden boxes that had been pried open to reveal weapons. Beyond the main room there appeared to be a much larger door, thicker than the others, and by looking at the vault like security it held—the extra bolts of metal and the strange mechanism over its locking device—there was no doubt that it held important information.

The locking device, too, was built and coated with iron. I narrowed my eyes on it and shook my head. As though an amount that small would deter us. Perhaps had I been from another Court, a more merciful one, it would have. It certainly had Roan and the others standing out of reach. Not me, though. I marched forward, assessing the lock.

In the Court of Midnight, iron had often been used to "strengthen" children, to develop a tolerance for pain. Nothing could be seen as a weakness. To be weak was to be easily killed. I recalled that all too well. Even the old scars along my back and against my chest seemed to tighten as I sucked in a breath. I had trained with shackles of iron on my ankles and wrists. I had tested myself for endurance, been weakened down to even less than a human and yet, I survived. In the Court of Midnight, only the strongest ever did.

Reaching forward, I clenched my hand around the lock. Several soldiers winced as they heard the sizzle as the metal touched my skin. I paid it no heed. Instead, I gripped tighter and then ripped the thing free. The door swung open outward and banged against the wall as I stepped back.

Almost immediately, I realized what we had found. Roan and I stepped inside and the others came in after us, moving gingerly as if fearing they might trigger a trap. But no, the humans—Amnestia's King and his Duke—had not planned on us coming here. They did not expect that, were we to infiltrate them without their knowledge, we would ever make it this far. Because had they done so, they might have realized just how dangerous it was for them to leave so much behind.

Maps covered the walls and notes were scattered over the large table that was the centerpiece of the room. They had been tracking our movements, that much was clear. Someone had been feeding them information. *Tyr.* A familiar anger rose within me and before I could stop it, small plumes of smoke began to fall from my arms and collect around my feet. Several soldiers noticed and were smart enough to avoid it.

I turned my attention to the maps along the walls. I recognized where the Court of Crimson had been and had a vague notion of where my home Court—the Court of Midnight—was last. There were several markings, though, and no way to tell where it actually was presently.

I looked over at Roan who was scanning the notes. He lifted one for me to see. Letters with the Royal seal, I realized. Sketches and diagrams and all one might need to plan another attack. What was more terrifying were the blueprints to build a castle—one like the Courts— and at the center of it, a Lanuaet.

Humans with the same abilities as Fae. The thought was preposterous and yet, with Tyr's help, possible. And all it would result in would be death and destruction. There were no limits to the humans' hatred whereas Fae were bound to protect the Earth as much as possible. We could not destroy without having to give back. Not like the humans.

Fury danced in Roan's gaze and it matched my own.

He raised an eyebrow at me in question and I nodded. I knew what he wanted. "Torch the supplies," Roan ordered. "Keep it contained, and when everything is destroyed make sure you put it out. We don't want this moving to the rest of the grounds."

As he and I stepped out the room, holding the documents we deemed most important, we turned back as a unit and watched as two Crimson Fae stepped up, lifting their arms and sending blast after blast of silent fire raging into the secret chamber we'd found. I felt the heat of flames warm my face.

"What are we going to do now?" Roan muttered.

"We go back," I said. "And show Groffet what we found. If anyone will know what all this means, it's him."

"This is too far," Roan replied. "Tyr needs to be taken care of."

"Yes," I agreed. He may have once been my blood brother, my past, but he'd lost all connection to me the moment he'd taken my future. Cress was my future and so was our race and I knew, beyond a shadow of doubt, that I would do what needed to be done to see Cress and our people safe. Even kill him.

CHAPTER TWENTY-SEVEN

Roan

A nxiety slithered across my nerve endings as I stalked the halls of the Court of Crimson. I could feel the tension in my shoulders. The mission had gone well—aside from the human child mishap, but I trusted Orion to have taken care of that issue.

No, there was a new issue at hand. Something far more devious, a new threat that now hung over our Court, our people, and our lives. Tyr was helping the human King build a fortress. The very moment we'd returned, Orion and I had headed for Groffet before anyone else. Before our people and men. Before Sorrell. Even before Cress.

Groffet was ancient. He had served my father and my grandfather during their reins as Crimson Kings, but something told me that my time as a King would be quite different from theirs. The past was receding. Traditions as we knew them were changing. The Fae, despite having the advantage in this war, were dying. Our magic was depleted and our people were fewer in numbers than they had been twenty years before when it had all started. Unlike humans, we did not breed so often for heirs and even more than that, no one in their right mind wanted to bring children into this world simply to fight a war.

I was brought out of my thoughts as the scent of smoke tickled my nose and drew my curiosity. *A fire within the walls?*

I followed the scent until I came to the training courtyard and beyond the entrance, as I stepped down the stairs and into the mini arena, I saw two familiar heads—one blonde and one a pale silver. Cress and Sorrell. My lips parted as I noted how close they were to one another, standing over a bale of hay that had been set aflame.

"I did it!" Cress shrieked and leapt at Sorrell, her arms encircling him. I half expected him to growl at her to release him, but he merely pulled her closer and leaned down, taking her mouth in a shocking kiss.

Sorrell, the ice King, himself, was kissing Cress. The Changeling, as he called her. Often refusing to even utter her name. And it was a true kiss, one filled with passion that I had not seen from him in many years. I stared in absolute stunned silence as he wrapped his arms around her, lifting her off her feet as he devoured her mouth with his own. Then, as if realizing they were no longer alone, he deposited her on the ground once more and lifted his head. His eyes clashed with mine and he froze.

LUCINDA DARK & HELEN SCOTT

"Sorrell?" Cress's trembling voice indicated she was oblivious to my entrance. Her cheeks were flushed and her smile confused until she turned and spotted me as well. "Roan!" she shouted. "You're back!"

And just like that, the spell of surprise I'd been under was broken. Cress raced from his arms straight into mine, slamming into my chest as her arms came around me and she practically climbed my body. "You're safe!" she said excitedly. "Oh, I'm so glad you're back. Look!" She turned and pointed to the still burning hay hale. "I did it! I blasted it!"

"I see ... well done, Little Bird." I glanced from her face to Sorrell's as he approached at a much slower pace. "I see the two of you are getting along as well."

Cress's eyes widened and though her smile remained, a hint of pink tinged her cheeks. Before she could say anything, however, Sorrell spoke first. "When did you return?" he asked.

"A few hours ago," I admitted.

He frowned.

"Orion and I went to speak with Groffet first," I told him, sliding my hand beneath Cress's body to hold her up.

His eyes followed the movement, lingering for a moment on where her ass was pressed beneath my fore-arms. I wondered, briefly, just how much closer they'd become in our absence. It didn't anger me. On the contrary, I was glad to see that he'd finally broken his abstinence. Without a moment to lose, as well, because with mine and Orion's return—there was only more problems waiting for us. My relief at seeing the two of them would be short lived, no fucking doubt.

"What did you find at the Duke's castle?" he demanded, lifting his gaze to meet mine once more.

"Nothing good," I replied. "Nothing good at all."

Cress pushed back away from me and wiggled. "What's going on?" she asked. I set her down between Sorrell and me, the two of us towering over her much smaller frame. She flicked a glance back to him before resettling her gaze on me. "Roan?"

"Orion is in the library awaiting us," I said.

"Then we must not keep him waiting much longer," Sorrell replied with a nod. "Cress?" She blinked as she turned to him, the flush rising curiously back to her cheeks. "Lead the way?" he suggested. I half expected her to snort and walk off—I'd become so accustomed to their apparent dislike of each other, especially his, it was odd to watch his gaze soften and hers to heat as she nodded.

Just as she strode past me and I moved to follow, Sorrell's hand came out and captured my arm. "A moment," he said. "We'll catch up."

She paused on the threshold of the corridor, narrowing her eyes at him before sighing and striding off. "Very interesting," I commented once I was sure she was out of hearing range. "When I last saw you two, I was beginning to doubt my assumption that you had any feelings for her at all."

He leveled me with an icy look and I lifted my hands in a placating gesture. "She is..." He trailed off, as if he didn't have the words to describe one single Changeling Fae woman.

"Yes," I said with a nod. "I know." She was sunshine and moonlight. Fire and Earth. Warmth that could melt even the coldest heart—now so much more obviously proven. "You finally gave in."

He nodded. "She makes it impossible not to." That comment I understood all too well. Cress was becoming more than just a Changeling. "Now." Sorrell's face shifted back to his serious expression. "Tell me what we're walking into."

"Like I said," I told him. "It's not good. Tyr has been feeding the humans information—on the Courts' whereabouts, ours and Midnight."

"That's treason," he growled.

"Yes, well..." I sucked in a breath. "I don't really think he gives a fuck anymore. He and the King are planning to build a castle—much like the Courts—with ... can you guess? A fucking Lanuaet at the center."

Sorrell's eyes widened and his face went from pale to dead white. "No..." It wasn't a denial, but a hope. A hope that what I said wasn't true. It shouldn't be, but it was.

"We have to end this war," I said, "and soon. We cannot let that thing be built. It'll spell nothing but disaster for all involved."

His eyes met mine and the weight of this knowledge settled over both of us. We were rulers, future Kings. The lives of our people were in our hands. It was a lot to bear—the weight of it could be stifling and almost murderous as time wore on. That was why the three of us had formed this outcast Court. Yes, it was necessary for more than one Royal to move the Court, but only one needed to truly rule it. Royals had been in such short supply since the war that having more than two at a time was a feat and a distinction of strength. But the three of us—Sorrell, Orion, and I—we were bound by more than our race or our Royal lineage. We were bound by more than blood because none of us were truly related.

The three of us were bound by honor. By trust. By hope. That one day this war would end and the dark clouds that hovered over us day in and day out would finally fade and the sun would rise once more.

I put a hand on his shoulder and squeezed. "I am truly glad to see you happy, to see you and Cress happy together," I said. "In the coming battle, I think you'll need her."

"She's not a fighter," he said. "Though she's been doing better, she is far from ready to take to the fields."

"I don't mean as a fighter, my friend," I replied. "I mean as a lover."

His brows lowered. "She's to be your Queen," he said slowly. "And yet you knew what would happen between us."

I shrugged. "Orion had her first, I second, and some-how, I just figured—we've shared everything since we were adolescents." I grinned at him. "Why not her so long as she agrees to it?"

He shook his head. "Sometimes, I forget just how truly hotheaded and insane you are."

"I think the bond between all of us makes us stronger," I argued. "Not just because we are all more connected, but I feel like my magic is stronger as well. Now"—I stopped and slapped him on the back as I pivoted and headed for the courtyard's exit—"let's head to the library and pray to the Gods that Groffet will help us find a way to win this thing before it's too late."

CHAPTER TWENTY-EIGHT

CRESS

Sorrell and Roan arrived at the library alongside each other. Though they noticed Nellie and Ash's presence with raised brows, neither of them said anything. Instead, Roan simply turned and closed the library doors behind him.

For a long moment, silence echoed throughout the chamber, and then Orion spoke. "Last night, Roan and I executed an incognito mission to destroy the King's supply storage at Norune Castle. While there, we uncovered some concerning information," he said.

"What kind of information?" I asked.

"The King has been tracking our Courts and is planning to build a moveable fortress much like ours," Roan stated.

"Movable?" Nellie shook her head. "That's not possible. Humans can't use magic."

"Humans don't *have* magic," Sorrell corrected her.

"They can, however, use magical items—this castle and the magic orb that controls it, for example."

Nel's eyes swung my way and I knew she was trying to determine if this was real, but this was the first I'd ever heard of such a thing.

"What does that mean?" I asked, focusing on Orion.

"It means," he said, "that our timetables must be moved forward. We can't allow King Felix to complete that castle."

Roan stepped forward and then leveled each of us with a look. The last person he landed on was Nellie, and I realized, now, why they hadn't immediately kicked her out of this meeting. They wanted to see what she would do, and how she would react to this information. I glared at him and stepped in front of her.

"Don't," I warned him.

"I'm sorry, Little Bird," he said. "We have to be sure."

"She's loyal," I snapped. "Whatever you have to say, she's not going to go blabbing it to another human. You keep her locked in here—there are no other humans in the Court of Crimson."

"Cress, it's okay." Nellie's words were soft, but my anger was still sharp. It wasn't until her hand landed on my arm and she forced me to turn and meet her gaze. "They're wise to be cautious—keep your friends close and your enemies closer and all that. I'm perfectly fine with anything they have to say."

"Brave words," Sorrell commented before I could respond.

I swung my gaze his way and stared him down.

"There is only one way out of this," Orion said, drawing my attention.

"Say it," Nellie offered. "I can take it."

"We must kill the King of Amnestia."

I watched as Nel's face paled, but she kept her lips shut. She was the daughter of doctors—of healers. Murder and war and bloodshed was not something she cared for. To be honest, the statement wasn't a shock for me. I wasn't even against it. Not after what I'd seen in the capital castle, but there was still a larger problem at play.

"Without a King, what will happen to Amnestia?" I asked.

Orion, Roan, and Sorrell exchanged a look. "We can't say," Roan finally replied.

"Then we can't do it," I said.

It was as simple as that. The King was corrupt and rotten, but without him, all I could see were the aftereffects. The people of Amnestia knew nothing but the monarchy. Dear Coreliath, if there was no ruler in place, chaos would take its place. Chaos was even worse than war.

"Cress, remember what he did to you—" Roan started, his face darkening. "Remember how you were held and almost—"

"I remember," I said, cutting him off. "I'm not defending him. I'm thinking of the people. What happens after he's dead?" I demanded. "Who will take his place?"

The three of them fell silent and I wasn't surprised that neither Nellie nor her Fae 'friend,' Ash, had anything to say. It was an impossible position. The King was the villain in our storybook, and yet, killing him would make us villains. It would destroy the country not to have someone in place to lead them back into the light, into a prosperous world without war and pain as the driving forces of their lives. I sensed the tension in the room, felt it rise as flames erupted at Roan's scalp. He turned and marched one way before swiftly pivoting and starting back.

No matter what, though, none of us had a clear answer.

We couldn't just kill the King and leave the Kingdom of Amnestia to rot. There would be nothing but chaos—the exact opposite of what we were trying to accomplish. We needed peace, not pandemonium. We needed to end this.

"There is another option," Groffet said suddenly. All eyes turned to him.

"Well, we're all ears, Groffet," Roan snapped. "Please, by all means..." He gestured to the rest of the group. "What other option do we have?"

Groffet eyed the red haired Prince and even though he was barely half Roan's size, he still somehow managed to look down his nose at him. "Humans—like Fae—believe in the line of succession," he began. "Therefore, if we can find a Royal of Amnestia who is willing to take over the crown and not the mantle of war, we may yet still have a chance for ending this bloodshed."

"The King never had any children," Nellie piped up. The Fae at her back, Ash, stepped closer as the Princes' gazes all turned to her. She shrank back slightly, but I watched as he lifted his hand and gently pressed it to her back. My eyebrows shot up when she appeared to sigh and lean into him.

"How do you know this?" Sorrell asked. "Is it common knowledge among your people? Do King's of the human realm not hide their offspring in case of an attack?

"It's common knowledge," Nellie said. "If the King had had a child, there would have been a celebration. Plus..." She paused as if unsure whether or not she should speak the next part, but one look from Ash and she lifted her gaze to meet Sorrell's head on. "The Queen was killed during a Fae raid many years ago. It's the reason why he's so hateful towards them now."

"Fae raids..." Orion's brows pinched as repeated those words. "Those haven't happened since the very beginning of the war."

"Then it's likely another reason why the war was started," Sorrell surmised.

Groffet grunted. "I did not say a child of the current King," he clarified. "I said a Royal of Amnestia— someone from his line. It doesn't necessarily have to be a child."

"The King had no children or siblings," Nellie argued. "There are no more Royals of Amnestia. He is the last of his line."

I stepped forward. "Shouldn't we try to find out anyway?" I asked. "Just to be sure? What could it hurt?"

For a moment, there was nothing but silence. Then, one by one, everyone agreed. Even Ash, though he looked more interested in Nellie than he did in the subject at hand, no matter its importance to our survival. Our eyes found Groffet's once more.

"What do we do?" Roan asked.

Groffet turned and waddled away, calling back over his shoulder as he moved. "There is a spell," he said, "that will determine if a person exists. We will use it and it will find them—wherever they may be."

"What if they're not even in Amnestia?" Ash asked.

Groffet went to a stack of books and pulled the top half off, using the stack as a step stool to reach the table. "*Wherever* they may be," he repeated.

My foot tapped with nervousness and I found myself wanting to pace—move—*something*. Anything but stand still. A cool hand fell on my arm and I nearly leapt out of my skin until I realized it was Sorrell. I looked up into his icy gaze and felt my whole body soften. "It will be alright," he whispered. "We will find a way for this blasted war to end with peace—even if we have to rule Amnestia ourselves."

"A Fae can't be the one to do it," I said with a shake of my head. "A Fae can't take over Amnestia." It might work for a time, but never for the long run. I could see the disastrous effects in my head. "Even if you have good intentions, they won't see it like that. The country's people would grow resentful, and eventually, even if you have peace at first, they'll rebel." There would be another war, and I could say with certainty that I was freaking tired of war. Exhausted by it and everything else.

"She's right," Roan said. Sorrell turned his gaze back

to him and so did I. Roan's eyes found mine and he nodded. "Think of it like this," he continued. "What would our people do if Fae were to be ruled by humankind?"

Sorrell scowled. "That's preposterous," he replied. "We wouldn't allow such a thing to happen. Fae are superior."

"No, we're not," I snapped. "And it's that kind of thinking that created this Gods forsaken war in the first place."

Sorrell's head whipped back to me and he narrowed his eyes. "Fae have magic that humans cannot even conceive of, much less use. They are born magicless. We are closer to the Gods."

"Yet the Gods abandoned us as they did the humans," Orion pointed out.

Sorrell gritted his teeth. "I am not the villain here. Tyr and that blasted King are!"

"No, you're not," I said, "but your thoughts are villainous, nonetheless. Thinking the way you do—that there are those who are superior and inferior is exactly what causes hate like this to build. It's wrong. How can you not see that?" When he didn't say anything more, I grabbed onto the lapel of his shirt and held it tightly in my grasp. "What do you see when you look at me?" I asked.

"I see a woman who is insane," he replied. When Sorrell shifted and tried to remove my arm, I held on.

"What else?" I pressed.

"Ugh." He tried again and again, but I refused to release him. "Fine! I see a woman who is far too stubborn for her own good. I see a woman who has time and time again gotten herself into trouble—who has refused to back down even when she knows she should. Who..." I stared up into those cold eyes of his and for a brief moment, they softened.

"What?" I asked.

For a long moment, Sorrell didn't speak. Then he lifted his hand and touched the side of my face, his palm curving to my cheek. "Who is far more brilliant than I ever gave her credit for."

I took a breath. "And am I any different from that girl you first met?" I asked.

A snort left him. "You're a little better at not almost dying," he conceded.

"Anything else?" I insisted.

He sighed. "No."

"You thought I was human when you first met me," I pointed out.

He frowned. "We weren't sure."

"No, but you thought I was human, and nothing else has changed about me since then except for the fact that —according to you"—And I wasn't sure that I liked this being the only thing—"I've gotten better at not almost dying. Nothing else has changed," I repeated, trying and hoping against hope that I was getting my point across. "I'm still the same. I'm still me. I was no different than when you thought I was human."

Sorrell's brows drew down low over his eyes. "That's a pointless argument," he said. "You are Fae. We know that now."

"But you didn't know it then," I huffed. "Please, at

least try to understand." I shuffled to the side and gestured to where Nellie stood. "Nellie is my friend," I said. "And she is, absolutely, without a doubt, human. Do you hate her?"

He lifted his eyes and looked at her across the room. His lips curled down, but he shook his head. "I don't particularly care for her either way," he stated, "but no, I don't hate her."

"Then it's just a race you hate," I said. "And I can promise you, they have been hurt just as much as you have by this war. Hating someone without reason simply for being something that they cannot change is worthless. Hate does nothing but perpetuate itself, but love ... understanding ... care. Those things can do so much more." I rested my hand against his chest and pushed myself against him. "You're a Prince of Frost." I lowered my voice so that only he and I could hear. "You will be a King someday. Don't be a King that perpetuates something so evil. Be the King I *know* you can be."

Sorrell looked at me, his icy gaze holding such uncertainty. I bit my lip and waited. "I don't trust humans," he admitted.

"I'm not asking you to trust them," I said. "I'm asking you to trust me—to trust Roan and Orion. You trust them, right?"

His gaze lifted and over the top of my head, he looked to them. Without looking back to me, he sighed. "Yes," he agreed, "I do."

"Then give this a try," I urged. "Don't let your hatred for humans color your view of what's right. They deserve to rule themselves just as Fae deserve the same."

This time, when Sorrell looked back at me, it was with a peculiar expression. Not exactly one I could pinpoint. It was as if he were looking at something new, something he didn't quite recognize, and yet he was trying to understand how it worked.

"You sound like a Royal," he said.

"A Royal?" I frowned.

Nellie was the one that answered. She stepped up alongside us and reached for my hand. "He means you sound wise," she clarified. Her eyes rose to meet his, but instead of hatred or disgust in Sorrell's eyes when he looked back to her, all I saw was begrudging respect.

The moment was disrupted, however, when Groffet waddled forward and slammed a book down on a nearby table. "Found it!" he called.

CHAPTER TWENTY-NINE

CRESS

"What do we have to do?" Roan demanded. He stepped up to look over Groffet's shoulder, towering over the small troll.

"A spell," Groffet explained. "One that will identify the closest lineal Royal heir to the Kingdom of Amnestia."

"Okay," I said as the rest of us gathered closer. "What do we need to do to pull it off and how are we going to get to them when we do locate them?"

"One thing at a time," Orion said gently as he came to stand at my side. With him against one arm and Sorrell against the other, I felt pinned, yet safe. I inhaled sharply and forced my attention back to the spell.

The words on the page were all a jumbled mess to me. Try as I might to read over Groffet's shoulder like everyone else, it was Fae language—something the nuns

definitely *hadn't* taught us in school. "What does it say?"
I asked.

"We will need a mirror," Groffet said, flicking his
hand out.

Ash rushed to the other side of the library and came
back a moment later, lugging a large covered object.
With a grunt he set it down several feet to the side of
the table and then pulled the sheet that had shielded it
away, revealing a tall, ornately carved mirror. Groffet
nodded in thanks and then went back to reading the
book.

He grumbled something to himself, turned, and
when he found the majority of his audience less than a
foot from him, he huffed and pushed his way through.

"It'll require magic, correct?" Sorrell inquired.

"Yes."

"Will it need the three of us?" Roan asked.

"No."

"What do we need to do?" Nellie asked.

"Nothing."

It was clear Groffet was growing agitated by all the
questions. I watched as he flitted about the room,
shoving books off of their carefully placed-though
haphazard looking-stacks. A wooden bowl was
scrounged from beneath another table. Dusty papers
were procured. A vial of something that disturbingly
resembled blood, and a bag that was as big as it was
shapeless also appeared.

"Uh..." I lifted a hand as Groffet set the bowl down
and leaned over the book, grumbling and reading as he
crumbled the papers and tossed them in the bottom of

the bowl. "Is that"—he uncorked the vial and upended what was definitely a red goopy liquid of some sort —"blood?"

"Yes," he grunted.

I grimaced. "Please tell me it's from an animal," I said, looking at Orion.

He cracked a smile, but it was not reassuring. "It's best not to ask," he replied.

Definitely not an animal then, I surmised. He was right. It was best not to ask. I didn't want to know whose blood it was, where it came from, or how they came to possess it ... scattered about like knick knacks in their Court's library. Nope. Definitely didn't want to know.

A split second later, I gasped. "Are those *bones?*" I hissed, as Groffet opened his bag and withdrew a handful of what looked like the bones of a small animal.

"Like he said," Sorrell answered. My eyes jerked to him. "Don't ask if you don't want to know."

"Roan," Groffet snapped. Roan stepped up and lifted his hand, curling each of his fingers down. All but one, and as soon as he did, a flame appeared at the end of his nail. Roan dipped his finger into the bowl, setting fire to the edge of the now soaked papers until it began to burn and ashes lifted upward. Setting fire to something in a wooden bowl seemed dangerous, but as I took a glance around ... maybe it was best not to ask? Or point it out?

The seven of us—the Princes, me, Nellie, Ash, and Groffet—stood back and watched as the contents of the bowl were incinerated by Roan's fire until there was nothing left but a black mixture. Whatever kind of blood it was that Groffet had poured into the bowl—it wasn't flammable apparently. It was the only thing left and it mixed with the ashes of the bones and papers.

Orion leaned down. "Roan's flame burns much hotter than the average fire," he whispered.

"Then why didn't the blood burn up?" I whispered back.

Orion's dark, midnight gaze locked on mine. "Because it's magic."

I absorbed that as Groffet lifted the bowl and turned toward the mirror. Without concern for whatever heat remained behind, he dipped two fingers into the bowl, stirring them around until his fingertips were coated in the mixture. Only then did he use them to paint markings in a line up the mirror's surface.

Halfway up, he had to stop, and Roan kicked over a stool for him to use. We watched as he clambered up onto the stool and finished the markings. They resembled some of the ones I'd seen in the book, but once more they were nothing legible. I shook my head, unable to make sense of it.

"What does that mean?" I asked, tugging on Orion's sleeve.

"They're glyphs," he answered. "The old written language of the Fae is close enough to the language of the Gods that the writing itself contains magic. The words are the spell, the question, the mirror is the conduit of the answer. Whoever appears within it is who we're going to be looking for."

I swallowed roughly and shivered as the mirror began to glow. Groffet backed up, tossing the bowl to the side without a second thought. We crowded closer, curiosity lingering in each of us. Whoever this person was, they would be the next King. We would need to find them as soon as possible, convince them to work with us, and then … a coup d'état.

It wouldn't be easy. That much was for damn sure. They would be risking a lot to help us. They could have a family. A life. Children. What were we about to ask of a total stranger? I looked around the room, my eyes leaving the mirror's surface to survey the faces in the room. I was so focused on my guilt and worry, that when Nellie gasped, I didn't immediately understand what had happened.

"By the Gods," she whispered, stumbling back.

My gaze shot to her and then to the mirror. *What was it? What had I missed?* When I saw the image in the mirror, my lips parted and my jaw dropped.

It was her. It was Nellie, but as a little girl. Playing alongside a tall dark haired man and a light haired woman. It was her running through a battlefield with gauze in her arms and tears on her face and blood in her hair. It was Nellie a few years later, solemn and quiet, as she washed dishes at the convent. The Nellie in the mirror paused, having heard something. Her head lifted and her eyes went to the window before her. A small smile appeared and then she shook her head. A moment later, I came in, covered in chicken feathers. I remembered that day. I'd been running from Sister Madeline through the chicken coup and had disturbed a very angry mother hen who'd nearly pecked my toes off.

"I don't understand," Nellie said, shaking her head. "It's broken. It has to be. My parents were doctors!"

Roan shot a look to Groffet. "Could there have been a mistake?" he asked.

Groffet shook his head. "No mistake," he replied. "She is the closest heir."

Silence descended and then, "Well," I said, drawing everyone's attention, "at least this saves us the trip."

Nel growled my way. "No, it doesn't," she argued. "Because it's not true. How can it be?"

Groffet waddled her way, his bulbous body swaying back and forth as he maneuvered around Roan and Ash to stand before her. "Doesn't matter what you say is true, girly," he snapped, his hands landing on his hips as he glared up at her. "The magic does not lie."

"Then you did the spell wrong!" she exclaimed. "You have to do it again. It didn't work."

"Nel." Ash reached out and grasped her hand, holding her as she began to shake.

"Ash," she said. "You have to know it's not true. I'm not related to the King. I can't be. I wouldn't have been in a convent orphanage if that were true." She looked at me. "You know me, Cress! You know I'm not some Royal Princess in disguise."

"Groffet is never wrong," Ash said.

I stepped forward, moving until I was right next to her. I took her other hand and held it in mine, squeezing as she had done for me so many times before. Then I turned to Groffet. "Is there a way to prove it?" I asked. "To make sure."

He sniffed as if the very idea was insulting, but when

I didn't take back my request and I met his beady little eyes with a glare of my own, he huffed. "I can do another spell, but it will only prove the inevitable; she is of the King's bloodline."

I looked at Nellie. "Do you want him to do the second spell?" I asked. Her face was pale, her eyes wide with shock, and she kept biting down on her lower lip, chewing it until I was sure she would bruise herself. "Nellie," I repeated her name when she didn't seem to hear me. Her hand jerked in mine and her eyes lifted to meet my gaze "Do you want him to do the second spell?" I asked once more.

She nodded. "He has to, Cress." Her words were whispered. "Because I'm not the King's daughter. There's no way. My father was a doctor."

"We'll figure it out," I reassured her. I turned back to Groffet. "What do we need to do?"

He eyed me for a moment but then he stepped back. "You don't need to do anything," Roan said as he moved forward and Groffet shuffled over to where Orion and Sorrell now stood, watching the proceedings. Groffet flipped through another book and uttered a few garbled words that sounded foreign and hypnotic all at once.

The language of the Gods? I wondered. As he did Roan lifted a knife from the nearby table and sliced his arm, running his fingers through the blood before painting glyphs around the outside of the mirror. Groffet then waddled forward and lifted Nellie's arm, eyeing her as if asking for permission. He gently took the blade from Roan and then did the same to her arm and used her blood to run over the markings.

"Why—" I began, confused.

"Roan's Fae blood will act as an accelerant," Orion said, answering my unfinished question. "While Nellie's blood will be used to trace her bloodline. It'll go fast, so pay attention."

She and I nodded and then, taking her hand once more, together, we watched the mirror shift and new scenes arise. Nellie's parents, each of them unique in their own way, but it was easy to see that Nellie took after each of them. Her father's large oval eyes. Her mother's petite nose and rosebud mouth. The strength of her father's chin and his coloring with her mother's hair. Nellie's hand squeezed mine as she stared at them. I could only imagine the mixture of love and pain she was feeling and a part of me wondered if I would recognize my parents if I were to see what they looked like.

The image in the mirror moved, slipping backwards from their deaths to their marriage to their meeting to their childhood. And then as they separated, the scenes focused on the father—so he was the true heir, I thought as we stared in quiet curiosity as his life ran down. From adulthood to adolescence to childhood to infancy. Until…

Nel's gasp sounded and rebounded around the room as she watched her father's mother—her grandmother —tossed from the capital castle. Hitting the mud as the King stood above her and guards threw her to the ground. Words were said, but we could not hear. All we could do was watch as she cried and begged, grabbing at the young King Felix's robes with pleas in her eyes. And it came as no shock to anyone to watch him turn away and walk back into the castle—leaving Nellie's grandmother in the streets.

"What does that mean?" Nellie's lips trembled as she asked the question and the images in the mirror went dark.

"She was likely his mistress," Roan said quietly and though he was normally so commanding in his tone, now his voice was soft and quiet, sympathetic. "And when he found out about the baby, he threw her out. Bastard children of Royals—whether human or Fae— are rarely looked upon with anything but disdain."

"He just threw her out like garbage," Nel whispered. "How could he do that?"

Because he was cruel, I thought, though I didn't voice it. When she turned into me and clutched my sides, I had no choice but to hold her and let her tears soak the front of my dress. I didn't care if she needed to soak a hundred of them. Her pain was my pain. When I lifted my head, I noticed that while Orion spoke quietly with Groffet, both Roan and Sorrell appeared to be watching Nellie and me. Of the two of them, Sorrell appeared contemplative. He now stared at Nellie with an open curiosity that I knew we all felt.

Nellie as the King's heir? It seemed too good to be true. Too unpredictable and yet … perfectly aligned with everything we needed. For a brief moment, I wondered … but no, the Gods had long ago stopped meddling in the lives of humans and Fae. There was no way they had set this up, was there?

CHAPTER THIRTY

ORION

My brother had once thought me broken, and perhaps, at one point, I might have agreed. The things I survived in the Court of Midnight—the most detestable of Courts—were not for children to understand. Yet, as a child, I had more than understood it. I had lived it, breathed it, and now, as an adult, I would vanquish it.

Hatred. Fear. Sorrow. Pain. The darkest parts of nature were in our blood—Tyr's and mine. These were also the very reasons I had left. Had I stayed, there was no doubt that I would have risen to my brother's side. I would have been a Prince of Midnight as wicked as he was, but in that dark hole where I'd been born and raised, two creatures had looked in and they had reached their hands down to help me out.

Roan and Sorrell. Each of us had our own pains. Our own lives had been fraught with nothing but Court politics, commanding orders from our parents, and control that we had only just managed to scrape back to ourselves before our fourth and final piece—a bright little Changeling—had fallen right into place.

As I gathered my weapons and strapped them to my body, preparing for the battle that was coming, I wondered what might have happened had Roan and Sorrell not come into my life. What might I have been had they simply acted as every other Crimson and Frost Fae before them—turning away in fear from a Prince of a Court known only for its darkness?

I would not be here, I decided, and I would not even consider helping the human King's heir take her place on the throne.

No, I may have been born as part of the Court of Midnight, but as far as I was concerned, I was no longer theirs. I was *hers*. My little Changeling. Sweet. Fiery. Unbreakable.

Even as my thoughts veered away from the darkness in my mind, I couldn't help but consider the other questions we had yet to answer. No messenger that had been sent to the Court of Midnight had yet to return. We could not expect their assistance in this war—if they were even alive.

There was no proof to lend to my gut instinct. No solid evidence. Nothing tangible that I could use to pinpoint why I had the thought that it—the Court of Midnight—was no more. Only something deep inside of me said that it was true. Something horrible had happened to my home Court. And worse, a part of me did not mourn them. My guilt for that seeped into my soul and reminded me that no matter how I gave myself over to my friends—to my new family—I wouldn't ever have their light.

Once all of my smaller weapons—daggers and the like—were attached to my body, my hand fell to my sword. Nothing prepared me more than the task of lifting this weapon. The weight of it never felt light, but today I lifted it and turned it against the light pouring in from my chambers above, letting the sun glint over its shimmering surface. In the surface of the blade was a reflection of a familiar and welcome face. I turned and met Cress's look. Her eyes fell on the sword in my grasp.

"You're preparing," she said.

It was not a question, but I answered it nonetheless. "I am."

Her lips pressed together. "I'm going with you."

My head began to shake, but before I could open my mouth and utter an argument, she was storming towards me. "Don't tell me no, Orion," she ordered. "I'm going. I've already talked to Roan and I'll be riding with him."

"It's not safe on the battlefield and you are not a soldier," I said.

"My best friend is going out there," she replied. "Nellie's human and she's going."

"She needs to be in the castle when the King is killed," I argued. "We have gone over this. The plan does not work without her presence."

"Which I understand." Her small, heart shaped face tipped up and those bright shining blue eyes met mine. "But I'm going to be there whether you like it or not."

I frowned, feeling the tingle of anxiety creep up my spine. My powers didn't just feed off of others' negative emotions. It fed off my own, and presently, the thought of Cress in the middle of a bloody battlefield with no way to defend herself made me swell and smoke began to lift from my form and curl around me. "I don't."

Cress laid a gentle hand on my chest and as if she had some will to dissipate the disturbing possibilities running through my mind, I felt my whole self soften. My shoulders came down and I moved closer, running a hand along her side as I tugged her to my chest.

"I'll be fine," she said, looking up at me.

I recalled thinking, the first time I met her, that females were such curious creatures and that she was no different. How wrong I had been. She was by far the most infuriating and contrary female I had ever come across.

"I would go into the depths of the Divine for you," I whispered. "Do not cross that threshold."

"I won't." Her promise was soft on her lips, and it was far too enticing for me to turn away. My head dipped and my mouth captured hers. A soft sigh escaped her as she burrowed closer to me. Her little hands wrapped around my body as I pushed my quickly hardening cock against her belly. The things I wanted to do to her. I wanted to pin her to my bed and make her scream as I licked her sweet little pussy. Then, when she would push my head away, claiming it was too much, that she had reached her peak too many times—I would merely grab her hands and hold them in mine as I devoured her core even more. Until she was so languid with pleasure and tender from all that I had done, she would never think of putting herself in harm's way again.

"Cress..." I said her name as our lips parted. Dark lashes fluttered against her skin. Despite the lightness of her hair, they were a stark contrast to her pale face. Those and the dark brows above her eyes. A wonder … a curiosity … I reached up and pushed a lock of her curls back.

Groffet had come up with the notion that she was of the Crimson Fae bloodline, but I had a suspicion he was only partially right. And if it was true—if our Cress was part of that long erased Court, the Brightling Court, then that meant she was the last one. Where the source of the Crimson Fae abilities came from blood and fire, Brightling Fae pulled their powers from light. Light could burn. Could set things aflame. But light could also drive out the darkness. And if it was true, then it was no wonder I was so drawn to her.

My little ray of sunshine. A blessing from the Gods of old. I didn't know how she had survived the purge, if I was right, but I was grateful. The only thing that made me hesitate, however, in sharing my theory, was the thought of her response. If she knew she was the last of her kind, that there were no others like her, that all of her family and potential friends had perished because of the Queens' and Court council's fears and animosity … it would break her spirit. And that, I couldn't let happen.

"Is there something else you're worrying about?" Cress asked, leaning away.

She was perceptive. I shook my head. "No, just your safety," I lied.

Her pretty eyes narrowed on me and then cleared. "It's about Tyr, isn't it?" she guessed.

"What?" I looked at her in surprise, but even as she said it, I realized it was true. Tyr's involvement and betrayal had been weighing heavily on my mind. So, too, was the knowledge that there was a likelihood I would face him again. That I would kill him. "I'll do what needs to be done," I finally said.

Cress watched me with thoughtful eyes for a long moment before she spoke. "It's okay to be sad about it," she said.

"Sad?" I shook my head. "There's no need. He betrayed not just me, but our people. He deserves his fate."

"That's true," she agreed with a nod. "But you can still mourn his loss. It's not a crime."

"Mourn the loss of a criminal and traitor?" I stared at her. "Why would I do that?"

"Because he's your brother," she said. Then she waved a hand through the air, sighing and turning away as she moved towards the center of the room. "You won't hear me say he was a great person or anything— I'm a realist like that—but he *was* your brother and you feel a connection to him. That's not wrong. Even if you don't mourn the person he was, you can mourn the person he might have been—should have been—a brother, a friend, and an ally.

"What I'm trying to say is that whatever you're feeling is allowed. If you're sad, it's okay. If you're angry, that's okay too." Her eyes settled on me with meaning. "No one has to live with the actions you take but you. No one can tell you what's right or wrong to feel, just you, and you have to trust that whatever you're feeling is valid. You can't punish yourself for someone else's actions."

My heart froze at her words, and at some point during her speech, I'd stopped breathing. She was a queen, or at least she had all the makings of one. It was stunning to see in action. Breathtaking. When I still hadn't responded, Cress raised her eyebrows at me expectantly.

All I could scrape out of my raw throat in that moment was, "Thank you."

Her eyes softened. "Always," she replied. It was both a response and an oath. Come what may, she would remain on my side even if I truly did have to play my own brother's executioner.

CHAPTER THIRTY-ONE

CRESS

The sun rose in the East, sending a kaleidoscope of colors washing over the sky. Dark blues turned to light and then oranges and reds and yellows as it slowly peeked above the horizon. Today was the day.

Roan's chest was warm against my back. I drew in a deep breath and looked up at him. "When does it start?" I asked.

Roan's eyes were on the castle in the nearby distance. The clomp of horse hooves beneath us rattled me as we continued forward in silence for a long moment more until…

"We will try our best to keep the casualties to a minimum," he began, his hand tightening on the reins. "But you should know, it will not be entirely possible."

I knew that much. My hand reached for the dagger Sorrell had given me. Strapped against the leather trousers beneath my purple skirts. It felt like a small weapon in light of all that was about to happen. A battle —a true one with swords and magic and fire and blood and death. I shuddered just thinking about it. As much as I knew this was necessary to end the war, it seemed a little counterproductive to fight to end the fighting, but there had to be one clear victor. This hatred had to come to an end.

"When the morning bells ring," Roan continued, "we will ride down to the castle's entrance."

"They won't let us in though," I said.

Roan shook his head. "They won't need to. We've already sent our scouts ahead and we have magic on our side. The humans can shore up their defenses all they like, but there's no way to truly deflect something they have no control over."

I pressed my lips together, looking up and spotting Nellie's head several paces away, her face tipped up as she talked with the man at her back. Her own rider, Ash. I watched the two of them together for a long moment, noting the gentle way he held her to him and how his eyes flickered down to meet hers as he both rode and listened to whatever she was saying.

"It may work, you know," Roan commented a moment later.

"What?" I asked. "The plan? I should hope so. Otherwise, this will be all for nothing."

"No," he replied. "Your friend and Ash."

A sigh escaped my lips. "I don't know how," I said honestly.

He chuckled, the sound vibrating against my back and sending a warmth through me that I didn't feel on the outside. "What happened to all that bravado and talk about not judging someone based upon their race?"

"It's not about his race," I replied. "It's about how long he'll live compared to her."

"I see." Roan straightened and our horse continued forward. "I understand your worries, but they're both in charge of their own hearts."

"I just don't want her to get hurt."

"Life is about getting hurt," Roan replied. "It is what makes living so exciting. You love and you lose. You fight and win. Without any dark, there cannot be light. Without death, there is no life. Without love, there is..." His words trailed off and I bit my lip.

"I get what you're saying," I said, "but Fae live far longer than humans. He'll outlive her by hundreds of years. How can he go into something with her, knowing that she'll pass long before he will?" My chest clenched at that thought. For the last several weeks, I'd lived with the knowledge of what I was, but it was just then that the reality of it hit me. I was Fae and my best friend was human. It wasn't just Ash who would suffer the loss when she died. I would, too. Tears pricked at my eyes and I squeezed them shut to ward off the pain.

Roan's heat moved closer as he leaned down and pressed his lips close to my ear. "Would you give her up now, knowing that?" he asked.

My eyes popped open. "Of course not." Every moment with her was even more precious because I knew that.

He nodded. "Then you understand how he feels," he said with a smug note in his tone.

I turned my head up and glared at him. He was smirking, the small curling of his lips making him appear even more handsome in the early morning light. I couldn't be too angry, though, because he was right. I sighed and turned back to face forward, adjusting myself in the saddle.

My eyes scanned the area. There were three main battalions of Fae soldiers on our side—with the Queens' soldiers coming in from the North. Each of them clad in chainmail and plated armor. Even the Princes. I looked down at the leather and metal plates that covered my upper chest. I felt woefully underdressed for a battle-field, but at the same time, I wouldn't be fighting. Though I was sure Roan was unhappy about not taking part in the battle himself, he, Nellie, Ash, and I would ride through the fighting into the main hub of the castle. It was our job to get to King Felix.

Sorrell would stay behind and lead both his and the rest of Roan's men. Orion would fight and search for Tyr. And ... Gods be with us, by the time this day ended, it would all be over.

"Get ready," Roan said a moment later, making me tense. I felt my back stiffen and my hands clench against the hump in front of me. My nails sank into the brown leather of the saddle as we picked up the pace. Our horse trotted to the front, rounding a line of Fae soldiers.

At first, there was nothing but silence. Not even the birds were chirping. As if nature, itself, sensed the violence that was about to happen. Then ... the bells. They rang once, twice, and then a few more times and by the time the last had faded into the morning quiet, we heard a battle cry and Fae were swarming forward. Hooves beating fast against the ground, dirt flying up in every direction.

Roan snapped his legs against his steed's sides and we galloped forward. Wind whipped at my face and I leaned forward unconsciously willing us to move faster, to get there before the blood began to spill. By the time we reached the wide open front gates of the village, the wood split and seared and smoking by some sort of fire magic, it was too late.

There were already Fae and human soldiers fighting and slashing. Fire was conjured. Water. Ice. Every element one could think of was being used during the battle. Dark smoke poured around the cobblestones street and I turned, looking back. as I realized that Orion had entered the fray. His face was expressionless as he rode through the streets, the dark clouds pouring from his body as he swiftly dove through a ring of soldiers swinging their swords.

I whimpered as he nearly got clipped. Roan urged me to face forward once more. "Don't worry about him," he ordered. "He knows what he's doing."

"But what if—" I tried, but Roan merely shook his head and forced the horse to move faster. We were flying over the streets now, dodging swords and screaming soldiers. Something occurred to me as we raced ever closer to the main castle. "Where are the people?" I asked, glancing around. "There are women and children that live here." *Even if they knew what was going on and decided to hide, wouldn't we have seen some of them?* I wondered silently.

Roan looked down at me and frowned. "Did you think we would risk innocents in our fight?" he asked, shaking his head.

"Then what did you do?"

"They're asleep," he stated.

I blinked and gaped up at him. "All of them?"

He nodded, steering the horse around another group of soldiers as they raced towards us. "Why didn't you just put everyone to sleep then?" I asked curiously. It would've been so much easier to just ride through the sleeping village and into the castle without all of this bloodshed.

Roan's head dipped and he grunted as the horse leapt over a fallen man, jarring the two of us. "This type of magic consumes a lot of energy, Little Bird," he replied. "You requested as little bloodshed as possible, and we agreed to spare the innocent. This was our compromise. Trying to keep a whole village asleep— especially one as big as this—would render us useless by the time we reach the castle. As it stands, the spell will only last for an hour or so. We must hurry."

Just as we were passing another group of village soldiers, he withdrew his sword and leaned over, swiping it across several men at once as they attempted to spear us. I winced when the end of one of their weapons struck at my leg, tearing into the leather and leaving me with a long cut.

Roan cursed and gripped the reins tight, pulling us

to a stop. "No!" I shouted. "Don't worry about it. Keep going."

He growled and glared backwards, but his legs kicked up and the horse stopped its deceleration and continued on. I released a relieved breath. Though my leg stung, it was nothing compared to what he would have unleashed against those men, and the best way to end it all was to just get to the castle.

"Yes," he gritted out. "They're all asleep. They remain unaware of what is happening and all of our men have been instructed to harm only those who wish them harm. The women and children will be safe. The sleep spells they remain under were cast over the village and it will ensure they're protected from all untoward harm —magical or otherwise. How's your leg?"

"It's fine," I said. "We have to keep going."

His eyes dropped down to meet mine and his lips pressed together, but instead of saying anything more, he merely spurred our horse even faster, catching up with Nellie and Ash. We made it into the castle's secondary main gates and beyond, stopping once we reached the entrance to dismount. As I listened to the sounds of the raging battle down in the village—the clashing of swords, masculine shouts, and the clomping of horse hooves—I stopped and glanced around at the empty courtyard.

The platform that had once been there was gone, apparently dismantled and taken away, but something more than the fact that this was where I'd nearly died made this place feel off to me. I shivered and rubbed my arms with my hands as Nellie and Ash stepped up to Roan and me.

"Where's the throne room?" Ash asked.

Roan and Nellie both looked to me and I realized that I was the only one who'd ever been there. Despite my circumstances of having been there, I could still recall the general layout of the castle when I'd been dragged before the King. I sighed and moved across the stones towards the entrance.

"This way," I called.

Roan moved ahead of me, his sword at the ready. He paused at the entrance, looking inside before conjuring a globe of fire and sending it down the first corridor. This ball of flame wasn't so much destructive as it just hovered in mid-air, giving off enough of a glow for us to see ahead and behind us. It fluttered along the hallway, illuminating the dark path and the drawn drapes on all of the windows that would have let in light had they been open. Nellie fell behind me, walking with unsure footsteps that faltered every once in a while. Ash was to the back.

"I'm not so sure about this," Nellie said quietly.

I glanced back at her. "About killing the King or about taking the throne?" I asked.

"Both," she said. "I'm not a fighter, Cress. I'm not a ruler."

I sighed and took her hand. I didn't know what to say to reassure her. To be fair, there was nothing I could say that would leave her with no doubts. She would always have them. Even if—Gods willing—this whole plan worked out and she was placed on the throne and the Kingdom of Amnestia finally ended the war with the Fae, she would still have them.

So, I said the only thing I could think of. "You care," I whispered in the shadows of the corridor. "You love. You believe. All of these things make you a great person, Nellie, and they will make you a wonderful Queen."

Even in the dark, I could hear the swish of her hair as she shook her head. "I'm not brave like you, Cress."

I wanted to stop and turn around and stare at her. The urge was there, fast and so very consuming, but I forced my feet to keep moving. We didn't have time. Instead, I just pushed as much of my emotions into my tone as possible. *How could she think she wasn't brave?*

"You are one of the bravest souls I know," I whispered harshly. "You gave up your life at the convent for me. Entered a Fae castle, even knowing what happened to your parents. You didn't reject me when you found out what I was. You still loved me."

She huffed out a breath. "Because it doesn't change who you are," she snapped.

I laughed, a low, quiet breathy sound. "Exactly," I replied. "And you realize that. You won't hold someone's abilities against them. You're not the type to see only what lies on the surface, but you hold what's underneath to the light. Someone's character, their actions, their intelligence." I shook my head. "Being willing to admit mistakes and working to correct them makes you brave. Not just holding a sword and cutting down enemies. Besides, I can't even do that."

"But you have magic," she said.

"A little," I admitted, "but I'm still weak by Fae standards. I'm not this great and powerful being, Nellie. I'm just me. Cress the orphan. Cress the Changeling. I'm stubborn"—I didn't have to see her to know she was grinning at that—"a little insane at times—"

"A little?" she countered.

"Hush when I'm complimenting you and telling you how amazing you are," I said.

"You're right, please continue."

"No," Roan said, stopping. I bumped into him and brought the three of us at his back to a halt. "There's no time."

He was right. We were here. The flickering of yellow candlelight beyond the throne room was visible in the darkened hallway. It was time to face King Felix. My hand squeezed Nellie's tightly. It was time to bring this Gods forsaken war to an end.

CHAPTER THIRTY-TWO

CRESS

T he doors of the throne room swung slowly open as we pushed against them. The room was just as I remembered it, stone floors and walls with a dais directly across from the entrance upon which were two thrones, one slightly smaller than the other. Fires lit each side of the room in a series of fireplaces and braziers.

Just as we entered, the King looked up. It was early in the morning, but it was clear he had not slept. There were deep, sagging shadows beneath his eyes and a scowl on his face that I was all too familiar with. Beneath him were a series of men—his Royal guard. None of this was shocking. What was shocking was seeing Tyr there alongside King Felix. He had to have known we would come here and that he would be outnumbered. Tyr seemed the kind of man who'd flee a fight he knew he couldn't win. So, why then, was he still here? The second he laid his eyes on me, just behind Roan, a sinister grin formed over his lips.

An uneasy feeling surfaced in my gut. I pressed it down as I flicked a look first to Roan—he held his sword at the ready as he strode forward—and then behind me to Nellie, whose wide eyes took in everything within the throne room with both awe and fear.

"So, the traitorous Fae bitch has returned," King Felix said as he rose from his throne and took a step towards the edge of his dais. Tyr hung back, content, it appeared, to watch the proceedings. I didn't like that. I didn't trust it.

"Roan..." His name was a warning on my lips but it was interrupted as Ash rounded Nel and me to come to his side.

"I am Prince Roan of the Fae Court of Crimson," Roan announced, his gaze scanning the Royal guard as they withdrew their weapons. They held back, though, waiting for the King's signal. "And you, King Felix of Amnestia, have been defeated. As we speak, my soldiers and those of the other Courts are laying siege on this very castle. The war is over, Your Majesty. You have lost."

For every beat of silence that reigned after Roan's words, I felt the tension in my body grow tighter and tighter. Then, with a bellow, King Felix began to laugh. His body shook with it. It was startling to see a man so much older be so capable of such a loud laugh. As his amusement waned, however, he lifted his head and fixed his gaze on the four of us.

"I agree," he said, sounding far too smug for my peace of mind. "The war is over—for you. Guards! Kill them."

As he brought his arm up and swept it downward, announcing his will to his soldiers, King Felix's voice was cold, devoid of any emotion other than fury and disgust. All at once, the Royal guard sprang forward—their weapons at the ready as they attacked. Nellie's gasp had me moving quickly to the side. With her wrist in my grasp, I yanked her behind me and backed her towards the side of the room just as Roan and Ash entered the fray.

Bodies went down under the slash of their metal. Fire erupted and in one fell swoop, Roan cleared half of the guard. Still, my eyes couldn't help but drift back to the King and Tyr. There was almost a child-like excitement on the King's face. A desire for bloodshed. It was disturbing.

Nellie's free hand sank into my arm, making me jerk my attention back to the battle before us. Ash was bleeding from his shoulder as he fended off two of the guards who were still on their feet after Roan's initial blast. I looked down at my hand. I had to help them somehow. But even as I willed my magic to spark to life, all that came forth was a puny ball of light.

Still, I thought, it was better than nothing. Without a second thought, I sent it hurling into the battle, straight at another guard as they crept up behind Ash, sword over their head, ready to cut him down.

The enemy guard took the hit and was flung across the room, slamming into the wall across from us.

Nellie's nails softened and she breathed a sigh of relief. "It's okay," I assured her. "They know what they're doing." Yet, my gaze remained rooted on the scene.

It wasn't until the last guard fell and a panting and bloody Roan stepped from the bodies of the fallen guard to stand before King Felix that I felt any kind of relief. Unfortunately, it was short lived as I watched the King withdraw his sword and throw off his cloak.

"Do you think that frightens me, boy?" he demanded, staring down his long aristocratic nose as Roan's fiery head tilted back. Sparks and embers danced at the ends of both his and Ash's hair as Nellie's friend moved forward to take his place at Roan's side. "I will go down in history known as the King who defeated the Fae. I will drive you from our land and wipe you from existence. You are a scourge upon this Kingdom."

"*Your* land?" Roan inquired. My back straightened at the deep, strange tone that overtook him. He moved forward a step. "You think that this land belongs to you? No." He shook his head, sending a rain of sparks flying around him. "This land was a gift from the Gods. It is *their* land, and a creature such as you has no claim on it. You may live on it and work it and rule it, but make no mistake, you cannot own it."

The King brought his sword up and darted forward —far faster than I'd expected from a man of his age. Roan and Ash spun out of the way, moving as if in sync with one another.

"You cannot kill me!" the King yelled, spinning to face them once more. "I am this country's heart and soul! My people will never respect you, they will never live under your wishes—they would rather die!"

"They won't need to!" I shouted. As if he'd forgotten my presence, the King jerked and spun towards me as I pulled Nellie forward. "The Fae aren't planning to rule Amnestia," I told him. "Unlike you, they just want this Gods forsaken war to end. They want the violence to cease as it should have years ago."

He laughed, the sound sharp and quick but not nearly as smug as he had been earlier, I noticed. "Foolish girl," he snapped. "If they do not plan to rule my Kingdom, then who will?"

I stepped to the side, revealing Nellie. "She will," I said. "Nelemente of Amnestia. Your granddaughter."

There was nothing but silence for a long moment, but as the King's eyes fell on Nellie's face, he paled. "I-I do not have a granddaughter," he spat back.

Nellie inhaled a breath as if realizing this was a crucial moment and, in true fashion of her character, she quietly moved until she was standing between me and the King. "We've never met," she said. "But you are my father's father. Perhaps you remember a young woman who you threw from this very castle several decades ago?"

"Eleanor..." The King stared at Nellie as if in shock. Yes, we'd seen the features of her parents and how she'd reflected them each, but what I hadn't noticed was how she, too, had looked so much like her grandmother. Her father's mother. "No..." He shook his head as if trying to ward off unwanted memories. "She was to get rid of her child."

"Your child," Nellie snapped, standing straighter. I blinked as she moved forward. "My father was your child too. He was brave and strong and kind and intelligent. He became a doctor for your war and he died for it—treating both Fae and humans alike."

The King's gaze jerked to the side as he glared up at Tyr, who had moved forward and now sat upon the King's throne as if he were enjoying a dramatic theater play. "You said the child would lead to my death!" he yelled. "You said it would be a girl."

Tyr shrugged. "And I have been proven right," he said.

My lips parted. "He told you?"

The King ignored my question and turned fully to face Tyr, gritting his teeth as his hand clenched upon his sword. "You lied! I cast my own son out because of your prophecy!"

"Prophecy?" For a moment, all I knew was confusion. Prophecy. Corruption. Power. Then it hit me, Tyr had been plotting this for far longer than any of us had suspected. I strode towards the King. "Don't you see?" I snapped, capturing his attention. "He's lied to you. You thought he was some prophet? He's a Fae! He betrayed us and he plans to betray you."

"He's my advisor," the King said, though he sounded far less confident.

Roan and Ash watched the two of us carefully and I stopped when Roan stepped forward. That was the line, I realized. The second I got too close to the King, he would move. Already I could tell that he was angry with me. His eyes were sparkling and glittering with retribution. I could only hope that he would spare my ass because I knew Sorrell wouldn't if he found out. Neither would Orion.

"Then why isn't he advising you now?" I challenged, gesturing up to the throne. "Look at him. He doesn't care about you or his people. All he cares about is power."

The King looked at Tyr. "But I..."

"Haven't you wondered why he hasn't aged?" I snapped. Seriously, just how far was this man willing to overlook. "Was he the same all those years ago?"

"She's right," Ash said gingerly, circling us. His eyes lingered on Nellie and her proximity to the King. In the distance, I could hear the clash of swords. The others had made their way to the castle, I realized, as Ash continued to speak. "Fae live for centuries longer than humans. We age at a much slower rate."

The King considered this and then he lifted his sword to point it at Tyr. "Explain yourself," he commanded.

All eyes turned to our enemy as Tyr sat and watched the five of us with a bored expression. "I do see the future," Tyr said after a beat. "Sometimes. It's part of my unique powers. Not many in my Court possessed it. I did see a girl usurper. Never did I imagine though that it would be your granddaughter!" Tyr's head went back and he laughed. No one appeared to notice the sounds of fighting growing closer and closer out in the corridor.

"You..." Shock coated the King's face and for a moment—a brief one—I felt sorry for him. Lied to. Betrayed. I knew that pain all too well. It lit a fire in my blood and made me feel a rage I'd never felt before. "You vile, loathsome creature!"

The King's outcry was followed by a jerk forward as he raced towards Tyr, his sword pointed and poised to strike the death blow. I stumbled back as Ash darted forward and grabbed Nellie, yanking her to the side. Roan's eyes followed the movement with horror and as I turned my cheek, I could see why.

Time seemed to slow and though I believed King Felix deserving of death for his crimes against Fae, in the moment, as I watched Tyr lift his hand, and with no weapon at all, send his head rolling with no more than a slash of darkness through the air, I wanted to take it back. I wanted to rewind time and figure out a less horrifying death. The only kind thing I could say was that it came quickly at least.

Nellie gasped right before Ash shoved her face against his chest, keeping her from seeing the King's— her grandfather's—head being severed from his body. It thunked upon the stone floor alongside his lifeless body and was consumed by Tyr's shadows for several moments. When the shadows receded, all that was left was a faceless and fleshless skeleton.

The doors to the throne room creaked and I spun as Orion and Sorrell both entered, their faces etched with war. Their bodies were covered in blood and gore, the red smeared on their skin. My heart seized with hope as

I saw their soldiers coming forward just before the doors slammed shut at their backs.

My eyes, along with everyone else's, moved to Tyr. "Now that we're all here," Tyr said with a smile. "The real fun can begin."

CHAPTER THIRTY-THREE

CRESS

Horror struck me. Tyr had planned this. Somehow, he'd known our plans. He'd watched us and he'd waited. He claimed that Nellie's presence was a shock to him, but in a way, it wasn't. *How could he have known?* I wondered. *When we had no clue?*

I edged backwards, fear making my heart pound even faster than it already was. I could feel it, a wild thing in my chest. My breath came in pants. Ash seemed to feel it too as with each step that Tyr descended towards the main floor of the throne room, he backed away, taking Nellie with him. I'd never been more grateful for him in my life. We didn't know each other beyond a few passing words, but his actions—the protective way he held my friend and guarded her against whatever Tyr was about to unleash—told me all I needed to know. He did care for her. He did love her.

And I could trust her to him if I didn't make it through this. Gods, I hoped I made it through this.

Tyr's feet made it to the main floor and as casually as if he were showing us a mere trinket, he withdrew a small dark globe from his pocket. Roan, Sorrell, and Orion each took a collective breath. I knew what it was. A Lanuaet—one of the very magical items that powered the Fae Courts. This was the thing that allowed them to move the castles and remain both a safe distance from the war and right upon their enemies.

Perhaps he wasn't intending to build a fortress around the Lanuaet, but to use it on the capital castle we were standing in. My body tensed as if preparing for such a possibility.

Instead, though, Tyr lifted it above the King's skeleton and the bodies of the fallen Royal guard and began to recite a language not all unfamiliar to us. These words were similar to the ones Groffet had uttered to show us who the Royal heir was and to show us how Nellie had come to be it. They were spoken in an ancient tongue, the words similar, though we couldn't translate them.

My lips parted on a gasp as I watched, transfixed by the sight before me. The King's bones crumpled under the weight of whatever spell Tyr was casting. He became nothing but dust that lifted and circled the miniature Lanuaet before being sucked into its core. The fallen Royal guard's bodies did the same. Their skin melted to nothing, their blood dried and the bones that remained were all pulled to the globe in Tyr's hand.

With each set it consumed, the glowing item grew in size.

"What are you doing?" Roan's horrified tone boomed throughout the room, making me jump at the suddenness of it.

As soon as the last of the bodies were retrieved, Tyr held it high and laughed. "I'm doing what I should have done years ago," he replied. "I'm claiming what is rightfully mine."

His gaze turned to his brother as Orion shuffled past me, striding towards Tyr without a single ounce of hesitation clear in his confident step. "No!" I reached for him, only to be pulled back as Sorrell's arms closed around me.

"Don't," he warned quietly. "He must do this for himself."

"He's going to get himself killed!" I argued, struggling, but all of my fighting was in vain. Sorrell was much stronger than I was and as his arms banded around me, they grew tighter and tighter with each attempt to break free until I could scarcely breathe. "Please, Sorrell," I begged. "Don't let him do this."

Tyr's grin widened as Orion moved towards him. "What is your plan, little Brother?" he taunted. "Do you truly think you can take me one on one? What an unimaginative approach. I'm disappointed in you."

"Tyrian Evenfall, first Prince of the Court of Midnight. You have been found guilty of treason against your people." The deep well of sorrow and rage combined in the sound of Orion's voice had my struggles against Sorrell's chest slowly fading until I stopped altogether. Everyone was spellbound as he stood before Tyr, sword in hand, dripping with the blood of those he had killed to get here. His face stoic and unfeeling. His appearance dispassionate—a direct contrast to the agony in his words as he spoke them.

"There's been no trial," Tyr replied haughtily.

"And there won't be," Orion said just before bringing his sword up and swinging it downward, straight towards the center of Tyr's head.

My limbs tensed as I watched with disbelief. It couldn't be that easy, could it? No, it wasn't. Tyr's arm moved far faster than I expected as he brought the Lanuaet in his grasp up and, the second Orion's blade hit it, a resounding boom echoed around the chambers. Orion's body was flung backwards—he flew past Roan and then Sorrell and me and then Ash and Nellie at the very back of our group until his back slammed into the closed throne room doors.

"Orion!" Sorrell released me to run to him as Orion's sword clattered to the ground. Blood poured out of his mouth as he leaned over and vomited.

Just as I reached him, the sound of Tyr's laugh rose and commanded the entire room. I went to my knees, my hands hovering over Orion, wondering if I shouldn't try to heal him by pouring more of my own energy into him. He was awake and though in obvious pain, he glared across the room at his brother.

"Did you think you would be fast enough to kill me, little Brother?" Tyr asked. With my hands finally settling on Orion's shoulders—needing to touch him in some way to assure myself that he was okay—I turned my gaze back to the man who had us all trapped. Tyr shook his head and lifted the Lanuaet. "Do you even know what this is?"

"Of course we know," Roan snarled through gritted teeth. He, too, glared at Tyr as he clenched his fist on the handle of his sword.

"Oh, you know that it's a container of magic, an item so powerful it can move entire Courts," Tyr agreed. "But do you know how it's made?" No one answered his question. I suppose no one did know—I know I didn't. Tyr's face split into a cruel smile. "Blood and bones," he said. "The Queens have been keeping so much from you, little Princes, things that would give you night terrors. Things that would make you cry tears of blood if you were to witness them firsthand."

His laugh chilled me to the bone. Orion shifted, pressing back against the doors as he slowly worked himself back to his feet, and my hands fell to my sides as my eyes remained on Tyr.

"It takes many sacrifices to make even a single Lanuaet," Tyr continued. "It's essentially, though, the perfect power source. They just didn't have the stomach to use it for what it could really do—not after what they'd done."

"What they'd done?" I repeated. "What are you talking about?" Out of the corner of my eye, I saw both Roan and Sorrell's faces blanch as they glanced quickly back at me—almost in unison—before refocusing their gazes on Tyr.

"You—" Sorrell began.

"Oh, you haven't told her?" Tyr asked, cutting him

off. Orion's hand touched my arm, distracting me for a moment. I didn't see it when Roan decided to rush him, but just as my gaze was lifting to meet Orion's, Roan's cry of outrage and subsequent grunt of pain jerked my eyes back to the rest of the room and I saw Tyr arch out a palm—sending Roan crashing into one of the side pillars. The post cracked under the brunt force of Roan's body slamming into it and he slid down and crumpled at the bottom. Strong, fearless, fiery Roan— knocked unconscious with one hit.

What kind of fucking monster were we really dealing with?

"Let me enlighten you, little Changeling," Tyr said as he glided forward. "Twenty odd years ago, there was a fourth Fae Court. The Court of Brightling. It was headed by a powerful, if not far too empathetic Royal family."

I remembered this. The guys had told me of a separate Court, but why did that matter here? What did that have to do with what was happening now?

"The Brightling Court adored humans, you see," Tyr went on. With every step in my direction, I could feel Orion tense further at my side. "And with the war starting, Fae grew mistrustful of them. The Queens sent out an order to have them exterminated, and thus, the Lanuaets that we now depend on today were born."

Realization dawned on me. The Queens had used the deaths and bodies of the entire Brightling Court to create their power source items. Sorrell chose his moment carefully. I hadn't even noticed that he had been preparing, but just as Tyr stepped past him on his way to me, he turned and lifted his hands. Bolts of ice shot up from the ground, crisscrossing over Tyr's legs and trapping him. Sorrell wasted no time, withdrawing his blade and slicing it through the space Tyr's body stood. Only...

The second the blade struck, Tyr was gone and the only thing that remained behind were the severed ice tips that Sorrell's sword had cut through in his stead. Tyr reappeared just behind him.

"Tsk. Tsk. I expected better of you, Sorrell. I expected you to learn from Roan's mistakes."

Before Sorrell could so much as turn towards him, he, too, was sent flying across the room. His sword clattered to the stone floor as Sorrell's body went crashing into the double throne chairs atop the dais. Once he was down, he did not get back up again.

"You need to get out of here, Cress," Orion said quietly. "I'll distract him when he gets close, but you need to get through those doors."

"Oh, I don't think that will be happening, dear Brother," Tyr said and, in a split second, he was right before us—wicked smile in place and a bloodlust in his eyes that made my chest clench with panic. "I'm not done with my story yet."

Tyr blinked in and out of existence for only a second —the Lanuaet, I realized. He was using it to move at will, far faster than he ever had before. When he was back, he held Orion's sword in his hand and I watched in horror as he slammed it right into his brother's chest.

"No!" I screamed as Orion's stunned shout of

surprise was disrupted by yet more blood choking up from his mouth.

Ash chose that moment to attack, moving up from behind to strike. Tyr chuckled, the sound twisted and grating in my ears. "I think we've had enough distractions, don't you?" he asked, looking at me even as he held the Lanuaet out. Power poured from the small globe and darkness began to creep up from the ground, encircling both Ash and Nellie. They struggled and fought as it wrapped its tentacles around their limbs, holding them secure until it consumed their entire bodies and they were left frozen in what looked like no ice I'd ever seen before. It was pitch black save for where their bodies were, pressed to the inside of the crystal—their faces awash in fear.

Tyr twisted the blade in Orion's stomach. "Stop it!" I screamed. "You're killing him."

"That's the point," Tyr said. "To get this Lanuaet to the power level I need it, it requires more sacrifices."

"Why didn't you just take the one from the Court of Midnight?" Orion asked as he gripped the blade, slicing his palms as he stopped the twisting motion Tyr continued to use.

Tyr's expression grew thunderous. "Our parents, it seemed, were well aware of my plans—I've been leading that damn human King on my leash for as long as I can remember. They knew, and they let it happen. The war only brought them more power, you see, but the second I turned my sights on them, of course, they destroyed their Lanuaet. The selfish cunts."

"Please," I begged, reaching for the blade. "Take it out."

Orion chuckled, though his slight amusement was only tinged with pain and more blood. "They finally saw you for what you were, eh?" he said.

Tyr shrugged. "I had to kill them for their betrayal, of course," he replied. "And then the rest of the Court— it was the only way to kickstart this new Lanuaet."

"But there weren't enough," Orion spat. "The Court of Midnight has been dying for decades."

Tyr ripped the blade free and Orion slid back down to the ground. I went with him, tears I hadn't even realized I'd started crying pouring from my face as I tried to clutch my hands over his seeping wound. "The Court of Brightling had been massive," Tyr said, glaring down at his brother, flicking his gaze to me. "And their power far stronger than Midnight's—the Queens hadn't needed so many bodies to create the three Lanuaet's they needed for the Courts left to live."

"Cress, run," Orion rasped.

"What?" I shook my head, pressing my fingers more firmly into his stomach. Was he insane? I couldn't run now. If I did, he'd die for sure.

"Go!" he barked. Before I could even get another word out, Tyr released the sword in his grasp and reached for me. His hand sank into my hair, ripping out several strands as he jerked me up from the ground. "No!" Orion's pain filled cry was followed by several dark tendrils wisping around both my body and Tyr's. Tyr glanced down at the powerful shadows and shook his head right before he lifted his boot and stomped their ends out of existence.

"At your level, Brother," he said, turning a sneer to Orion as I fought to free myself from his grasp to no avail, "you couldn't even defeat a pixie."

"Not ... her," Orion panted.

"Oh, yes, her," Tyr said with a laugh. When he turned his attention back to where I was trying to kick and punch at his side, he moved his face closer. "Do you know why I've told you all of this?" Tyr asked.

Shivers danced up my spine. I had a sinking feeling. One that I didn't want to admit to.

"I knew it as soon as I saw you," Tyr continued. "You look just like the Brightling King and Queen. Their daughter. Their precious little Princess. Oh, how I thought you'd died with your clan, but to see you in the Court of Frost. To see how you'd ensnared my brother and his friends with your beauty and your bumbling ineptitude. It was hilarious. And I finally knew what I needed. It was simple really. One single Brightling Royal can bring this Lanuaet to complete and utter God level power."

I gasped as he released my hair, his hand going instead to my throat before I could drop from his grip. My air was cut off and I struggled, growing weaker and weaker as I fought back. I kicked. I punched. None of it had an effect.

"But..." I tried to gasp, "the execution?"

He laughed again. "I was serious when I said I could foresee parts of the future. I knew those men would come for you and that you would be rescued—all of that talk of watching you dangle and die in front of a crowd? I just wanted to play with you. This was the path that guaranteed me the highest chance of success. Now, here we are, and you will die to serve my purposes." My lips parted, but no more words came. I was out of time and air. "So, thank you, dear little Changeling," Tyr whispered as he leaned down and pressed his lips to my ear. "I know it's been a long journey to get here. All I need now is for you to die."

His hand crushed my throat and the darkness crept in on either side of my vision. Soon, my struggles waned and then stopped altogether. It was no use. He had won and I was about to do exactly as he said.

I was going to die.

CHAPTER THIRTY-FOUR

CRESS

L ife. Death. Sex. Love. All of the things you would expect to cross a girl's mind right on the verge of death crossed mine. So did all of the self deprecating questions:

Are you really going to let this happen?

What kind of wuss gets choked out by an evil Fae intent on taking over the world?

Wait, I'm a fucking Princess? Like a real one?

Okay, so that last one didn't really have much to do with the death part so much as it had to do with the life part. I couldn't help but be shocked, though. I mean, who would've thought that I'd be a Princess? Kind of had me wondering why I always imagined Princesses to be these elegant, fragile little flowers who couldn't lift a spoon to their lips if it wasn't pure silver.

The only spoon I'd ever eaten off of was wooden. The only thing flowery about me was my winning personality. And elegance? Definitely not my style. But fragile? Until this moment, I'd never considered myself fragile. I'd nearly died half a dozen times since I'd been led to the Court of Crimson and the Fae. I'd been almost murdered, shoved off a castle wall, chased by an angry mob, attacked by unknown shadow creatures in Alfheim, and glared down by the Queens who had— apparently—ordered the slaughter of my entire Court.

It all sounded like a bedtime story gone horribly wrong.

And yet, Tyr thought that there was some hidden power inside of me that would complete his magical murder orb? No. I could hardly toss a fireball at a bale of hay. There was no hidden talent, no power reserves deep within me. If there was, I would know it … wouldn't I?

It's not inside, a voice suddenly said, *but on the outside...*

I froze. The voice was familiar and feminine. It sounded like a dream I'd had long ago. No, more recent. It sounded like the woman from my dream in the prison tower. The one who'd been running from something with a man...my mother?

Power is all around you, the voice continued. *It's steeped in your skin. In the air you breathe. In the flowers that grow. Call for it and it will come. All you need to do is trust in the Gods and give over to them. They will guide you.*

Kind of difficult to take power from breath when I had none, I thought sardonically, but at this point, what was there left to lose? Nothing.

Roan and Sorrell had been knocked out cold. Ash

and Nellie frozen in some strange black ice-like crystal. Orion... if I didn't at least try, he would die right along with me. And that, more than anything, made me focus.

All around me, I thought. All around me. I ... just ... needed ... to ... breathe ...

I cried out as air rushed into me and my eyes shot open. Tyr stood above my prone body, the Lanuaet in his fist raised above me. All around us, black powder swirled. When he noticed that I was awake, a dark scowl overtook his face.

"I should've known that wouldn't be enough to kill you," he snarled. Once more, he disappeared and then reappeared, this time with a dagger in hand as he held it over me.

"Not this time," I shot back. The second his arm descended, the dagger aiming straight for my heart, I lifted my arm. The blade pierced my forearm, making me scream at the pain it sent—but pain was better than death. It was better than not breathing.

The Lanuaet was glowing, hovering between us. "It won't matter!" Tyr screamed at me. "It will take your life force anyway!"

An idea formed. I didn't know if it would work and there was no time to figure out a second plan of action. If the Lanuaet wanted power, then I would give it power. All of it. My skin glowed as I reached up and yanked the dagger out of my forearm. Blood oozed from the wound before being lifted and sucked right into the glowing orb's spinning sphere.

I panted as I closed my eyes and focused on the space around me. Power was everywhere, the voice had claimed. In the air. In the stone. In the breath we breathed. I conjured it, calling it forward. Focusing as Sorrell had taught me. Only instead of flames, I was pulling *everything*.

My body felt hot—sweat beaded on my brow and that, too, was taken into the Lanuaet's dark globe of magic. I pushed more and more out. Like I was trying to heal Orion all over again. I pictured the sun within me and let it burn outward. I would give until there was nothing left. I would make Tyr regret this.

"What are you doing?" Tyr demanded as the Lanuaet began to vibrate in his palm. He screamed and the sound of burning flesh reached my nostrils. I didn't care. I had to focus.

More and more power was thrust into the orb Tyr tried to keep hold of until finally, it became too much for him. He released the sphere with a shout, holding his shaking burned hands out in front of him as he gaped at the thing he'd created, hovering all on its own.

"Stop!" he screamed.

A white light blinded me as a fissure cracked across the surface of the orb, emitting the power that it had consumed. Tyr jumped towards it and, just before his hands touched it, another crack formed and the power that slipped out slammed into him. Blood spurted out across my body, raining down over my chest. I turned my face to the side only to watch as Tyr's severed body fell to the stone and his unblinking dead eyes met mine.

In the next instant, the Lanuaet shattered and a brilliant white light crashed into me, sending me straight back into the same oblivion that I had almost let myself die in. *At least this time,* I thought just before my mind winked out, *the others would survive.*

❦

I woke to someone rattling metal not very far from where I laid. My thoughts were murky and my head felt as though someone had slammed it into a stone wall more times than I could count. A groan left my lips seconds before my eyelashes fluttered open.

"Miss?" A round faced woman with large eyes and wearing a white apron stood alongside the bed I lay in holding what looked like a fireplace poker. "You're awake?"

I looked from the poker in her hand to the look of shock on her face and back again. "If you're planning to kill me with that, can you wait until I have the energy to defend myself?" I asked around a groan.

"I must tell the Queen!" she half screamed. I winced as the high pitched sound of her voice ricocheted into my skull, but before I could say another word the maid was gone, leaving the door on the bedroom chamber hanging open as her fast footsteps faded down the hall.

I doubted she'd even heard a word I said. Slowly, as gingerly as possible, I rose from the bed and stared down at the gown I now wore as well as the growth in my hair. The dress was a silk nightgown with puffy sleeves and lace on the cuffs. Though I couldn't remember getting into it, even stranger than that was the fact that my hair was no longer cut short. It was far lower than it had been the last time I'd been awake.

Instead, it now reached almost to my collarbone. I tried to recall something—anything that might have led to the dress or the hair change—but I could hardly remember anything at all aside from the last image I'd seen right before I'd passed out. Tyr's cold, dead eyes staring me in the face. A brilliant white light. The Lanuaet exploding over my body.

What in the name of Coreliath had happened?

More footsteps sounded outside of the chamber and I groaned again, not ready to face another contingent of confused, screamy maids. "Please, just—" I stopped as I turned towards the doorway. It wasn't a maid. It was Nellie.

She looked ... different. Her face was smoother, her hair pulled up into an elegant chignon that made her appear older. Her shabby peasant girl dresses that she normally wore were replaced with a fabric that was such a deep burgundy that it resembled expensive wine.

"Cress?" Her voice shook as she entered the room. "It's really ... I mean, you're really awake. You're here. You're alive."

"Yeah?" I arched a brow even as I wavered on my feet. "Why wouldn't I be?"

"Y-you've been asleep for weeks," she confessed. Tears formed in her eyes. "I didn't know if you'd ever wake up again. None of us did."

"I was?" I blinked at her for a moment before scanning the room. "Where are the guys?" I asked.

"They're being informed," she replied. "I just need-ed..." She sniffed as the tears came crashing down and suddenly she was in front of me. Nellie's arms wrapped around me and she clutched onto me as she sobbed. "Oh, Cress, I thought we'd lost you."

I didn't know what to say, but when your best friend held you like she was afraid you'd disappear, crying her eyes out, there was only one thing to do—you hugged her back.

"I'm okay," I whispered as I wrapped my arms around her slightly shorter frame. "I'm alive. I'm here."

"You stupid," she sniffed. "Arrogant. Dumb. Selfish." Nellie pulled back and punched me in the arm. "Don't ever do something that stupid!" she screamed.

"Ow!" I rubbed the place she had hit. "What'd I do?"

"You almost got yourself killed!" she yelled. "Just because I was trapped inside that ice thingy doesn't mean I wasn't aware of what was going on! I saw what you did. You almost—" She broke off and for a brief moment, I was honestly worried that I'd survived Tyr's murder attempt only to be killed by my very own best friend. She looked ready to strangle me. "You almost died, Cress. You scared the Gods damned shit out of me."

My eyes widened. "You don't curse," I blurted.

She shot me a glare. "I do when my best friend is being stupid," she snapped back.

"Hey," I replied, "be nice to me, I saved your butt."

There was a brief moment of silence and then she sniffed again. "You did, Cress. You really did."

"So, that's it then?" I asked. "Tyr's dead. The King's dead. The war is over?"

"The war is over," she agreed with a nod.

I remembered what the maid had said just before

bolting out of the chamber. "And you're the Queen now?" I asked.

A light flush touched her cheeks. "Not yet," she confessed. "They call me that—it was … there was a lot that happened after your men woke up—the dark one, Orion, had to be healed, and they helped me explain things and convince the rest of Amnestia's army and nobles. I wanted to wait, though, to be crowned until … well, until you woke up."

I sagged back onto the bed, my butt hitting the mattress and sinking down. "It's over." I said the words more for my own ears than hers. I just couldn't believe it. Exactly what we wanted. The war was over. Nellie was now the Queen—or would be very soon. It had worked. It was finally…

Tears pricked at my eyes and I lifted my gaze to Nellie's. Before I could say a word, however, there was a loud bang at the doorway and three men crashed into the room. Their eyes wild. Their bodies tense. And then they saw me.

Alive. Awake. And crying my eyes out like a blubbering baby. Nel smiled at me. "I'll give you some time," she said. "But now that you're awake, I hope you'll come to my ceremony. I wouldn't be here if it weren't for you. None of us would."

I didn't respond—she already knew my answer.

As soon as the door shut, though, I turned to the three men waiting on me. "Well?" I asked, sniffling as I wiped away the snot dripping from my nose with the lacy cuff of my sleeve—which was not as easy as it sounded. "What now?"

Three pairs of eyes landed on me. One cold as ice. One hot as fire. And one as dark as midnight. And one by one, they moved closer.

"Now, Little Bird," Roan said as he leaned down and took one of my hands before lifting it to his lips, "we get married and we live."

"All of us?" I asked, looking between the three of them.

Both Orion and Sorrell nodded. "All of us," they agreed.

EPILOGUE

CRESS

I t was over. Well and truly over. After all of the fighting, the years of war, of loss, of hatred, it was almost ... impossible to imagine, but here it was. The end of the war that had ripped apart the lives of so many.

Months ago, when I'd been nothing more than an orphan, preparing to age out of the convent's good graces, I'd known so little about the rest of the world. Back then, even though it was such a short while ago, the idea of war had been a distant one.

Sure, I'd known it was happening. I'd been aware of it, but because it had never affected me—never caused me loss or grief—it'd been almost like a fairytale. Told in whispers before bed. Holding a wealth of warnings and lessons to learn. Do not go too far from the convent. Do not trust the creatures who would use magic to hurt you. Now, here I stood on the balcony of Amnestia's Royal castle overlooking the large courtyard where mere weeks ago, I'd nearly died.

So much had changed.

I had changed.

The world had changed.

And Nellie, too, had changed.

My body turned towards the sound of footsteps on the stone floor as they approached and my best friend rounded the corner, dressed far differently than I'd ever seen her. She looked up and spotted me.

"There you are!" Nellie rushed forward, nearly tripping over the red and gold skirts that appeared massive on her petite frame. As the end of the dress's train came into view so did the two lady's maids who were attempting to hold it up off the dirty floor. Nellie turned back to them as soon as she realized they were there. "You don't have to do that," she said quickly.

"Your Grace," the older of the two women began, "your gown—it will be—"

"Fine," Nellie insisted. "Please." She gestured to me. "Would you give us a moment?"

The older women frowned, obviously very displeased, but what could they say? Nellie was about to be crowned a Queen. Another thing that I hadn't predicted would ever happen.

As soon as the lady's maids were out of earshot, Nellie whirled back towards me. "Do you believe this thing?" she said with horror as she waved a hand down to the dress she wore.

I bit back a grin. "It's beautiful," I said.

"It's heavy," she complained.

"It's fit for a Queen."

She grimaced and then gestured to my attire. "I'd rather wear what you're wearing," she said.

I glanced down to the mass of dark purple skirts beneath which I wore tight fitting leather trousers that molded to my frame. I shrugged. "Next time find out that you're a Fae rather than a would be Queen," I told her.

"You better be careful," she said. "Or I'll command my new guards to cut off your head."

I lifted a palm and conjured a ball of heated light. It sparked and danced between my fingertips. "Just try it," I challenged with a smile.

There was a beat and then both of us burst out laughing. By the time we managed to calm down, my light had faded and I was wiping the tears from beneath my eyes. For a moment, the two of us just remained silent after catching our breaths. And as I stared into her eyes, I could see the trail of emotions as they collided into one another. I understood it. I was feeling them too.

Nellie's eyes softened and gently—as gently as she'd always been and likely always would be—she reached for my hands and took them in her own. "I want to say something," she said. I waited, but when it appeared she wasn't yet ready for whatever it was that she wished to say, I decided it was an opportunity for me to say what I was thinking.

"You're my sister, you know," I told her. She lifted her eyes away from our hands and met my gaze. I smiled softly. "You've always been. Ever since we met at that stupid convent."

She rolled her eyes. "It was not stupid," she retorted. "You just have an issue with authority."

I laughed. "Now that you're Queen are you going to hold it over my head?" I asked.

She smirked. "Perhaps I will."

"Ha." I shook my head. "Good luck with that. I've got three Princes to contend with and they've got magic."

"Yeah, but they also have the poor intelligence to be in love with you, too," she shot back.

"Yes," I said, unable to stop the ridiculously wonderful smile from overtaking my face. "They do."

"What I wanted to say," Nellie began again a moment later, "was thank you."

I blinked and frowned at her. "For what?" I inquired.

A sigh left her lips and she shook her head lightly. "For ... it's hard to say what it is, it's more than one thing," she confessed. Her hands squeezed mine tightly as she beseeched me with her gaze. "Thank you for being my friend," she said.

"You don't have to thank me for that—" I started, only to be cut off as she kept going.

"Thank you for being my sister. Thank you for believing in me. Thank you for coming back for me, and Cress..." She paused and then dragged me forward —with far more strength than I expected in her small body—into a hug. As her arms wrapped around me, Nellie turned her cheek and pressed it to my shoulder before whispering the last of her thank yous. "Thank you for being you."

Tears assaulted my eyes. My tongue swelled and stuck to the roof of my mouth. There was nothing more

I could do but accept her hug. I tightened my hold around her and reached up to cup the back of her head, stroking my fingers lightly through the curls her new lady's maids had no doubt spent all morning trying to perfect. I was sure she wouldn't mind if I messed them up a smidge—this was an emotional moment after all.

I sniffed hard as one of the tears escaped to cascade down the side of my face. When we pulled away from each other once more, I realized I wasn't the only one affected. I touched her face, grinning as her tears overlapped my fingers. Her face, even splotchy and red, was lovely.

"You are going to make the best Queen Amnestia has ever seen," I promised her.

Nellie's hands reached up and slipped over mine. "Will you be with me?" she asked.

It was an impossible question with a bittersweet answer. Because after what had happened on the battlefield ... after the full breadth of my powers had been awakened, Roan, Orion, and Sorrell had explained what that would mean for me. An average Fae often outlived the lifespan of several humans. I wasn't an average Fae. I was the last of the Royal line of the Court of Brightling. Nellie was wholly and completely human.

My lips parted and I uttered an oath to her that I would take into her grave and then my own. No matter what else happened to this world, I would keep this vow unto my dying breath.

"I will be with you for as long as you need me," I said to her. "And when you no longer have that need, I will pass it on to your children and your children's children.

For as long as your blood remains in this world, I will honor and protect it."

More tears came, pouring down both of our cheeks and, when the last of the words of my oath—sealed with an unspoken magic, a promise to a friend—Nellie pushed forward and hugged me again. We stayed there like that, for several long moments—clinging to one another until the lady's maids came back and the sound of their outrage and horror over Nellie's ruined hair and makeup forced the two of us to part with laughs.

"You're still coming to the coronation, right?" Nellie asked quickly, her eyes seeking reassurance as she was gently prodded back towards the corridor.

"I wouldn't miss it for the world," I said. She paused on the threshold with each of her arms engulfed by one of her maids and then with a brilliant smile, she nodded back to me and disappeared to ready herself for one of the biggest days of her life.

The coronation of the new Queen of Amnestia.

I remained behind on the balcony for a long time after that, watching the proceedings down below as people flitted back and forth in preparation for the after coronation celebrations. It wasn't until I felt a chill down my back that I realized I was no longer alone. Turning back to the entrance to the balcony, I spotted Sorrell leaning against the stone wall there.

"Thought I might find you here," he commented, pushing away from the wall.

"Oh?" I asked lightly.

He approached quickly, not stopping until my hips were pressed right up against the stone railing and his arms were on either side of me, caging me into his embrace. "You've been gone for quite a while," he said.

"I've been thinking," I replied.

Cold, blue eyes no longer devoid of emotion met mine. "About your friend?" he guessed.

"Yes and no," I answered. "About what the three of you told me."

"You knew that Fae lived a long time, my love," he said.

"Yes," I replied. "I guess I just hadn't given it much thought." My hands slipped up the black and blue coat he wore. It gaped open revealing a snow white shirt underneath. I gripped the lapels and used my hold to drag him closer. "I've been a little preoccupied," I admitted.

"Yes, you have," he agreed.

"Everything's changing." My words dropped to a whisper as his head dipped and he drew dangerously close.

"You won't be alone, my love," he said.

No, I wouldn't. I'd always believed that I would be just fine on my own. I'd always been an independent soul. Now, though, it was nice to think that I'd always have someone. Someone to live with me, laugh with me, love me as I loved them in return.

As if he sensed the direction of my thoughts, Sorrell pressed forward and kissed me. My eyes slid shut and my arms lifted, winding around the back of his neck as I let myself sink into the great passion that I'd learned he'd been hiding from everyone—including himself, I suspected.

However long our kiss lasted, when we parted, I was left shivering and laughing as I flicked frost off of my shoulder. He grinned ruefully—so unlike him and yet becoming more and more the norm that it made my heart swell.

"We should hurry," I suggested. "It'll start soon."

Together, Sorrell and I headed away from the balcony towards the center of the castle—a giant throne room in which I'd once been paraded before the previous King Felix in the hopes that he'd kill me. All of that was behind us now. The King was gone and so was Tyr.

My head lifted as soon as we entered and I found Roan and Orion waiting for us near the dais where the castle's highest ranking officials—those that had survived the war and not been charged with war crimes —and the priest of the Gods waited.

"You made it," Roan said as we approached. "We were worried we'd have to go looking for you."

I scoffed and rolled my eyes. "I wouldn't miss this," I told him, the same words I'd said to Nellie. "If I did, I have a feeling the new Queen of Amnestia would try to kill me. Can't have her starting another war, can we?"

"That's not funny," Roan said dryly.

"Get ready," Orion announced. "Here she comes."

I hurried to move to the side, facing the front as the doors to the throne room opened and music began to play. In the time that we'd been separated, Nellie's makeup and hair had been perfectly restored. She lifted her head and held it high as a parade of people lined up behind her. The long gold and red train of her gown drifted across the stone surface. I could tell that Nellie had ordered her lady's maids to let it because as they followed behind her, they stared down at it with pinched, broken looks.

I smiled and lifted my fingers, flicking them towards my friend as she strode by. The skirts lifted and hovered over the ground, trailing behind her as if she were gliding on air rather than walking. The maids' eyes widened and I heard the gasps before they jerked their heads up and to the side. I met their stunned looks with a wink as Nellie proceeded to the front of the throne and knelt before the Priest.

As I stood there, staring at the delicate shoulders of my best friend as she was blessed with the water of the Gods and an ornate golden crown was placed upon her head, I realized … this was more than just the end, this was a new beginning.

For Nellie and her Kingdom

For me and my Princes.

For all of Fae and humankind.

THANK YOU FOR READING!

We hoped you enjoyed the Twisted Fae series. This is the third and final book in this series, but please still consider leaving a review. If you're dying for more books, we have an extensive backlist which you can turn the page and find, but here are our recommendations if you loved this series.

Lucinda Dark —> Barbie: The Vampire Hunter Series

Helen Scott —> Immortal Hunters MC Series

ABOUT LUCINDA DARK

Lucinda Dark, also known as USA Today Bestselling Author, Lucy Smoke, for her contemporary novels, has a master's degree in English and is a self-proclaimed creative chihuahua. She enjoys feeding her wanderlust, cover addiction, as well as her face. When she's not on a never-ending quest to find the perfect milkshake, she lives and works in the southern United States with her beloved fur-baby, Hiro, and her family and friends.

Want to be kept up to date? Think about joining the author's group or signing up for their newsletter below.

Website
Facebook Group
Newsletter

ABOUT HELEN SCOTT

Helen Scott is a USA Today Bestselling Author of paranormal romance and reverse harem romance who lives in the Chicago area with her wonderful husband and furry, four-legged kids. She spends way too much time with her nose in a book and isn't sorry about it. When not reading or writing, Helen can be found absorbed in one video game or another or crocheting her heart out.

Website
Facebook Group
Newsletter

Heart of Tartarus

Shadow of Deception

Sword of Damage

Dogs of War (Coming Soon)

Contemporary Series:

Sick Boys Series

Pretty Little Savage

Stone Cold Queen

Iris Boys Series (completed)

Now or Never

Power & Choice

Leap of Faith

Cross my Heart

Forever & Always

Iris Boys Series Boxset

The *Break* Series (completed)

Break Vol. 1

Break Vol. 2 (coming soon)

Break Series Boxset

Contemporary Standalones:

Expressionate

Wildest Dreams

Criminal Underground Series (Shared Universe Standalones)

Sweet Possession

Scarlett Thief

ALSO BY HELEN SCOTT

Legends Unleashed

(Cowritten with Lacey Carter Anderson)

Don't Say My Name – Coming Soon

The Wild Hunt

Daughter of the Hunt

Challenger of the Hunt – Coming Soon

The Hollow

(Cowritten with Ellabee Andrews)

Survival

Seduction

Surrender – Coming Soon

Salsang Chronicles

(cowritten with Serena Akeroyd)

Stained Egos

Stained Hearts

Stained Minds

Stained Bonds

Stained Souls

Salsang Chronicles Box Set

Cerberus

Daughter of Persephone

Daughter of Hades

Queen of the Underworld

Cerberus Box Set

Hera's Gift (A Cerberus Series Novella)

Four Worlds

Wounding Atlantis

Finding Hyperborea

Escaping El Dorado

Embracing Agartha – Coming Soon

Wardens of Midnight

Woman of Midnight (A Wardens of Midnight Novella)

Sanctuary at Midnight

The Siren Legacy

The Oracle (A Siren Legacy Novella)

The Siren's Son

The Siren's Eyes

The Siren's Code

The Siren's Heart

The Banshee (A Siren Legacy Novella)

The Siren's Bride

Fury's Valentine (A Siren Legacy Novella)